THE
LITTLE LIES
WE HIDE

FRANÇOIS HOULE

Dawn Rainbow Books
OTTAWA, ONTARIO

Copyright © 2019 by François Houle

For permission requests, email: francois@francoisghoule.com

www.francoisghoule.com

The Little Lies We Hide/François Houle. -- 1st ed.

ISBN: 978-1-7750490-8-1

Published by Dawn Rainbow Books

Cover Design: KD Design

Cover Art Image: CrazyD©123RF.com

Editor: Ethan James Clark, SilverJay Editing

In Memory of My Dad

André Houle (1933 – 2005)

ONE

"W hy are you behaving like a dumbass?"

"I'm not!"

"Of course you are."

Bradley glared at Kate from across the living room, the black leather couch between them acting like a bored arbitrator. Behind him, a wall of windows looked out at the Vancouver skyline from the seventeenth floor.

This was Kate's three-million-dollar condo. He had a tiny apartment about a tenth of the size in the old part of downtown. It was within walking distance of the radio station he worked at as the Program Director, so the location suited him fine.

Besides, Bradley didn't own a car.

Kate, on the other hand, had a brand-new BMW 4 Series Convertible in a gorgeous Melbourne Red Metallic. It complemented her high-powered position as Executive Vice-President of the conglomerate that owned, amongst many things, the radio station Bradley worked at.

"We're going to be late for work," he said. "Can we talk about this later?"

"Well, *you're* going to be late for work as I can pretty much come in as I please, and no, we're going to talk about this right now."

"Oh, pulling the old boss trick on me."

Kate crossed her arms and focused her emerald green eyes on him. He could feel the sharp intensity radiating from them cut him to pieces. He hated it when she pulled rank. Didn't make for fair play.

But damn it if she didn't look beautiful. At forty, she put to shame girls half her age, and in the boardroom, she ate grown men whole with her sharp tongue and sharper intelligence. Why she was with him, he still couldn't quite figure out. And this argument they were having left him even more confused. Had she really just asked him—?

"Whatever it takes," she said.

"Whatever it takes? You make it sound like I'm some deal you need to close before breakfast. And I haven't even had a cup of coffee. Why can't we get a damn coffee machine in here?"

"If that's what you need to say yes, then I'll have one installed this afternoon."

Bradley ran a hand through his longish auburn but slightly greying hair. A few weeks back, he'd told Kate he was thinking of getting his hair cut short, but she hadn't liked the idea. She'd told him the long hair, the goatee, and the earrings fit his radio persona to a T. And then she'd added *makes me weak in the knees.*

Nothing made her weak in the knees, as far as he knew. They had met about three years ago when her company had bought the radio station he'd been working at. The station had gone through different ownerships over the years, changed format a few times to try to cater to new markets, and there had even been rumours of being shut down. But then Kate had showed up one Monday afternoon and gathered the staff and told them they'd been bought. No surprise there for anyone, and of course all the mumbo-jumbo coming out of Kate's mouth about them turning a corner and becoming *the* radio station of Vancouver had fallen on deaf ears. They'd heard it before, including Bradley.

Except that he hadn't been able to keep his eyes off this tall brunette wearing a power suit that probably cost more than his monthly wage, and the faint aroma of her perfume had been just strong enough to make him imagine that her smile was filled with hidden messages and possibilities.

Not the first time he'd been fooled so easily.

And as quickly as she had materialized on that day, he'd barely seen her the next three months. The station still sucked, the format was still awful and dated, and just like before, rumours of being shut down floated through the stale office air like a bad cold.

Then things started to change, and fast. The previous Program Director was shown the door, Bradley was told he was the new PD (he'd sensed he couldn't refuse, unless he viewed being unemployed as a better career move), and Kate became a permanent resident of the station. Three months later, the station had been well on its way to becoming *the* radio station of Vancouver and Bradley had found himself falling hard for Kate.

So why was he freaking out at her marriage proposal?

CG ᘓᘓ

He should have known something was up this morning when he found Kate still in bed at five. She never skipped a day to run her 5k before work. He'd thought maybe she was sick, but he'd never known her to be sick. The woman was all about healthy lifestyle. She popped vitamins like they were M&Ms. Probably when they then made love, that should have told him that something was definitely up, but when Kate O'Grady made love to him, she was like a drug that left him completely and utterly in her possession.

He wasn't complaining.

He really did love her.

But why did they need to get married? Hadn't she been the one who had said two years ago that although she wasn't looking for a fly-by-night fling, marriage wasn't on her horizon either? That had suited him just fine. This was 2018 and no one needed a marriage certificate to *seal the deal*. He hadn't needed a piece of paper to confirm his feelings for her, and neither had she.

Until this morning.

"Marriage? Why now? What's changed?"

"Not exactly the response I'd expected," she said and softened her stance. A little. "What's changed? I guess *I* have. I'm not twenty anymore."

"So?"

Kate looked at him as if he were a bad puppy who had just peed on the floor, and she was about to reprimand him. He hated feeling so inferior to her. Maybe that's why he didn't get the marriage thing all of a sudden. She really didn't need him, but he hoped that she still wanted him. Of *course* she did. Why else would she want to marry him?

Well, he knew one person who would be thrilled at the news: his mom. It had been a long time since he'd spoken to her—last Mother's Day, he thought. It was September. Crap, he'd let time fly.

"You here?" Kate said with a flash of annoyance. "Bradley Knighton?"

He was in trouble now. She only used his full name when she was getting pretty pissed with him. "Just thinking about my mother."

"Seriously?" she said, now totally irritated. "I ask you to marry me and your mom is what pops into your head."

"Yeah," he said, getting defensive. "I was thinking that if anyone was going to be thrilled at the news, it will be her."

"Well, that's exactly why I've asked you to marry me," Kate said with a hint of irony. "So I can meet her and the rest of your family."

Bradley became distantly quiet.

"What is it with you and your family?" she said, softening her tone. "You never talk about them. When's the last time you actually went home?"

"A while," he whispered.

"You might need to right whatever is wrong there," she said. "I won't put up with any family ill will at my wedding."

"So, it's a done deal?" he said, sounding like a six-year-old. "I don't even get to say what I want?"

"Jesus, Brad!" She closed the distance between them and stood a foot away. "Do you love me?"

"Of course."

"Then what's the holdup?"

He tried to step away but she grabbed his arm. He looked down at her grasp, a sudden burn churning deep inside of him in a place he couldn't reach. "I don't know. I guess it's not something I ever thought we'd be discussing. I didn't think we needed it to be together."

She let go of his arm. "I didn't think I needed it either before . . . before I met you. You're special to me. No other man has ever made me feel this complete before. I guess . . . I guess I don't want to lose you."

He looked into her eyes, the depth of her love pulling him in and driving it home that he was a fool not to put a ring on her finger. Still, he couldn't silence the nagging burn. "Marriage is no guarantee. We both know that."

She stepped into him and rested her head in the hollow of his shoulder. She was the strongest woman he'd ever known and it always caught him by surprise when she showed that she had fears and insecurities; that, like everyone else, she had vulnerabilities.

He wrapped his arms around her and took in the scent of her perfume. Why couldn't he say yes?

The answer was nineteen years in the past and thousands of miles east.

Ɒ Ɒ

Bradley was standing at the massive kitchen island, a glass of orange juice in hand. He set it down on the granite countertop, his hand running against its smooth surface, not finding any of the chipped edges that were so prominent along the worn laminate countertop at his apartment. The more time he spent in Kate's condo, the more he realized the huge gap between their lifestyles.

When is the last time she's been in my apartment?

"Don't worry about it," Kate said, back from the washroom. She looked ready to take on the world for another day. "You obviously don't feel the same as I do."

"It's not that," he said in a voice full of regret. "I'm crazy about you."

"But?"

"There's no but," he said, his hand still running across the granite. "Look at this countertop."

Standing on the other side of the island, she crossed her arms. "What about it?"

"It's gorgeous."

She sighed. "Brad, really? And your point?"

"I make about sixty thousand a year. I live in a shabby apartment in a downtown area that's not the safest. You live along the waterfront in this luxurious condo. I know what these condos sell for."

"Again, what is your point?'"

He rubbed his goatee. The grey in it was starting to bother him. Why was he getting so much grey lately? He was only thirty-eight. Then again, Dad had been mostly bald by forty, so maybe grey wasn't so bad.

"I'm not with you because of your money. That's not who I am."

"I know," she said. "But it's never bothered you before that I have a slightly higher standard of living."

He raised an eyebrow. "Slightly?"

Her embarrassed yet slightly coy smile was framed by unchar-
acteristically blushing cheeks. "Touché."

They stared at each other, two people madly in love but being
held back by baggage that should have been tossed long ago. Was
he afraid that if he finally said yes, he'd be closing that door from
his past forever?

"Talk to me," Kate said. "You need time to think about it?
Then take it. I know I blindsided you a little . . . okay, a lot."

"I just don't quite get it. Why now?"

"I turned forty back in May."

"It was a great party."

She smiled. "It was."

"So?"

She reached for his hands and took a moment before she
looked at him. "I'm forty and I want to have a baby with you."

The look on his face was that of a man who'd been shot and
hadn't realized just yet that he was bleeding out.

ᘓ ᗭ

Bradley pulled his hand away like he'd just touched something
hot, and backed away. He looked at Kate as if she were a stranger.
"A baby?" he said, sounding as horrified as he felt. "You want to
have a *baby*? You? Do you know what that will do to your career?
Are you going to become a stay-at-home mom? I can't afford to
keep us in this condo, and my tiny apartment is going to get real
cramped real fast with three of us living in it. A baby! Really?"

He started to pace the length of the island like a dog needing
to go out for a pee. Or in his case, flee.

"Brad, stop!" She waited until he stood still and looked at her. "No, I'm not going to become a stay-at-home mom. I don't know the first thing about babies, I admit. But there are lots of great nannies out there. I'm not giving up my career, but I'm willing to make concessions. Having a baby with you is the purest sign that I know of to show how much we love each other. And I want our child to have married parents. That's important to me. My parents are still together after fifty-one years."

"And they already have ten grandkids thanks to your brother and sisters."

"But not from me and you," she said. "You know they're very fond of you."

They were great people who'd been good to him. Her entire family was what he thought families should be like: lots of laughter, innocent ribbing, and a ton of love and support. And they had accepted and welcomed him into their stronghold instantly, easing the estrangement from his own family.

But a baby?

At this point in their lives?

Boy, she was full of surprises today. First, she proposed to him, and now she wanted a baby. None of these things had ever crossed his mind before, and he was pretty sure they had never crossed her mind before either. The last thing he'd ever seen himself as was a married man and a father.

And then it hit him, the irony of his predicament. If—and that's a big if—things had worked out all those years ago, he'd probably be married now and odds were that he'd have at least one kid, probably more. Maybe what had happened was a blessing, because he wasn't convinced that he was cut out for either of those.

So, what exactly was he cut out for? What did he want?

What he was cut out for and what he wanted was what his life already was: Program Director of the most popular radio station in Vancouver, and sharing his life with the most wonderful woman he'd been lucky enough to find. That was enough for him.

Apparently, it was no longer enough for her.

"We can't have a baby for your parents' sake."

"That's not why I want one."

"This is coming out of nowhere. You can't return it after it's born, there is no thirty-day money back guarantee. A baby comes out screaming and turns everything upside down. Not unlike the Tasmanian Devil."

"You're comparing our child to the Tasmanian Devil?"

"Our child?" A worried frown wrinkled his forehead. "Are you already pregnant? Because if you—"

"Relax," she said with that tone she used at the office to take control of a situation just before it got out of hand. "Take a breath. I'm not pregnant. Give me some credit here. I'm not trying to trap you into a situation that would be based on a lie. I want you to be as committed to us as I am."

Bradley clenched his jaw and gritted his teeth, a habit he'd developed long ago to control his anger when all he'd wanted to do was take a baseball bat to David after another humiliating prank by his brother. Like then, he now felt trapped and helpless; he loses and someone else wins. He'd really believed that twenty-year-old loser Bradley had been left behind in Ottawa, that finding Kate had been meant to happen all along, that finding her had been the biggest win of his life, a win that big brother David couldn't ever take from him.

But now he feared that if he didn't go along with Kate's plan, he'd lose her. No David to blame. Just himself.

He was so damned tired of being on the losing end.

"I am—"

His cell phone began to play *Time Bomb*, a song that had resonated with him as a teenager and had seemed fitting as his ring tone—the perfect anthem to his chaotic and messy life. Definitely fitting for today.

"Who is it?"

Bradley looked at the number on the screen and his face folded into a questioning frown. "My sister."

TWO

Cassandra Knighton watched her husband David back his Audi Q5 out of the driveway—an extravagance he'd told her he deserved after busting his ass building a successful career for nearly twenty years—and waited until she could no longer see the taillights through the spaces in the branches of their neighbour's gigantic maple tree on the front lawn before she let the curtain fall back. It wasn't even six in the morning, the dawn sky just starting to pink, and her husband was already heading to the office.

Or somewhere else.

That was more likely. She wasn't stupid. She knew what was going on. What had been going on for the better part of their marriage.

Why would he need to go into the office, a real estate office, this bloody early? Some agents barely ever went into the office, doing most of their work from home using their cell phone and a laptop. Spending time with their family.

But not David. David was all about David.

She touched the necklace around her neck, a simple C-shaped golden pendant. Life had seemed so full of possibilities and hope when she had seen that future through the eyes of a naive teenager. David had intoxicated her with his charm, made a young girl believe that she was special because he had picked her over all the others. Everyone would have traded places with her to be David Knighton's girlfriend.

Cassandra doubted any of them would want her life now.

She wasn't oblivious. Oh, she pretended that everything was fine. She had mastered the art of pretend. But she noticed things, like how his once passionate kisses were now barely a peck on the cheek, and the way he could barely look her in the eye when he was lying, and of course, she'd become quite good at detecting the unmistakeable scent of another woman on him.

She let herself drop on the edge of the king-size bed they shared and although she could feel her eyes burning, she didn't dare shed a tear. Tears were for weak women. She had never been weak. Angry? Yes. Pissed off? Definitely. But not weak. Still, as she sat there contemplating the rest of her life—at some point she would need to decide what was best for her—she cursed herself for all the wrong decisions she'd made.

What a stupid fool she had been to fall for all of his lies and promises. She had been so sure that he was the better choice, that he would be good to her and for her, that he'd been sincere when he'd told her that his straying had been an expected young man's mistake that would never happen again. She had believed him when he'd vowed he would spend a lifetime making it up to her.

Lies, lies, *lies*.

Fool, fool, *fool*.

What would her life have been like if she had followed not just her heart, but her gut? And of course, by the time she'd found out what she would be forced to keep a secret forever, it had been just too late to change anything.

As she'd heard her mother say time and time again, *I made my bed and I must sleep in it no matter what.* Cassandra had never understood what her mother was talking about, until her father had walked out on them the day before her tenth birthday. On that day, she had understood that her dad wasn't a nice man. Neither of them had really been sorry to see him go. He had been a selfish man who'd gambled away their money—what little he hadn't spent on liquor and other women.

How ironic that she had fallen into the same trap.

Ironically sad.

If only she could go back to the summer of 1999. Would she really change anything, take that chance?

Cassandra noticed that the left side of the bed hadn't been slept in. He'd probably slept on the couch again in the room he used as a den, but since she had gone to bed long before he'd come home, she had no idea what time that might have been. Long gone were the days she stayed up for him, waiting so they could reconnect, both eager and hungry for physical release.

Maybe that had been a lie too, or she'd simply been a convenience. Either way, she'd been used.

Cassandra stood and walked to the ensuite that was probably twice the size of their old apartment, and brushed her teeth. She could still taste last night's bottle of wine pasted to the back of her mouth.

At least his money was good for something.

But she hated that it had become her crutch, her way of burying the grief and regret that consumed her. That's what falling in love with the wrong man had done to her. She had once been an independent and determined young woman full of energy and dreams, but as she wiped her mouth with the back of her hand after spitting in the sink, she didn't like the heartbroken and shattered stranger who stared back at her from the mirror.

Cʒ ʒⱳ

Cassandra Blackburn was seventeen, a senior, when she hooked up with David Knighton at a party. It was a bit of a surprise, considering all the years she'd been hanging out with his brother Bradley, and not once had David showed any interest in her until that night.

Everyone had gone to this party to celebrate the Forest Creek Cavaliers winning the Carleton-Goulbourn Hockey League finals in four straight games over the Carleton High Leafs. David, for the fourth straight year, was named MVP on the strength of his dominating performance: twelve goals and nine assists.

All the girls at Forest Creek High, from freshman to OAC— the Ontario Academic Credit formerly called Grade 13— dreamed of being his girlfriend. He was tall, gorgeous, had a smile to melt hearts and the lines to hook them, which had landed him a string of girlfriends during his high school years. Some lasted a month or two, others a day, but that was enough to give these girls bragging rights.

Cassandra felt sorry for these poor souls, especially knowing how David really was when there was no audience. Bradley had spilled the goods on his brother as often as he could, so much so that she'd once had to tell him that David didn't interest her in any way so he could stop worrying about her.

And here she was at this party unable to resist David Knighton's dimpled smile and charismatic charm.

What an embarrassment.

But David didn't seem to be the jerk Bradley had painted him as. In fact, he was attentive, witty, and truth be told—and she hated herself for thinking that—much better-looking. It wasn't just the hair colour and eyes that were totally different; there were features David had that were just simply more refined, almost feminine, yet he was the one bashing guys into the boards, while Bradley looked more rugged, was quiet and didn't care for the attention, and preferred to read books and work on his studies.

The two brothers couldn't be more different.

Bradley was going to kill her. They'd been friends since she and her mom moved to Forest Creek after her father left, and as she was sitting on the edge of the hearth beside David, who'd taken her hand into his—how warm and soft his hands felt—all she could think was how in the world she was going to convince Bradley to forgive her.

She was going to have to beg big time.

The smart thing to do would be to pull her hand away and tell David that she was flattered, but that she wasn't interested in being part of his long string of girlfriends. But those eyes . . . nothing really as striking as Bradley's blue eyes, just plain hazel eyes, but the depth and intensity they radiated, the pull she felt, like no matter how badly she wanted to go, she just couldn't look away.

Maybe that was how those others girls had all felt? Cassandra had heard all the rumours of how dreamy David was, and she was starting to believe it.

What was it that made Bradley dislike his brother so much?

She would have to ask—

The thought was interrupted by David leaning into her and meeting her lips with his, a soft, gentle pressing of flesh on flesh that made her want more.

A lot more.

Which made her face feel warm, and her mind quickly filled with shame. Bradley was going to be so mad.

"Stay here," David said.

Cassandra looked around and noticed that everyone was looking at her. This would be the perfect time to disappear. Nothing good could come from this. Whatever this was. If Bradley had come tonight, she wouldn't be sitting here getting seduced by David. She could simply get up and leave.

So much of her wanted to stay.

"Here," David said and handed her a beer.

She frowned. "Kind of underaged."

David laughed softly. "You're legal in Québec."

"Not until July twenty-fourth," she said. "And this is Ontario."

"Technicalities," he said. "Cheers!"

He tapped his bottle against hers and she raised the bottle to her mouth and had her first taste of beer. A grimace chased the bitterness across her face.

"You'll get used to it," he said.

"Probably not."

"Feisty," he said. "I like that."

She didn't know what to say so she took another swallow of beer. The bitterness didn't seem to crunch her face as much.

"Want to get out of here?" he said.

She should have said no.

CB ଃ

There was no point trying to fall back to sleep. Her mind was reeling, full of anxiety and fury, and the best remedy for that kind of turmoil was a strong cup of coffee and a generous shot of Baileys. Oh, she had come a long way from never having had a drink before that end-of-season hockey party; that young and naïve girl was just a memory that seemed more fictitious than real.

Cassandra headed down the stairs toward the kitchen at the back of their three-thousand-square-foot home—much too big for just the three of them—and made a pot of coffee. As she waited standing in front of the garden doors that looked out into the vast back yard lined by a forest at the very far end, she recalled a conversation with her mother the morning of her wedding.

"You sure you don't want to wait?"

"A little late for that."

"You look beautiful."

"Thanks, Mom." A pause. "Am I making a mistake?"

"We all make mistakes, honey."

In the mirror, Cassandra shot a look at her mother, eyes rounded and full of desperation.

"Not exactly a vote of confidence."

"I'm sorry."

"David isn't Dad."

"Didn't say he was."

"You don't like him?"

"I'm not the one marrying him."

"But?"

Her mother took her time to find her words. "I married too young. I was pregnant, and back in those days, even in the carefree 1970s, girls like me didn't have many options. So I married your father. I knew in my heart that I didn't love him, that a careless night of too many drinks and too much smoking up had landed me in the trouble I was in, but I also knew that I didn't want to give you up. Marrying your father was the compromise that I made so that I could keep you."

Tears stung Cassandra's eyes.

"Don't you go wrecking your makeup now, Cassie girl. You put those tears right back where they belong. I never shed a tear for my choice, and neither will you. I don't have much in my life, but I got you and you've always been more than I needed. Maybe your David will be everything your father wasn't."

"And if he's not?"

Her mother put a hand on her belly. "She'll be all you need."

"She?"

"I have a feeling."

Cassandra pulled a mug from the cupboard and filled it with coffee. She dropped about an ounce of Baileys into it and took a long sip. "Looks like we both failed at choosing the right man," she said to the empty room and took another sip. "Oh Mom, what should I do now? Angel is almost all grown up. She starts college Tuesday and soon she'll be moving out and I'll have nothing but this empty house and a cheating husband."

She moved back to the garden doors and saw a fading reflection of herself as the sun was slowly rising, a mirror of her faded life. At times like these, her mother's absence dug deeply into her core. They hadn't always gotten along, especially when her mom had pushed and pushed and pushed for her to work harder, get better grades, be the best at all the sports, as if somehow that could set her free, but even in those moments of friction, they'd had a special bond, them against the world.

You can be anyone you want to be, honey. Be better than me. Be someone.

Cassandra snorted.

Some someone I am. I'm Mrs. David Knighton, housewife, alcoholic, and all-round useless human being.

Except when it came to Angel.

For her daughter, she had settled for a life full of regrets.

CB EO

Cassandra always loved September, especially the way the morning freshness whispered promises of renewed hope, a chance to revisit the shortcomings of the last two months while also keeping the upcoming cold dread of winter as distant as possible. Days were still long and warm, even hot at times, and the evenings were perfect for that favourite sweater that hadn't been worn since the spring. Fall had a way of making all of life's follies fade away.

The summer of 1999 had been like that: full of turmoil, lies, and promises colliding and severing hearts. What she had yearned for and what her common sense had told her were as opposite as winter and summer, and looking back, she knew she had thrown away a hint of love as if it were a disposable inconvenience. She had not trusted her intuition, instead believing that it couldn't last, wasn't real, that it was a mistake. Going back to David had been the only right thing to do.

But then she had convinced herself that no, she wasn't going back to him, that he didn't deserve her after all. He'd cheated on her one too many times.

But David, master persuader, knew how to say the right things.

Cassandra refilled her coffee mug, eyeballed about an ounce of Baileys, and went out back. She stood on the two-tier composite deck that had cost more than Angel's entire college tuition was going to be, and walked towards the glass railing. She rested her forearms against the top, stared at the inground pool—she sighed at the thought of needing to close it soon, once the weather turned too cool to enjoy a dip—and breathed in the scent of Labour Day weekend.

The doorway to autumn.

Just like she remembered, the air smelled sweet and promising, but also deceitful. What waited after autumn were months of bitter cold, long dark days, and never-ending loneliness.

Cassandra raised the cup to her mouth and took a sip of coffee. She let out a sad breath. If only she had read her mother better on her wedding day, truly listened to what she was telling her.

You didn't really want to hear it.

That was true. It was too late to change her mind. Almost two hundred people had come to see her, *her*, walk down that aisle and marry whom everyone thought was the love of her life.

Even at the cost of her friendship with Bradley, she had fallen in love with David at that party. And, for a while, they were *the* couple. For most of her OAC year, their relationship was solid.

But then rumours started to circulate as summer of '99 approached.

Josée Dubois.

Cassandra and Josée had been number one and two on the volleyball team since their sophomore year, and when her friendship with Bradley cooled, Cassandra began hanging out more and more with Josée.

Her best friend.

How could Josée have done that to her? She simply hadn't been paying attention, the way Josée seemed to laugh too hard and too long when David was around, the way Josée never took her eyes off of him, the way she was always asking Cassandra how her dates went. She caught none of that because Cassandra was head over heels in love with David Knighton then and nothing could have changed that. Not even when he came grovelling back to her and promised that his thing with Josée had been a mistake, that he would never cheat on her ever again because he loved her, and he couldn't bear to lose her.

So, she took him back for the first time just before the end of her OAC year. But then a month later on her birthday, he was a no show. How she wished now that she could have seen into her future! What a foolish and gullible girl she had been. As smart as her mom had told her she was—as far as academics went—she hadn't been that smart with her heart. Guys like David Knighton weren't the guys you married.

Cassandra touched the pendant around her neck again. She hadn't worn it in years, had sort of forgotten it until she'd gone looking into her old jewelry box two weeks ago, the one that was lodged at the back of a shelf in the walk-in closet. It had just caught her attention as she was looking for something to wear. Her heart had seemed to shrink even more when she first saw it, but then, as if on autopilot, she'd put it around her neck and hadn't taken it off since. Angel had noticed and asked her if it was new.

"No," she'd said. "I just haven't worn it in a long time."

Cassandra took a big sip of coffee and felt a warm trail of Baileys slide down her throat. Sad that this was the highlight of her day; even sadder that she hadn't done anything about it for years. Her excuse had always been Angel: her daughter needing her, her daughter needing her father, her daughter needing the illusory perfect family that Cassandra had fabricated. She felt horrible for being so deceitful, but she'd convinced herself long ago that living the lie was better than the pain the truth would bring.

Lately, though, she wondered whether that had been the right decision. She figured if she was still debating it today, that it must mean it had been wrong. There was no *must*. She knew, not just in her heart but in her soul, that she had messed up her life, and probably Angel's too.

A robin landed about four feet from her on the railing, chirped away without a care in the world, and took off. Cassandra followed it until it veered sharply and flew over the house.

She was still young enough to salvage the years that lay ahead without compromising the lie. She could divorce David. God knew he had committed enough adultery to warrant her demands. Angel wasn't a baby anymore, and yes, she would be hurt to see her parents split up, but Cassandra had lived long enough for her daughter. Wasn't she allowed a little happiness?

CR ♌

Angel was born four weeks premature and those first few days when Cassandra was still at the hospital, she walked the corridor to a shine, pacing back and forth, unable to care for her daughter as she was kept in the NICU. Nurses kept telling her that Baby Knighton was all right, that she could go back to her room, but she simply couldn't. All Cassandra could do was stare at her tiny, beautiful, and fragile baby and cry until she was too exhausted to shed another tear, and then somehow, from the depth of her grief, she'd find more tears. It was during that time that she finally found the right name for her precious little girl.

Angel.

Angel Doris Knighton.

Doris was Cassandra's mom's name. She had died of lung cancer just two weeks before Angel's early arrival, the hardest day of Cassandra's life. When her mom had finally told her after the wedding that she was dying, Cassandra had been so angry that her mother had hidden her sickness for so long. In her defense, Doris had told Cassandra that she hadn't wanted to put undue stress on her as she was already planning a wedding and handling a pregnancy.

The day her mom died was emotionally draining and everyone feared that the cramps Cassandra felt were early labour, which wouldn't be good, but it turned out it wasn't labour.

Just a broken heart.

She spent the week following her mom's burial in bed, consumed by loneliness. Her mom, her only living blood relative, was now gone. How was she going to go on without her? Who would be there to help her with the baby? She wasn't even twenty yet. She knew nothing about taking care of a baby. David knew even less. How were they going to raise a baby? Everything was happening too fast.

Her life was out of control.

Then one morning, on her way to the bathroom, her water broke. David had already left for work and her mom was gone and her new mother-in-law lived way out in Forest Creek, so she'd dialled 911. All she could think on the way to the hospital in the back of the ambulance was that she couldn't lose her baby, she couldn't lose her baby, she couldn't lose her baby.

Angel had looked porcelain-breakable in her tiny incubation pod. That's what it had looked like to Cassandra—a pod keeping her baby safe. And alive.

Her daughter had lived the first four weeks of her life in a pod before she was allowed to take her home. Cassandra would spend all of her days at the hospital while David attended the real estate courses he'd enrolled in through the Ontario Real Estate Association, telling Cassandra that their future depended on him becoming a successful real estate agent. He would come visit afterward, and in those precious moments David held Angel, Cassandra had seen a boy turn into not just a man, but a father.

It had given her hope that her husband wouldn't be like her father.

 beginnin

It took several weeks before Angel finally started to gain weight, and several months before she slept through the night. The doctor had explained to Cassandra that she shouldn't compare Angel to other babies of the same age.

"Angel was born four weeks early," the doctor had said. "When she's sixteen weeks, compare her to babies who are twelve weeks."

"Forever?" Cassandra said.

"Just for the first couple of years," the doctor said. "But stay alert to any sort of slow development."

The conversation confused her at first but then it finally made sense to her after about three months. She told herself that those first four weeks in the pod were as if Angel had been in the womb, so they didn't count toward her normal development. But even though Angel did seem to be doing fine, Cassandra had become somewhat afraid to leave her daughter alone. One of the things she had kept of her mother's was this really old rocking chair that might have belonged to her grandmother, which Cassandra placed just beside Angel's crib. It wasn't great for sleeping in, but it gave her peace of mind.

Just in case.

She'd heard of SIDS, and because Angel was so tiny, well, her mind wandered off like that of any overprotective new mother. But Angel was a fighter and every day she got stronger and Cassandra got more and more attached, and soon she understood why her mother had settled for a marriage without love. The love of a child could fill any void.

Another thing Cassandra noticed those first few weeks was that Angel wasn't taking to David, but he kept trying. The love in his eyes for Angel was undeniable. But it still left him frustrated.

She'd told him it was probably because Angel didn't see him enough, that it might take some time for their bond to take. Eventually, it did, and they were a happy family.

For a short while.

Cassandra finished her coffee and headed back into the house. Angel was eighteen now, just beginning the first year of culinary studies at Algonquin College—she really wanted to partner with her aunt Emily and grandmother Irene to run the family bakery and maybe bring it into the twenty-first century—and Cassandra knew Angel couldn't be her excuse for staying with David anymore.

Her life had been put on hold for too long.

THREE

Angel dragged her butt out of bed after hitting snooze the third time. Why she had agreed to take the early Friday morning shift eluded her as she tried to rub sleep from her eyes on the way to the bathroom.

Her dad had made her get a job for the summer. He'd said she needed to learn the value of making her own money, that way she wouldn't spend it frivolously.

Like his big fancy new car wasn't frivolous.

Life at home reminded her of a UFC fight when the combatants circle each other first, to get a feel for when to strike. She knew her parents didn't love each other—she'd have to really be deaf, dumb and blind not to notice—and lately, her mom looked like she was ready to jump off the ledge. Angel wasn't exactly sure that there was any one thing that gave her that impression, just that her mom appeared drained and defeated.

And she had no idea if there was anything she could do. She and her mom were close, but talking to her mom about her marriage felt like stepping over a line she wasn't sure kids were allowed to cross. It's not like she could just go *hey mom, how's your love life these days?*

Besides, she sort of knew. Her dad was gone all day and her mom was home alone all day. And when her dad was home, he was usually locked up in his den while she and her mom whispered so as not to be heard, like they were planning some great conspiracy against him.

They really weren't. It was more basic than that. Her dad had become a sort of stranger to them, at least to her, and naturally, people typically try to keep their personal business from a prying stranger's ears.

Sad, really.

On the surface, he appeared to be a great guy. He could talk the paint off the wall, and on many occasions, Angel had noticed that people were actually captivated by what he was saying, all along knowing real well that he was just bullshitting. That's what really burned a hole in Angel: that he could be so fake while seeming so sincere.

So she called him out on it as often as she could.

Of course, she hadn't been that bold when she was younger, mostly because she hadn't started to see her dad as he truly was until about two years ago. Being phony to others she could let go, but when he put her mother down or made her feel like she didn't matter, Angel no longer put up with that.

Which of course was hard because he was her dad and she did love him even if he was being an asshole.

He hadn't always been that way. When she was four, he took her and her mom on a ski trip to Mont-Tremblant, about two hours from Ottawa. She had never skied before and was petrified, and he'd been by her side the whole day while her mom went up and down the big hills like it was the easiest thing in the world to do. She'd been envious of her mom being so good, but also so grateful that her dad stayed on the little hill with her and did his best to teach her.

Later, they'd gone over to the tobogganing hill and she'd had a blast with her dad while her mom had relaxed in a hot tub. Best weekend ever. They had seemed so happy, or at least it's what she remembered. Thinking back, even then her parents hadn't spent a lot of time together. She was always with one or the other, never both, as if they couldn't be in the same space at the same time.

Four-year-olds didn't notice such things, but eighteen-year-olds did. It wasn't fair that she needed to take sides, that her entire existence was the result of two people whose love had seemingly died long ago, if it had ever existed at all. Lately, she was really pissed off at her dad because of the way home life was, and it bugged her because that four-year-old girl still remembered how great he could be.

Or had he been faking that too?

She wouldn't put it past him. She guessed when his business was selling people their dream home, even when it was a piece of crap, he'd learned to embellish things, to make them look better—much better—than they were. And maybe along the way he'd become so used at making stuff up that he could no longer tell truth from lie.

She wasn't a kid anymore, and she understood that people did fall out of love, but it sucked when it happened to your parents.

Angel stepped into the shower and stood under the hot water until she felt like her worries had been peeled off her skin from the heat and had been sucked down the drain and out of her life for good.

⊗ ∞

Angel used the towel to clear a circle on the steamed mirror so she could see herself while brushing her long dark auburn hair, just like Grandma Irene. Her grandmother's hair wasn't naturally auburn anymore, but Angel had seen pictures of when her grandma was younger. Grandma Irene had pictures everywhere in her house, pictures of her dad and Aunt Emily and Uncle Bradley when they were younger. She loved spending time with her grandparents and working at the bakery, but her dad hadn't wanted her to work there, saying that working with family wouldn't give her the same experience and appreciation as working for a complete stranger.

Well, that was going to change soon because she wasn't studying culinary arts not to work with her aunt and grandmother. She'd already made plans that she would join them when she graduated and they were all for it. Her plan was to use her education to bring something new to the bakery, hopefully make it even better than it was.

"Honey," her mom said from the other side of the bathroom door, "want me to make you breakfast?"

Angel looked in the mirror and wasn't entirely pleased with the round-faced girl staring back. Both her parents were tall, so she was too, but she was soft. She didn't care for sports and preferred a good book to television. Of course, hours on Snapchat could entertain her as well.

"I'll just have some fruit."

"You're going to be on your feet for the next six hours," her mom said. "Fruit isn't going to cut it. I'll make some pancakes."

No sense arguing. Pancakes sounded a lot better than a stupid banana or apple, and she knew that she'd be fighting a headache halfway through her shift if she didn't eat something of substance.

Pancakes are nutritious, right?

She could throw some strawberry jam on them instead of syrup. That could count as a serving of fruit. *Right?* One down and a bunch more to go. Blah! She hated all the stupid advice as to what was considered eating well. Her idea of eating well was one of Aunt Emily's Double Devil Chocolate Walnut Brownies. Good God, that was like a piece of heaven.

Maybe she'd bring a yogurt for lunch and some carrot and celery sticks. *Yummy!*

Not.

From the corner of her eye she saw the white scale lying on the white tiled floor like a camouflaged enemy. She turned her back, wrapped the towel around herself, and went back to her room to get dressed. She worked at a second-hand thrift store so a lot of her own clothes came from there. The manager encouraged the staff to buy and wear clothes from the store when they worked, serving both as free advertising and proof that retro clothes were in fashion.

Plus, it bugged her dad that she chose to wear clothes that had been worn by other people. He'd said that it didn't make the best impression and Dad was all about best impressions.

"You know," he'd said just last Monday afternoon as she was getting ready for her evening shift, "I'm pretty sure I don't have a son, so why do you dress like one?"

She'd been wearing ripped black jeans, a grey tank top and a plaid long-sleeve shirt. And tan-coloured Timberlands.

"It's bloody hot outside. You're going to fry."

"It's my pan, Dad."

He'd mumbled something incomprehensible as he eyed his phone while heading for the front door.

"Have a great evening," Angel had shouted sarcastically as the front door closed. "Thanks. I'll have a great one too." Then she heard the sound of his new Audi Q5 gunning up the street like the devil was chasing him.

"Does he even care?" she'd asked her mom, whose only response had been a slow, forlorn shrug.

Today, she was dressed in black leggings and an oversized sweater. The store was always cool so she knew she wouldn't be overdressed, and since they had a bunch of fall clothes that had come in over the summer months and this being Labour Day weekend, they expected to be busy with back-to-school kids coming in to grab whatever fancied them.

That's why she was going in early. Karen, the manager, had scheduled extra staff today because she expected a very busy day.

Angel headed down to the kitchen for breakfast. Her mom had poured her a cup of coffee—she wasn't sure if she liked it yet but she kept drinking it every morning in an attempt to convince herself that she did—and had put out the strawberry jam as if she'd read Angel's mind.

"They look good."

She devoured two pancakes and eyed a third one, but she caught sight of her mom sitting across from her staring away, lost in her own world. She looked so sad, like someone had just run over her cat.

If they'd had a cat.

Dad didn't like cats. Didn't like dogs. Didn't like anything that needed attention and care. You didn't become successful in life if you couldn't concentrate on what mattered. Limit the distractions, work hard, succeed.

Guess they were a distraction.

"Mom, you okay?"

Her mom bit at her lower lip, the way her mom did when she was about to lie. Angel couldn't remember exactly when she'd come to that conclusion, but she'd figured it out a while ago.

"I'm fine, sweetie."

Yeah, and I'm Nicole Kidman. She had fallen in love with Nicole Kidman's acting in the HBO series Big Little Lies, loved the way she finally killed her sadistic and abusive husband (well it wasn't exactly Nicole's character who pushed him down the stairs, but Angel changed that part to suit her admiration). Angel's father wasn't *that* horrible of a man, but he definitely fell way short of being a great husband and father.

Angel watched her mom and it pained her to see this beautiful woman who had such a unique laugh—barely heard these days—fade away like she was, like her life didn't matter, her happiness didn't matter, her pain that she tried to hide so badly didn't matter.

Of course it mattered. It mattered to Angel, and it should matter to her dad, but he was just too damn self-absorbed to notice. Angel wanted so much to ask her mom why she had stayed married to her dad all these years, but she knew why.

Because of me.

Because of her, her mom lived in the shadow of her dad, eclipsed by his ego and his drive to succeed. How much more could the man succeed? Huge house, new fancy Audi, and her mom drove a BMW that he'd bought last Christmas not because she'd wanted it, but because her dad hadn't wanted her mom to drive in that old beat-up minivan that she'd had ever since Angel was born. After all, her dad was all about making good impressions and a rusty 2000 Chrysler Caravan didn't exactly impress anyone.

Angel had loved that minivan. Her mom would pick up four of her friends and drive them all to dance lessons. That had been her favourite activity when she was younger. She'd taken ballet, jazz, and hip hop, the latter being the one she preferred and excelled at. She even did competitive dance until she was fourteen, and then one day, that was it, she'd had enough. Dance no longer held any interest for her. Looking back, she felt pretty certain that her mom had pulled further into herself when she no longer needed to drive Angel everywhere. Those activities had been as much an escape for her mom as they had been a social outing for Angel.

She suddenly shouldered a moment of guilt as she realized that although it was easy to blame her dad for her mom's misery, maybe she was a bit to blame too. Her narrow-minded teenage selfishness had played a part in contributing to her mom's isolation.

"Maybe you should get a job."

Her mom took a long sip from her cup. "I never went past high school. I was supposed to go to college that September, but you had different plans for me."

"Sorry," Angel said. It wasn't the first time she'd apologized for something she'd had absolutely no way of preventing from happening.

Her mom looked at her and she could tell she had no regrets. "I love you. Don't you ever think otherwise."

"I know," Angel said. "But I keep wondering if you and Dad would have gotten married anyway if it weren't for me, and maybe you'd be happier—"

"Stop right there," Cassandra said and put her cup on the counter. "I loved your Dad and you are the result of that love."

"Past tense, Mom."

Cassandra lowered her eyes.

"You don't need to stay together for me," she said. "Not anymore. You could go back to school. It's not like we can't afford it. Go study something. Get out. Meet people. Live."

Cassandra picked up her cup in both hands and looked toward the garden doors. "I'm too old."

"Seriously, Mom," she said. "You're not even forty yet and you know forty is the new thirty."

A tired smile shadowed Cassandra's lips. "I wouldn't know what to study. I have no idea what I'd be good at."

"And that's why they have school councillors."

"Why the sudden concern?"

Angel took a sip of coffee and grimaced. Maybe she should put sugar in it like most people did, but then they're not really drinking coffee. She was either going to learn to love it black, or give it up.

"I'm starting college Tuesday. In a couple years, I'll probably move out, so I won't be here anymore and you need to do something. Being in this house all day long isn't good for you."

"You going to major in psychology?"

Angel gave her a look. "You know what I'm studying."

"Well, in case you end up hating culinary arts, maybe that could be your backup plan. You might just be really good at it."

"Or maybe you," she said. "I don't want you to waste the rest of your life."

"Who's sounding like a parent now?" Cassandra said. "I've been nothing for so long—"

"You're not nothing!" Angel nearly screamed. "Don't *ever* say you're nothing. You've been my mom for eighteen years and have been incredible at it. Maybe you could learn early childhood development and work in a daycare."

"Oh, I don't think so," her mom said in a voice that sounded so defeated. "I barely made it through alive with you." Again, that sad smile.

"Kind of being overly dramatic," Angel said. "As far as I can tell, I'm a fairly straight-headed young woman."

Her mom reached across the island and patted her hand lovingly. "You are a lovely young woman and you deserve most of the credit. I simply steered you in the right direction."

"Well, that's more than Dad did."

Her mom pulled back and seemed to be nodding in agreement, but it was so subtle that Angel wasn't entirely sure. She often wished her mom would just lose it, let her anger explode.

Her parents' arguments when she was young had been epic, like two combatants literally fighting to the death, but those fights were gone now. As much as she'd hated the shouting, the accusations, the four-letter words, their silence now was somehow worse. It meant they didn't care anymore, that whatever had become of them was a *fait accompli* and there was no reason to fight anymore.

The corpse of their marriage haunted their lives, but neither one was quite ready to bury it. Dad was too proud to admit failure, and Mom was too tired to dig the hole.

"I'm going to get ready for work," Angel said and left her mom alone in the kitchen.

ೞ ೱ

Angel sat at the small table in her room that she used as a makeup station, and put on a little foundation to hide her blemishes—lately she seemed to be getting more of them than normal and it was really annoying her because she had to lay on the foundation thicker than she liked—and then continued by lining her eyes with a thin black pencil before finishing with her mascara. She used to really overdo the black—her black phase, her friend Lilly had called it—but over the past summer, she had slowly cut back on the black. Besides, she was going to work, not a party, so she didn't want to look too goth.

Her black combat boots had been replaced by tan Timberlands, her black shirts by plaid button-down shirts, her black hair back to its natural auburn. Her mom had never given her a hard time about how she dressed or how her makeup looked, but her dad had disapproved, not in words, but in the shake of his head and the annoyance in his eyes.

So she had upped the black as much as she could just so she could see the judgemental expression on his face. If he'd said something to her, had had some kind of interaction with her instead of that standoffish glare of dislike, then maybe she would have gone through her black period much quicker. Or maybe he'd known that she would eventually outgrow it but wanted to make sure she knew that he didn't approve every chance he got.

All that did was make her feel like she was doing something horrible when all she was doing was expressing how she felt. Good God! It's not like living in this house had been a picnic at the end of a rainbow.

Lilly wasn't a friend from school, but from work. She was a tiny oriental girl who made Angel laugh so hard that her sides would ache, especially when she pretended not to speak English very well, which wasn't the case since she'd been born in Ottawa. If you closed your eyes when she spoke, you'd never be able to tell she was Chinese.

They weren't always scheduled together but today they were, so Angel knew it was going to be a good day. Being the last Friday before school started, the place was going to be a zoo, so having Lilly there—making faces behind a difficult customer, or talking in her broken English to a girl their age who felt she was better than them even though she was the one shopping at a second-hand store—would make the day fly.

And then they were going to a party tonight, which she looked forward to.

"You look so grown up," her mom said, standing in the bedroom doorway. "And beautiful."

"I'm fat."

"Oh, honey, you are so not." Her mom moved into her room and stood behind her. "Any boy would be lucky to have you as a girlfriend."

"Not really interested," Angel said. "All the guys at my school are a bunch of morons."

Her mom kissed the top of her head, like she'd been doing since she was little. "Plenty of time, anyway. No need to rush into it like I did."

Angel didn't say anything.

"You driving me?" she said. "Or do I get to drive the Beamer today?"

"You need to get your G2 first," her mom said. "Then we'll see."

"Maybe Dad will get *me* one," she said with a teasing grin. "To keep up with the Joneses."

Her mom's entire face actually smiled. "You little troublemaker. I'll go get dressed. I need to get groceries anyway."

೮೩ ೮೦

They rode in silence most of the drive, which was about seven minutes from their driveway to the front of the store. Angel put her hand on the door handle but turned to her mom instead of getting out.

"Are we going to Grandma and Grandpa's for Thanksgiving?"

"Of course," her mom said. "Grandma is all about tradition. Why? Don't you want to go?"

Angel was quiet for a moment.

"Could I bring Lilly?" she said. "I'm the only one my age there and it gets a bit boring sometimes."

"I don't see why not."

"Cool," she said and let go of the handle. She sat, quiet and rubbing her hands. "Mom, will Uncle Brad ever come back to visit? I've never even met him."

Her mom was pensive for a long time, and Angel wasn't quite sure, but it seemed that her mom had gotten even sadder.

"It would take something catastrophic for him to come back, I think."

"What happened?" Angel said—a question she'd asked a few times in the past, but which had never been truthfully answered. "Why did he leave?"

"Why the interest all of a sudden?"

"We're going to Grandma and Grandpa's," she said matter-of-factly. "They've got pictures of him all over the walls. That's all I know of him. No one ever talks about him. Did he, like, kill someone?"

Her mom actually broke a tiny fragile smile that was full of pain. "No honey, nothing that sinister."

"Then what?"

With a big and heavy sigh her mom said, "I broke his heart."

FOUR

Emily Knighton always showed up at the bakery she operated with her mom at four in the morning. There was a time when her mom would have already been at the shop, but over the past year, she'd listened to Emily and didn't show up until around seven.

Mostly, it was because they couldn't leave Dad alone anymore. His behaviour was worsening quickly and he couldn't be trusted not to burn the house down or get lost if they let him out of their sight and he went wandering.

Henry Knighton had been diagnosed with Alzheimer about fifteen months ago and at first, he'd just seemed forgetful, like losing his keys, or being unable to remember the names of people or things, but over the last three months, he'd really deteriorated and he now hallucinated frequently and could barely take care of himself.

Emily had broached the subject of putting Dad in a home but Mom wouldn't hear of it.

So, for now, Emily worked solo from four to about seven, when Mom crossed the road and Dad tagged along. They had cleared up a room in the back, set up a television, and installed a child's safety gate in the doorway so that it kept him confined. Unless he was having a moment of clarity, he couldn't figure out how to open the gate or had yet to realize that he could simply step over it. Emily and her mom were thankful, but it was also very sad.

Dad had been an electrician in his day and Mom had run the bakery since she was about fifteen, when Grandma Alice had needed help because her arthritis had gotten pretty bad at the young age of forty-four, and because Aunt Margaret, who was older than Emily's mom by five years, wasn't cut out for the bakery—she was right into the hippie movement that had been taking over the 1960s with their love, peace, and drugs—so Mom would get up early before school to put in a solid three hours before she went to class, and then again after school she'd come in and work another two hours before going home to do her homework. The bakery had been in the family for a hundred years now, since Emily's great-grandmother Sarah MacDonald had opened it in 1918, at the young age of twenty-three.

Great-Grandma Sarah had died in 1995, three weeks after she had turned one hundred and a month before Emily would turn thirteen. Emily was now thirty-five, the youngest of the Knighton kids, unmarried, and with no prospect in sight. It wasn't from a lack of dating, nor because she was unattractive or overweight. Quite the opposite. She was tall, maybe a little too thin, and had the most stunning piercing ocean blue eyes anyone had ever seen. The problem was her standards. No one she had dated could ever meet them.

Emily Knighton was a modern-day spinster.

And she was the only sibling Bradley talked to. Well, they hadn't actually spoken on the phone in a long time; most of their conversations occurred via text, email, or Facebook. She knew he was doing well, was happy with his job, and had a girlfriend that he loved—she'd told him she was happy for him, maybe a bit envious, but glad that he'd found someone.

Finally.

Even if he had never told her how he'd felt about Cassandra when they were growing up, she had known, maybe even before he'd realized it, that he loved her.

Cʒ ৪১

Henry Knighton was a seventy-one-year-old behemoth of a man, standing just shy of 6'5" and weighing a rock-solid two-thirty, and with the mind of a forgetful ten-year-old, he was quite a handful.

Back before the disease started gnawing away at his intellect, he'd been a good-natured blue-collar type of man who had believed in working hard and playing hard. Pushing the kids to be their best had been ingrained in him since he was a child and his father, who had grown up during the Great Depression of the 1930s, had drilled into him that only the strongest survived, so don't ever feel sorry for yourself. Instead, work your butt off.

Henry had finished high school at the age of seventeen and had immediately begun his apprenticeship as an electrician. A good, sensible trade, and one that always seemed to be in demand no matter how the economy was going, but definitely better during construction booms.

So today, when he got up and went tearing through the house to find his hard hat and tool box, frustration quickly set in when he couldn't find them. And like a six-year-old not getting his way, he was currently standing in the middle of the low-ceilinged basement—for a man of his stature, seven-foot ceilings weren't exactly giving him a lot of head space—with his arms crossed against his barrel chest, a scowl on his face hot enough to burn the house down, stomping his feet, and making growling noises not particularly flattering for a man of his age.

"Irene," he shouted. "Where'd you hide my hard hat and tool box? George will be here any minute to pick me up and I won't be ready." He waited a beat for a response. "Irene!"

And that's when he saw them again, the two black young men standing in the far corner of the basement holding his hard hat and tool box, egging him on to come and get them. He'd seen them just yesterday trying to steal his money, so now he was hiding it all over the house. He couldn't remember their names, but he thought George might since they were the first two black electricians the company had hired. Henry had no problem with that—a man had a right to take care of his family—but what he couldn't understand was why they were in his house stealing his things.

That he had a problem with.

He called out to his wife one more time, and, getting no answers, he went back up the basement stairs to find her. If anyone knew why these guys were here, she would.

CB EO

Emily and Bradley had always been close, their bond having formed quickly as a way to cope with having to live in the overbearing and obnoxious shadow of David, who demanded everyone's attention when he entered a room. Even as kids, if David wasn't the centre of attention, he'd do whatever it took for everyone to notice him. One time, when he was eight, David had set the back yard on fire—dry autumn leaves had covered the entire yard and he'd thought it would be a good idea to light them up—because everyone had brought presents for Emily's fifth birthday party and no one had brought him any gifts.

Bradley, on the other hand, had made Emily a card showing the two of them riding their bikes down the street like they liked to do—always under the watchful eye of their mother—with David obviously missing from the card. Bradley had also written that she was the most wonderful sister in the whole wide world and that he loved her very very very much.

Nothing from David.

Which hadn't been unusual in those days. That tension with David had pushed Bradley and Emily to stick together, and when Bradley had moved away, it had left a void in her life. If it hadn't been for her managing the bakery with their mom, she might have moved away long ago too, but if she were honest, she knew she was a homebody and had a need to stay close to home.

Might also be why she couldn't find someone with whom to settle down. Part of her had yet to become completely independent and the other part felt responsible for looking after her parents since neither brother was going to.

Emily did enjoy the bakery. She'd been helping her mom since she was ten and had graduated with her culinary arts diploma from Algonquin College in 2003. A few of the desserts that people drove all the way from Stittsville and Kanata and Barrhaven to bring home were her creations. A couple of years ago, they had done extensive renovations to the shop: brand new equipment, a fresh clean customer area, and a new front façade that looked modern but had kept the charm of the early twentieth century.

At least, for once, David had come through and had provided the funds so that they didn't need to borrow from the bank. Business had risen twenty percent since, which proved that appearance did matter. If you looked successful, people tended to flock to you, which made you more successful. She'd heard David say this more times than she cared for over the years, and it annoyed her that he'd been right.

Okay, so the guy wasn't entirely ruthless, just self-centered and a real pain in the butt most of the time, but he knew how to make a business succeed.

Emily pulled the last of the breads from the ovens and looked up at the clock. It was almost eight o'clock and her mom hadn't made her way over yet. She peeked out the front window and saw no sign of her parents crossing the street. It was no coincidence that her great-grandparents had built the house and the bakery across from one another on Main St. Back then, Forest Creek had been a small village of just two thousand souls, people like her great-grandparents establishing businesses to cater to the surrounding area farmers, and a hundred years later it was still a little hidden gem of a community in the south-west end of Ottawa with just under eight thousand residents, most of whom commuted to downtown Ottawa for work.

The bakery—the signage above the front door simply stated *bakery*, all lower caps—of Forest Creek was well known across the surrounding towns and neighbourhoods, and over the last two years, since the renovations, Emily had managed to build a nice presence on Facebook, which she liked to think had had as much to do with the new growth as had the reno.

They now had five employees, and Jeanine, a homely grandmother type of fifty-nine with a penchant for baking, was first to arrive.

"Where's your mom?" she said.

"Not sure," Emily said. "Maybe she's having her hands full with Dad this morning."

"Why don't you go check on them," Jeanine said. "I'll be fine here."

Emily took her apron off, hung it on the back of a chair, and headed towards the front door.

"I shouldn't be long."

03 80

Henry closed the basement door—mostly to keep those guys from coming up, forgetting that without a lock, it wouldn't be much of a deterrent—and stood just outside the kitchen, unable to remember what he was going to do.

He shrugged and headed up to the second floor, but when he reached the landing, he froze. Those two guys were there again, but this time they weren't black, they were Germans, dressed in Nazi uniforms, spewing something he couldn't understand, nor cared to.

Henry pivoted and hurried down the stairs. He dashed into the sitting room to the left of the reception hall—years ago when the kids were young, Henry had taken part of the spacious reception hall to build a powder room because Irene had gotten tired of seeing mud tracks all the way upstairs to the only bathroom in the house—in search of hidden money. A small section of the sitting room had built-in shelves full of books and he hid all his money inside those books. Henry had loved to read when he was of right mind: Bram Stoker, Jane Austen, Ernest Hemingway, and F. Scott Fitzgerald, to name a few of the classic authors he admired, but he could just as easily grab a Stephen King or James Patterson novel. That's something he and Bradley shared—their love of books.

He pulled The Great Gatsby from a shelf and pocketed a crisp one-hundred-dollar bill, but five other books proved moneyless. He scratched his stubbly chin and pulled two more books, again coming up empty.

"Irene! Where'd you put my damn money? We've got thieves in the house and I've got to hide my money so they won't steal it. IRENE!"

Henry kept pulling books out and not finding any money hidden inside their pages. He became so agitated and overwhelmed at the real possibility that the thieves had already robbed him of his hard-earned money that he began to cry, first just single tears stringing down his wrinkled cheeks, and then a full-blown sob with his chest heaving and his shoulders shaking.

"Irene," he said in a distressed and frightened child's voice. "Please help me. Please help me find my money."

He stretched the word *money* into a very elongated two-syllable utterance that was full of agonizing distress. After what seemed like an eternity, his tears subsided, his mind cleared up a bit, at least enough so that he no longer felt threatened. It seemed like the thieves had disappeared.

With one great sigh, Henry stepped over the pile of books that littered the floor at his feet and left the room in search of something to eat. His stomach was growling and he hoped that Irene had made blueberry pancakes.

His favourite.

☙ ❧

Emily walked into her parents' home and while looking at a Facebook post on her phone, she called out like she always did, out of habit more so than necessity. Normally, her mom would call back that she was in the kitchen, but not this morning.

"Mom? Dad?"

She peeked into the sitting room and saw the pile of books on the floor. She frowned.

"Mom? Dad?"

She headed to the back of the house where her dad had blown out the back wall to add a new kitchen extension the spring after Great-Grandma Sarah had passed away. The house had once been a beautiful home, a place for gathering and being entertained, a place a young Great-Grandma Sarah had cherished and shared with friends and family. The kitchen had always seemed too small, though, and the extension had been overdue. Unfortunately, the house had been neglected since Emily's father had fallen ill and now it had begun to look old and tired. One more thing she was going to have to take care of.

"Mom? Dad?"

Still no answer, which she felt was odd, unless her parents were upstairs and Mom was busy with Dad, washing him up or dressing him. Sometimes, he'd put his pants on backwards and Mom would try to explain to him that he had to reverse them, which he didn't always do—until he had to go to the bathroom and couldn't find his zipper and then he'd yell at Mom, accusing her of removing the zipper from his pants. He was getting worse, Emily knew that, and so did her mom, but Mom wasn't ready to have him in a home. He was her husband, a good man, a proud man, and she knew he wouldn't do well away from her.

Emily hadn't brought it up in a while but she knew that sooner rather than later she would need to convince Mom it was the best thing to do, if for no other reason than to keep both of them safe. Dad stood a good foot taller than her mom and a few times lately he'd been a bit physical with her, grabbing her arms a little too tightly and leaving bruises.

"It's nothing," Mom would say every time.

"He could really hurt you," Emily would say back.

Mom simply dismissed it, but Emily worried. He was her dad and she loved him. He had never shown any violence toward anyone, but the man inside that shell of her father was a bit of a stranger now, and Emily was concerned that someday, whether he meant it or not, he would hurt her mother. She hated what was happening to him; this disease had made victims of them all, and it broke her heart to feel so helpless.

There was nothing anyone could do and that was the worst part. She had read all the literature, visited the websites, and there was no cure. It seemed to her that the disease was still a mystery to the medical community and it appeared it was going to stay that way for a long time.

Emily reached the kitchen and saw her dad standing on the other side of the island that had been part of that major renovation when she was a teenager. He seemed to be kicking something.

"Dad, where's Mom?"

Her dad made a kicking motion again. And again. He didn't look at her.

"Dad!" This time she said it with enough authority to make him turn his head and look at her. "Where's Mom?"

He looked at Emily, a confused frown on his face that Emily was seeing more often lately, his mind trying to construct the reality that surrounded him, and most times he surfaced from the fog.

Not today.

Her dad did the kicking motion again.

"Dad, where is Mom?"

Emily saw him point at something. "She's sleeping on the floor and won't wake up. Why is she sleeping on the floor? I'm hungry. I really wanted blueberry pancakes but she didn't make any. Why is she on the floor? I'm hungry."

Instantly, Emily felt her breath catch as her chest shrank. Her dad wasn't making sense, yet he was. Suddenly, Emily was five again, running down from upstairs to come help her mom make breakfast on a Saturday morning before Dad and the boys woke.

This is where she had fallen in love with baking. Being with her mom always made her feel safe and special.

"Dad, you go over there and sit," she said as she came around the island and saw her mother on the floor. "I need to help Mom."

"But—"

"Dad, I need to help Mom and I need you to listen to me. Please, just sit on the stool."

He did as he was told and Emily kneeled beside her mom, putting her cell phone on the floor. She put two fingers on her mom's neck, feeling her own heart stop for a moment as she couldn't find her mother's pulse.

Come on.

Nothing.

Come. On.

Emily grabbed her phone and dialled 911. She gave the operator all the information she was asked, and now all she could do was wait.

Her whole world, the only one she'd known and loved, had instantly collapsed—she had just lost her mother, her friend, her business partner. Emily looked up at her dad who sat quietly on the stool, the crease of his brow above his eyes matching the confusion that was building inside of her.

Her mom was gone.

Gone.

Emily couldn't catch her breath.

Tears escaped the corners of her eyes.

What would she do now? But there was no time to wait for an answer.

Her father slipped off the stool and walked away.

"Dad!"

Emily wiped her tears, kissed her mother on the forehead one last time. Then she stood and went looking for her dad.

F I V E

B radley held his phone in his hands for just a second, a second that stretched forever and allowed him too much time to think the worst. Why else would Emily be calling so early?

"Hey little sister, what's up?" he said, trying to sound casual but hearing the strain in his voice.

There was a long pause followed by a loud intake of air.

"I really wish I was calling you for no reason whatsoever," Emily said, a slight tremor in her voice, "but Mom . . . Mom died this morning. Mom is gone, Brad. Mom is gone."

Bradley felt the way he always had when David would slam him against the wall for no other reason than to just be the idiot that he was: stunned, out of breath, close to tears. There had been times, while growing up, that Bradley really thought his brother had mental problems. And if Bradley was dumb enough to run his mouth, it only made David do even more stupid things.

Emily was as level-headed a person as could be.

"What? How?" He saw the questioning look on Kate's face and he gave her the wait-a-minute index finger signal with his left hand. He was still trying to process what his sister had just told him. "What happened?"

"She had an aneurysm," Emily said and Bradley could tell she was struggling to keep it together. "I found her in the kitchen, on the floor. Best guess is that she died instantly, before even hitting the tiles. She had . . . she had this twisted horrific gaze in her eyes, as if she knew what was happening to her just before she di—"

Emily broke down and Bradley fought to keep his own composure. He lowered his head and rubbed his forehead so that Kate wouldn't see the grief and panic on his face.

"Are you and Dad okay?" he said.

"Yeah," Emily said and started to laugh, a crazy sort of laugh-cry. "Dad was standing over Mom in the kitchen when I came to see what was taking them so long this morning, and he was trying to wake her up by kicking her."

"Are you kidding?"

"Oh, Brad," she said. "Dad . . . isn't Dad. His mind is going away so fast. I'd been trying to talk Mom into putting him into a home, but you know Mom."

"She wouldn't hear of it."

"Exactly." A pause. "At least I'd gotten her to cut back at the bakery, but I feel I didn't do enough. She had her hands full with Dad."

"Don't do that," he said. "Don't blame yourself."

"I was so sure Mom would live to a hundred, like Great-Grandma Sarah."

"Great-Grandma was a tough old bird," he said. "I think the Big Man upstairs didn't want to deal with her and that's why she lived so long."

He heard Emily laugh a sigh of relief. He felt horrible for her, for being the one to find their mother that way. He'd also thought that Mom would be around for a lot longer. She had been tough like Great-Grandma Sarah, the two a lot more similar than different. Great-Grandma Sarah had still been helping at the bakery when she was ninety, making sure that her recipes were followed to the letter. Even David had been a bit afraid of her, his shenanigans stopping abruptly whenever she entered a room.

"I can't believe this," Bradley said.

Guilt flooded his mind. He hadn't seen his mom in nineteen years and now she was gone.

Mom is gone?

The words stung. They felt cold and unimaginable. His mother couldn't possibly be dead. She was just sixty-five, a month shy of her next birthday.

"I can't believe this," he said again.

"Me neither," Emily said. "If only I'd paid more attention, maybe I would have seen some kind of sign."

"Em, there aren't any signs."

"I just—"

"You did your best," he said. "You know you did. This wasn't your fault."

"Easy for you to say," she said, sounding a bit bitter. "Both you and David left me to take care of them. No one ever asked me. Everyone just assumed I'd do it. Not that I minded, but you know, it would have been nice to get help once in a while."

"I'm sorry," he said. His sister wasn't wrong; he had fled, leaving a seventeen-year-old girl behind who might have had plans of her own but felt obligated to stay close to home, knowing that someday she would be needed in a reversed role, the caregiver instead of needing care. "I'm sorry I never came home, I'm sorry I waited until five years ago to get in touch, and I'm sorry I missed out on a lot of years with you."

"I didn't mean to get all David on you," she said and that got both of them laughing cautiously. "You know you need to come home?"

Bradley took a moment for it to sink in. "I know."

"We're all adults now," she said. "David isn't as big of a knob as he used to be."

"I doubt that."

"I had to try," she said. "It will be nice to see you. Just wish it was under better circumstances."

"Me too," he said. "I'll be on the first flight available."

C3 &0

As soon as he ended the call, Bradley found a chair. All of his energy had suddenly disappeared and he really needed to sort out his thoughts.

He was going home, home to face not just his brother David, but all the painful memories that had been the catalyst for his departure. He had never told Emily why he'd left, but he felt pretty sure that she had figured it out over the years. He had tried so hard to fool himself into believing that more than three thousand kilometers could make him forget.

The past was something no one could outrun.

And now he was going back to it.

The guilt of having been away so long, of only calling his mom on special occasions like her birthday, Mother's Day, Christmas and the odd other time, was something he was going to have to live with now. How many times had she asked him to come home for a visit? He'd always made up some lousy excuse why he couldn't get away.

Sadly, he had never thought that he'd run out of time before he'd run out of excuses. And by the sounds of it, Dad was in pretty rough shape; he might not even recognize his own son.

And there was Big Brother. Ah, yes, the tormentor of his childhood who'd thought that it was funny to send him roses for Valentine's Day when he was a high school freshman and included a card signed Vickie Marsh, knowing full well that Bradley didn't like her that way—they were friends, but that was all—and then he'd had to make a fool of himself when he'd had to let her down as gently as he could and she'd had no idea what he was talking about.

When he'd gotten home, Bradley had totally lost it on David and tried to take him down, but unfortunately David had been six inches taller than Bradley at the time and maybe he hadn't intended to hurt him, but Bradley ended up with a broken arm and six long weeks in a cast.

Bradley rubbed his left arm as if he could still feel the break. It wasn't the worst thing that would happen throughout high school, but each fight or torment he suffered at David's hand had made it harder and harder to feel anything for his brother but fear initially, and hate eventually.

And to think that David had saved his life once was almost impossible to believe.

CB EO

"Brad, honey," Kate said as she put an arm around his shoulder. "What's going on?"

He looked at her, this beautiful woman that he loved as much as his heart allowed, knowing that he was truly lucky to have found her and that he could have a wonderful life with her, baby and all, but he was afraid of what waited at home, afraid that once he went back, he wouldn't ever leave again.

"My mom died this morning."

He felt her head rest against his. "I'm so sorry."

Neither said anything for what seemed an eternity, Kate holding him, Bradley tormented by all the what-ifs from his past.

What if I hadn't left?

What if I had gone back?

What if I had stood up to David instead of fleeing like a coward? Would it have changed anything?

Would it? He really couldn't be sure it would have, and why did it matter now? He'd lived the life he'd chosen, buried his pain, and in the process had cut off the rest of his family. Looking back, it was easy to see the errors of his decisions, but letting guilt second-guess everything that had been done was pointless.

The past was the one thing carved in stone. Nothing could change it. What *could* be changed was what lay ahead.

"I have to go home for the funeral," he finally said, the last word coming out in a whisper that died in his throat. "I should have . . ."

"It's not your fault that—"

"No, not for that," he said. "For never visiting, or even inviting them. I was embarrassed by my lack of success. I didn't want my parents to see how I lived."

Kate pulled away just a tad, but remained close enough to keep her hand on his back. "They wouldn't have cared, I'm sure."

He gave her a sideways glance. "Probably not. But I did. I came here with nothing, not even a plan. It took me three years of doing crap jobs to scrape enough money together to go to college and earn my radio broadcasting diploma. I still had no idea if it's what I wanted to do, and I honestly don't know why I enrolled in it other than I love music. It was always my escape, the one place I could lose myself."

"I'm glad you did," she said. "And you should be proud of what you've accomplished."

"I just never got to share it with Mom and Dad," he said. "I mean, they knew about my career. I filled them in when I called home, but I kept my distance, as if I were afraid that if my old and new lives mixed, it would all come apart somehow." He was silent for a beat. "I think I didn't want them to tell David anything, so I didn't tell them much either."

"You know I don't have a very good impression of your brother," she said. "You don't paint a pretty picture."

"We were mortal enemies," he said, a hint of regret in his voice. "I was smarter, but he was the muscle and he used it to get what he wanted."

"He was scared of you."

"I don't think so. He's taller and a lot bigger. He spent all his time in the gym while I devoured books. I didn't have much of a chance."

"People who feel inferior to others will typically bully them," she said. "It was a long time ago. Brothers and sisters fight."

"Did you?"

She hesitated. "I'm the baby by quite a few years, so no. But I had friends who were like you and David. People grow up."

But David? From what Emily told him, sure he wasn't the petty teenage boy he'd been, but instead he'd become the self-centred man who seemed to care only about himself. He felt sorry for Cassandra and Angel.

Angel.

He had never met his niece. She was the only one of the next generation of Knightons and he barely knew her. He occasionally checked her Facebook page, but she didn't seem to use it much. Kids her age were more into Snapchat or Instagram. If there was a positive angle to his upcoming trip back home, his niece was it. He bet she was beautiful and witty like her mother. That's one thing he always remembered about Cassandra—her off-centre sort of humour.

Which made him wonder, not for the first time, how she had ended up with control-freak David? While he and Cassandra had hung out as friends, he'd told her all about David, but that still hadn't deterred her from dating him. Girls had simply been attracted to David. He had been tall, muscular, and as he'd heard enough times in the school hallways, *dreamy*, so Bradley got that part, but he had also been very shallow, possessive, mean. He'd gone through girlfriends like a kid eating Pez, so why had he gone for Cassandra and why had she not said no after everything Bradley had told her?

She had seemed way too smart for David, way too smart to put up with his immature and selfish behaviour. How many times had he cheated on her and then begged for her to take him back? Bradley and Cassandra had had many late-night talks about

David, and she had often asked Bradley why she couldn't say no when David came grovelling.

He'd had no answers for her. He'd tried in the past to warn her off his brother and that hadn't worked. So, if she was going to break up for good with David, he had been determined that it was going to be because it's what she really wanted, not because he'd talked her into it in any way.

He remembered the night of her nineteenth birthday. She had been so excited all day but when she had come to find him in St. John's Quiet Garden where he'd gone to be alone, he had hoped that his brother had finally messed up bad enough and that, finally, she was going to break up with him for good.

But she didn't and a month later Bradley was on a plane to Vancouver. Too bad, because from what Emily had told him not long ago, David and Cassandra's marriage only seemed to exist for appearance's sake. Not that Cassandra had confided in Emily, but his sister had told him that back in the early days of their marriage David had always been possessive, putting his arms over Cassandra's shoulders in a *she's mine* gesture or always making sure they sat together, again to make sure everyone knew she was his—but that had stopped long ago, possibly years. It was just one of those things that had gone unnoticed as time passed, probably because it had become rare to see David and Cassandra together. A lot of Sunday dinners, David didn't even come with Cassandra and Angel, only showed up minutes before food hit the table, and dashed out right after it was done.

Emily had told Bradley how irritated their mom was every time he did that, so much so that one Sunday, about a year ago, she'd told David that if he was going to pull that on her tonight, he might as well just leave right now. She wasn't going to be disrespected again, working all day to create a beautiful meal only to have him beat it out of there once his belly was full.

Bradley had laughed at that. It was so Mom. She was never afraid to call it like it was. She had put David in his place plenty when they were young, but she had missed a lot too as she'd worked so much at the bakery, and Bradley had never been one to tell.

"Somehow, I think my brother is incapable of growing up," he told Kate.

CB ED

Bradley was on his phone looking at available flights to Ottawa and found one that afternoon leaving at two. He'd be at his parents' place around midnight.

"I'm going with you," Kate said.

"This isn't the right time to introduce you to my family," he said. "I just want to fly out, attend my mom's funeral, and come back before anything develops between David and me."

"You can't just fly in and fly out," she said. "You haven't been home in a long time."

Bradley looked at her, hating that she was right. He'd have to stay a few days and help Emily sort things out with Dad, if nothing else. How was he going to get to know Angel if he didn't stay a few days?

But he really didn't want to bring Kate. It just didn't feel right to bring her, a stranger to everyone else. This was his mom's funeral, someone Kate didn't know. But she was his girlfriend, frig, maybe even his wife soon if she had her way, so why didn't he want her to come?

He knew why.

"I really need to do this alone," he said, a plea in his voice. "Please, Kate."

"I could be your moral support—"

He fidgeted on the stool. The last thing he wanted was for the old love of his life and the new love of his life to be in the same room. He was afraid of what would happen.

He was afraid of making the worst mistake of his life.

"Maybe we'll go back for Christmas," he said. "A bit of time will have passed, so it will be easier."

"Fine," she said.

But Bradley heard the undertone. She wasn't fine with it at all and when she walked away, he knew he was making a mistake. Kate never gave up that easily. He was going to pay for this some-how, but right now all he could concentrate on was getting back home as soon as he could.

He pulled out his credit card and booked a one-way ticket to Ottawa, not because he wasn't coming back, but because he just didn't know when that would be. He had no idea what was really waiting for him back home, and the more he thought about it, the more unsettled it made him.

SIX

When Cassandra got home after dropping off Angel at work, she unloaded the groceries and put them away, gathered all the dirty laundry from her daughter's floor and put in a load of dark colours, fixed herself a salad, poured half a glass of red wine, and parked herself on the sofa. She found one of those made-for-TV Hallmark movies and soon lost herself in the romantic story that was nothing like her life was now.

She had loved David. Like the lead male in the movie, David had come after her, wooed her, made her feel special. He'd started to show up at her field hockey games after that party, cheering her on so loudly that it was almost embarrassing.

Almost.

She had loved the attention the other girls suddenly gave her. Rumours had started to go around that she was dating David after that party, but they actually hadn't even gone on a proper date yet. That had changed the following weekend when he picked her up in his dad's old Ford F150—it had looked at least twenty years old but in mint condition—and they had driven all the way out to Cumberland to the only drive-in theatre left in Ottawa. She couldn't remember the movie because, to be honest, they hadn't watched much of it. The first movie had been for the kids, so they'd hung out in the arcade section for a while, eating pizza and drinking pop, but once the main movie was about to start, they got a bag of popcorn and headed back to the pickup. David fished two beers from the cooler hidden in the back bed of the truck under heavy tarps, and before long her head was spinning a bit and things got pretty hot.

Two hours later the credits were rolling on the screen.

And she was falling in love with David Knighton.

CB ВО

Fall came and went, then Christmas—David bought her a Grays field hockey stick she knew was rather expensive, while she'd gotten him a less extravagant gift of two hockey tickets to the Ottawa 67s—and when the year turned to 1999, the last year of the century with all its Y2K doom and gloom gaining steam, Cassandra's life had never been better.

The one regret she did have was that there was no way to keep both Knighton brothers. As much as she'd wanted to, neither could be in the same room with the other, let alone share her. She had tried to talk to David about that, but he'd wanted no part of that conversation, so she had broached the subject with Bradley.

Same reaction.

And that really upset her because she and Bradley had been friends since Grade 5 and she really didn't want to lose that.

"Guess you should have thought of that before you decided to date my weirdo brother," Bradley told her.

"I don't know why you say that," she said.

"Just wait," he replied.

Just wait. She had been so sure Bradley had simply been jealous that she'd found someone and he hadn't, but she couldn't have been more wrong.

Or stupid.

CӠ ഉᴐ

She had planned to go to college after high school, but that was before she became pregnant and before David asked her to marry him. She had always wondered if he'd married her because he loved her or because she had become an obligation. There had been signs during the spring and summer of '99 that he was cheating, and then when on her birthday he was a no show—no call, no present, nothing—she had been madder at Bradley than at David because dammit, Bradley had been right.

Still, on Saturday December 4, 1999, at just a little over four months pregnant, she walked down the aisle of Saint John the Baptist Anglican Church, said her vows, accepted David's, and walked out of that church as Mrs. Cassandra Knighton.

An early winter storm had greeted them as they came out, like an omen of what was to come.

The Hallmark movie finished and instead of lifting Cassandra's spirit, it unceremoniously disappointed her. She poured another glass of wine and started surfing the internet. In the back of her mind, her conversation with Angel this morning poked at her, like someone trying to get her to do something.

She found herself looking at the Health Science programs at Algonquin College, remembering how she'd once thought of pursuing a career in sports injury—she'd twisted a few ankles and broken a thumb and pulled a hamstring more than once—and the college did have Occupational Therapist Assistant and Physiotherapist Assistant programs that intrigued her. But she soon saw that it was two years of full-time studies and the thought of going to school with a bunch of late teens and twenty-somethings quickly deflated the tiny bit of enthusiasm she had.

Who was she kidding?

She closed the lid on the laptop, filled her wine glass again, and took it with her to the laundry room where she hung the heavy clothes like shirts and pants to air dry, tossed socks and undies into the dryer, and put in a load of colours. She then pulled out her Dyson and vacuumed the floors, and by the time she was done it was nearly four in the afternoon.

Her eyes wandered toward the laptop.

Maybe she shouldn't be so quick to dismiss college. Two years, immature twenty-year-olds as classmates. She shook her head. Maybe she could just get some menial job, anything to get her back out there, be part of something, contribute, feel needed.

Feel wanted.

That's what she was most tired of: not being wanted. Sure, Angel still needed her, and Cassandra felt fulfillment in helping her daughter, but the biggest void was not being wanted by David.

Intellectually, physically, sexually. She missed the way he used to touch her, made her feel desired, made her feel like she mattered to him. They hadn't been intimate in . . . she actually couldn't remember. Years, probably. She knew she could lose twenty pounds at least, but she still looked good. Didn't she?

Okay, maybe she should get rid of the grey in her hair. It had been a while since she'd had it done. And the wrinkles around her eyes were becoming more noticeable, but they had creams that sort of helped for that. She was only thirty-eight, not a hundred.

Cassandra made her way to the family room with her wine, thinking of watching another movie. Angel was going over to Lilly's tonight and she wasn't expecting David anytime soon, if at all. She stood in the middle of the room, eyeing the expensive leather couch and two matching chairs, the two-thousand-dollar area rug over the maple hardwood floor, the abstract artwork on the walls she had never liked, the seventy-inch OLED television—she had to admit she did like that—and the unlit gas fireplace. All the makings of a happy, comfy home life.

A happy, comfy, *lonely* home life.

She sighed and thought about Bradley, about what happened the night of her nineteenth birthday, about her decision to break up with David after that day . . . and about the secret she had been hiding ever since.

She'd been blaming David for everything that had gone wrong over the last twenty years, and he did deserve part of the blame, but it was time that she stopped lying to herself.

She'd messed up and it was time that she finally started to take responsibility for it.

SEVEN

E mily felt the tension in her shoulders and the back of her neck, a sign that soon she'd have one of her unbearable migraines. So much had happened today and she really didn't have time for one of those.

She popped three extra strength Tylenols into her mouth and chased them with a glass of water—something stronger would be preferable, but with everything she had to do on top of being responsible for her dad, it wasn't an option. She knew the pills probably wouldn't help, as they rarely did, but what else could she do?

There was no one else to handle things.

Her phone call to Bradley had gone better than expected. She'd been dreading the argument of convincing him that he had no choice, that he had to come home, but the argument had never happened. He'd agreed. She realized that he hadn't mentioned anything about Kate, and now she wondered if that was part of the reason he hadn't argued or made excuses why he couldn't come.

She'd have to ask him if everything was all right with them.

She took a breath.

Mom was gone. When the paramedics had arrived and tried to revive her, Emily could tell that it was pointless, but a tiny part of her—the little four-year-old in her who had once found her mother sitting on the end of her bed, crying, and when she'd asked her mom why she was crying, all she'd said was that sometimes grownups made mistakes and it made them sad—still wished they could have saved her.

Mom is gone.

It wasn't something that she was ready to accept, so best to keep busy and not think about it. If she had to pretend to get her through the day, then that's what she'd do.

Ah, to hell with it. She knew her mom always kept a bottle of whiskey in the hutch in the dining room, which they hadn't used since last Christmas. Damn it, this coming Christmas was going to be the worst.

Mom won't be here.

Emily poured a generous amount in a glass and gave it the old one-two down the hole it goes. It burned as it went down her throat and she could feel her nerves loosen.

One thing the Knightons were good at was enjoying a stiff drink or three. Usually more. Then, not only did nerves loosen, but tongues too. A lot of truths can be spoken with a loosened tongue.

Bradley was coming home because Mom was dead. Bradley and David and Cassandra in the same room for the first time in nineteen years.

The thought of it made Emily reach for the bottle again but she stopped herself. Not right now. She had so many more phone calls to make and she didn't want to sound like a drunk. Family might not believe what she had to tell them if she sounded half sloshed.

She grabbed her phone, and since she didn't want to talk to David, she phoned their home number instead, fairly sure he wouldn't be there. The guy was never home.

She got their voice mail.

"Hey, it's me," she said, a tiny quiver in her voice. "I've got some . . . news I'd rather not leave on voicemail. Cassandra, call me ASAP."

She hung up and heard something crash in the kitchen. Her shoulders sagged. With all the commotion of the day, she realized that Dad had not had anything to eat all day—a quick glance at her watch told her it was already three in the afternoon—and he was probably trying to make something for himself. If he was having a good moment, he could actually make himself toast or fill a bowl with cereal and milk.

She needed to breathe.

How was she going to cope without her mom? Take care of the bakery and her dad? Her mom had been her best friend. They'd worked together every day, planned new desserts or breads to bake, and shared secrets with each other—like her mom had recently told her that she had never intended to marry Henry, that she had dated some guy named Lucien, but Grandma Alice had hated him because he rode a motorcycle, smelled of booze and cigarettes, and cursed like it was everyday language. Grandma Alice was quick to point out that Henry Knighton, who was an electrician, a good trade job that would allow him to take care of a family, was still available.

Irene had known Henry for years, but had never thought of him as someone she'd wanted to date, but not long after that conversation with her mother, Henry had come calling.

Emily had been surprised by her mom's openness. Kids never thought of their parents as ever being young and foolish, and if not for Grandma Alice meddling, Emily realized she might never have been born.

Emily choked back her grief.

Her mom, her friend, her confidante.

Gone.

Emily wanted to cry. But she couldn't.

Because the man in the kitchen that her mom had never intended to marry was her father and he had become her responsibility.

CB EO

Emily made her dad an omelet and toast with strawberry jam, poured him a huge glass of chocolate milk—something he'd apparently loved as a kid but wouldn't have touched a few months ago—and joined him with a large coffee and a small helping of eggs. She hadn't eaten today either, usually grabbing something once everything was done at the bakery—

The bakery!

She'd totally forgotten about it. God! She didn't have the energy to go back. Instead, she grabbed her phone and called over.

"What's happening?" Jeanine said, her voice rising an octave. "We saw the ambulance and—"

"Mom died," Emily said with little energy. "When I got home, she was lying on the kitchen floor."

"Oh no!" Jeanine said, obviously fighting to stay composed. "Not Irene. My God! Not Irene. What happened? Oh no."

Emily waited until Jeanine stopped crying, not trusting her own voice, but needing to be who Jeanine needed her to be: her boss.

But they were more than that. All the ladies that worked there—Beth Welker, Suzie Prudhomme, Valery Belofsky, and Violetta Tonelli—had all become part of the Knighton family and each one was going to be devastated, Emily knew, and she was going to need them more than ever now to help her get through this and keep the bakery going. It was hers now, and she wasn't about to let a hundred years of history die with her mom.

"She had some sort of aneurysm," Emily said and filled her in as best she could, her throat growing thicker with each word. "I really need all of you to just take over the bakery for a few days."

"Of course, of course," Jeanine said, her composure returning. "Don't worry about a thing. We'll take care of everything. You take as much time as you need."

"Thank you." Emily heard voices in the background and Jeanine shushed them. "Once I have the funeral details, I'll let everyone know. We'll close for the day so everyone can come."

"Yes, we'll all be there," Jeanine said. "I can't believe this happened . . . I'm so sorry, Emily."

"I'll talk to you later."

She looked at her plate and pushed it away. What appetite she'd had was gone. She just sat beside her dad, drinking her coffee, wondering how she was going to find the energy to start calling the extended family and the gamut of friends they'd accumulated over the decades.

CB BO

By five-thirty Emily ended the last call, relying on those she spoke with to make their own phone calls and pass the news along. She had told everyone to check her Facebook page for when the funeral was going to be since she didn't have those details yet. There was no way she was going to call them all again. She was exhausted; each time she spoke to someone she was pulled into their grief and relived the morning all over again.

After feeding her dad, she had moved to the sitting room to make those calls and now she sat with her feet up on the coffee table, two fingers of her mom's Canadian Club in a glass. She twirled the whiskey around gently, but didn't drink it. Her dad was sitting in his worn recliner, snoring away like a man without a care in the world. She couldn't fault him. He really didn't know what was happening.

And that saddened her. She had just lost her mom, and each minute that passed, she was losing more and more bits of her dad.

Could her life suck any more?

I'll have none of that feeling sorry for yourself, she heard the voice of her mom echo in her head. *I didn't raise a quitter.*

Emily was about to protest, about to point out that Bradley running away from his life here sort of was quitting, but then she realized there wasn't any point thinking it, let alone saying it. Arguing with a ghost made no sense.

"Love you, Mom," she said and raised her glass. "What am I going to do with Dad?"

Since no answers came, she downed half her drink, hitting her empty stomach with fiery fierceness that shot right up to her head and made her dizzy. She couldn't get drunk because her dad needed her, so she put the glass on the side table and went to the kitchen to find something to eat. She came back a couple of minutes later with two pieces of toast smothered in peanut butter.

Not exactly a gourmet meal, but her stomach seemed thankful. Emily reached for the remainder of her drink and, holding it in hand, wondered whether the mistake her mom had told her of back when she was four was the secret she'd told her not long ago about marrying her dad instead of that Lucien guy. What other secrets might her mother have had? What other secrets might forever be lost in her father's failing mind?

Emily raised the glass to her lips and finished her Canadian Club as thoughts ran through her mind, thoughts that made her question how well she really knew her family.

EIGHT

Bradley sat in the back of the Uber looking out at the house he'd grown up in, thunder slamming the inside of his chest as memories crowded the back of his throat. The place looked a lot older than he remembered, but the memories stung with freshness.

His hand, which had been on the door handle, let go and he rested it on his thigh. Getting out of the car would end his exile and force him back to a time filled with anxiety and broken possibilities, into a past that he really didn't care to go back to. That life was long gone.

So why was he so afraid to face it?

Back home, Kate waited for him. She was the one he'd been meant to find, he felt sure of that. The next few days weren't going to change that. He'd visit, say goodbye to his mother, then hop back on a plane and go back . . . *home?*

Yes, Vancouver was home. It had been for years. Ottawa was where he'd grown up, but it wasn't home anymore. Sitting in the idling car, he had no doubt that this house wasn't his home anymore.

That home belonged to a boy that no longer existed.

Bradley looked out the back of the Ford Focus and saw him and Emily riding their bikes up Main Street toward the Jock River Bridge where they'd go and sit by the water and skip stones across the surface.

"He always does this," Bradley said. *"Whenever I'm better than him, he wants to fight me to prove he's* better."

"David's dumb," Emily said.

"He just thinks because he's older and bigger that he should win all the time."

"That bugs me," she said. *"He never lets me win."*

"He doesn't let *me win,"* Bradley said. *"I just beat him. He's the one who wanted to play Monopoly so I don't know why he's so mad that I beat him. It's just a stupid game anyway."*

"David's stupid."

They both laughed hard. And then they were silent for a few minutes.

"He just doesn't understand real estate."

"And you do?"

Bradley bobbed his head. *"Remember when I was sick a few weeks ago? Mom and I played it while I was home and she explained it all. She said I was such a smart boy because I understood right away. She said David didn't get why he needed to get all the properties of the same colour to monopolize the board and win."*

Emily looked at him like he had three eyes.

"That's why they call the game Monopoly. It means you own everything so people have to pay you rent and stuff."

"Oh!" she said.

"You'll get it when you get older."

"I'm eight," she said.

"And I'm ten."

"But David is eleven so why doesn't he get it?"

"Because David is dumb," he said. "And he doesn't like math. He only cares about hockey. I don't know why he wanted to play a board game he's not good at. We haven't played in a long time, like three years, so it was weird that he wanted to play. He never wants to do anything with me anymore."

"Maybe he needed to beat someone at something."

The memory faded and Bradley looked at the house again, this time focusing on the passage of time. The front porch light was on and even though the lighting was poor, he was able to see that the stain on the porch had peeled away, leaving behind weathered boards that showed signs of decay. The shutters on either side of the front sitting room window were rotting, and the swinging love seat he and Cassandra used to sit on and talk for hours was all rusty. The front steps had shifted over the past nineteen winters and seemed to dip to the right; shrubs were untamed and in need of pruning, and the Crimson King maple tree on the front lawn was now at least thirty feet tall and Bradley couldn't see the second storey.

He assumed it was probably in as bad a shape as the main floor appeared to be.

"Hey, you getting out?" the Uber driver said. "I have another ride to pick up back in Barrhaven."

"Sorry," Bradley said. "I've been away a long time."

ㄷㅈ ㄸㅇ

Bags in hand, Bradley made his way up the steps and stopped in front of the door. He didn't feel right about walking in, especially at two minutes to midnight, and then he wondered whether his old key still worked or whether his parents had changed the locks since he was a kid. He decided to knock and wait.

This felt so weird, standing outside the family home, a place he used to come and go as he pleased, waiting for someone to come to the door and invite him in.

The door opened and his little sister—who wasn't so little anymore—stood in the doorway, tears spilling down her cheeks. Without a word she wrapped her arms around him and he had no choice but to drop his bags and hug her back. They must have stood like that for a good two minutes, silent, decades of absence somehow disappearing in that moment of physical reconnection. He had really missed her and he felt his throat get small.

"Why'd you have to wait for Mom to die to get your sorry butt back home?" Emily said as they pulled apart.

Home?

There it was again. Home. Was the family home always home no matter how long you'd been away? Was where you were born always going to be home no matter how many years have passed since you last lived there? Wasn't there a cliché that said that *home is where the heart is*?

Bradley suddenly questioned where his heart had been all these years and wondered if it was the reason he hadn't been able to accept Kate's proposal.

Home?

Such a powerful four-letter word. It could define who you were, who you had been, and possibly who you were going to be.

Home could also be an anchor that held you back against your will and made you forget about your dreams. He looked at his sister and wondered if his leaving had forced her into staying. Had he killed her dreams?

Maybe that was why he'd stayed away: so that he wouldn't have to answer for his actions.

"Hey, little sister," he said, a weary smile trying desperately to form on his lips. "You look like—"

"Don't you dare say it," she said. "This has been the worst day of my life, no thanks to you."

"I was going to say you look great," he said.

"You're such a little liar. I have sleep in my eyes, my hair is probably a tangled mess, and I drank myself to sleep. And that couch isn't very comfortable."

"You didn't need to wait up."

"I really wasn't," she said. "I was just too tired to make the bed in my old room. You look beat too."

"It was a long flight. Too many hours to think about everything."

They stood looking at each other, siblings who had kept loosely in touch now uncertain what came next.

"Just get in," she finally said. "I'm too tired to stand."

He grabbed his bags and followed her into the house only to drop them on the floor. He took in his childhood home as if he were seeing it for the first time.

The walls were still painted that pastel yellow he'd always hated, the same row of framed pictures of him, David, and Emily followed the staircase to the second floor, and the furniture in the sitting room was more ancient than it had been back then.

"Hasn't changed much."

"No, it hasn't," Emily said. "Hungry?"

"I could eat something."

They made their way to the kitchen and Bradley grinned when he stepped on the floorboard about halfway down the hall, the one that had always sounded like it was complaining when you stepped on it.

It still complained.

David had never been able to sneak up on him because of it. His brother could never remember which one it was.

Emily pulled out a chicken casserole from the fridge. "Jeanine, who works at the bakery, brought it over earlier."

"Looks good."

Emily scooped some into a plate and heated it in the microwave. "Coffee? Beer?"

"I'd love a beer." He took a long swallow. "How's Dad?"

Emily pulled out his plate from the microwave and put it in front of him along with a fork. "I don't know. I'm not sure he really understands that Mom is gone. He kept asking me when she was coming home."

"That's got to be hard for him," he said and scooped some casserole into his mouth.

"Like I said on the phone, he's getting worse." She took a seat beside him. "His moments of true awareness are dwindling much faster now. I have a feeling that soon he won't comprehend anything. He won't know who we are. He won't know who he is."

Bradley put his fork down. "Wow. That really sucks."

Emily nodded.

"And Mom didn't want to find him a home?"

She shook her head. "I tried to talk to her about it, but she wasn't ready to deal with it. Now she won't have to."

"Ouch!"

"Sorry," she said. "That was harsh. I can't think straight right now. It was a rough day."

He took her hand. "Sorry I couldn't be here sooner. Couldn't Dave and Cassandra help?"

"I never heard back from either one," she said. "I left a message on their home phone and then got so busy calling everyone and looking after Dad."

As if on cue, Emily's phone began to ring.

"Hey Cassandra . . . don't worry about it . . . well, I don't have great news to tell you. Mom died this morning . . . I know she was . . . I don't know . . . I called everyone . . . no, I didn't call Dave . . . yes, he just got here . . . yeah, we should all get together tomorrow . . . yes, I'll be staying with Dad for now . . . okay I'll see you later."

"Kind of late to be calling."

"She apologized for not getting back to me sooner," Emily said. "She's been home since dropping off Angel at work this morning, but . . . well, she started drinking and before she knew it, the day was done and she fell asleep watching a movie."

"You mean passed out?"

Emily made a face, like she was trying to deny it. "She and Dave aren't doing well."

"And she's become a bit of a boozer?"

Emily shrugged. "I'm not her mother."

"I guess I always assumed they had the perfect marriage."

"Why would you say that?"

He looked away. "Just that, you know, after she decided to marry him after all the times he cheated on her, I figured they must have something special."

She snorted. "Far from special. Far from perfect. Far from loving."

Bradley remembered the day he'd left. It had been a chaotic day. He'd thought he was doing the right thing, getting out of the way. Saving himself.

"Not what I expected," he said. "You and Mom never really mentioned it."

"Cassandra did an exceptional job of pretending all these years. I think she was doing it for Angel. It's only in the last few months, maybe a year, that I've noticed the cracks in the lie of their marriage. David hasn't been faithful to her for a while now."

"Not surprised." He shoved more food into his mouth. "What else did she say?"

"Just that Mom was like a mom to her since hers died shortly after she got married. She asked me if she could do anything. Asked if you were here."

"So has anyone told Dave? What about Angel?"

"She said she was going to tell Angel in the morning. She's spending the night with her friend. As for Dave, she said if he comes home, she'll tell him."

"If? Jesus."

"Our big brother is quite the sweetheart."

Bradley ran a hand across his weary face. Technically, it was just nine in Vancouver, so he shouldn't feel so tired, but then again, it wasn't every day that your mother died. He'd been wired up since this morning when Emily called, and sitting in the kitchen now with her, he felt his exhaustion take over. He couldn't even begin to think how tired she must be with everything she'd had to do today.

"Let's not worry about him tonight," he said. "I think we both need to get some sleep. Think our old rooms are available?"

"Mom did use them as storage," Emily said. "It was more convenient than having to go into the dark and dungy basement."

"Man, I hated that basement when I was young."

"This house is a hundred years old. Basements weren't built for usage like new homes are. It's still creepy down there and the ceiling is too low. Makes me feel like the house is trying to swallow me." She shrugged and goosebumps ran up her arms. "Remember that time David locked us down there and I was freaking out, screaming like something was trying to get me?"

"I wanted to kill him," he said. "Two hours before Mom came home and heard us screaming. He was such a dick."

"I shouldn't say this," Emily said, "but I often wondered if he had mental issues, you know, like that boy wasn't all there at times."

The smile that licked his lips was full of sadness.

"I think he just got off jesting us. He always thought he was so clever and funny."

"I didn't," Emily said.

"Me neither."

Bradley finished his beer and thought of getting another, which he normally would at home, but decided not to.

"You okay?"

Emily was rubbing her temples. "Yeah. I thought I was going to get a migraine earlier, but then I fell asleep. I have a bit of a headache, though."

"You need to get to bed."

"I don't want to deal with making a bed or clearing my room. I'll just take the couch for tonight."

"I'll go check out my old room," he said and got off the stool. "How do you think Dad's going to react if he sees me?"

Emily's face became a big question mark. "I have no idea. He might think you're one of his hallucinations."

"Seriously?"

"Yeah, and that's not good," she said. "He can get a bit violent."

"Great."

"Just call me," she said. "So far, I've been able to deal with him."

"But?"

"I have no idea for how much longer," she said. "Like I said, he's not getting any better."

Bradley pulled her into a hug and then kissed the top of her head. "Get some sleep. You look like the walking dead."

"Not funny."

"I wasn't thinking." He headed towards the stairs but stopped before climbing. "It's nice to see you."

"We'll catch up tomorrow."

"Night, sis."

"Night."

CB ⊗

Bradley climbed the staircase and with each step the years seemed to fade away. By the time he reached the top, he was fourteen and trying to be quiet as he sneaked in past curfew. He always got caught by his mother.

But tonight, she wasn't calling out to him.

Bradley heard his father snoring, just like he'd snored back then. He'd always wondered if that was the reason why his mother was always awake when he came home late. The man sounded like a wheezing giant with a bad cold.

Bradley stuck his head in the open doorway and waited for his eyes to adjust to the darkness of his parents' room—his dad's room now. All he could see was the back of his head sticking out from under the sheets.

"Good night, Dad," he said quietly.

He pulled the door almost closed and then walked down the hallway to his room. His was on the right, David's was on the left. Mirror images of each other. His room faced the front while David's faced the back yard.

Bradley stood in front of his door, a warm feeling rising inside of him. The sign he'd put up on the door when he was twelve was still there.

Keep Out!

Twelve was the age when boys started to change, and when boys wanted some privacy. Unfortunately, his brother had never respected it and would barge in all the time, hoping to catch him doing God only knows. All he'd wanted was to have his space, have a quiet room to do his homework and read.

Bradley had loved to read, especially sci-fi. Asimov, Clark, Bova, and a slew of others he couldn't remember now. He'd been a huge fan of Star Trek: The Next Generation. Data was his favourite.

Bradley pushed the door open, flipped the light switch up, and even though his room was full of totes and a mountain of old clothes covered his single bed, everything else had been left as is. He'd been nineteen when he left, so this wasn't the room of a young boy—most of those things he'd gotten rid of as he'd travelled through his teenage years—but a few things remained. His old twenty-inch CRT television was still there, collecting dust and cobwebs apparently; his alarm clock radio still sat on the night table to the right of his bed, and the two posters of Shirley Manson were still up on his walls. Man, he'd had such a crush on her. David couldn't stand Garbage and had even snapped Bradley's CD of Garbage Version 2.0 in half.

That was the only time Bradley had ever beaten David in a fistfight. His anger had turned him into a madman and if not for his dad pulling him off David, he might have done more damage than just the bloody nose David got.

He looked at the posters and noticed for the first time ever that there was a bit of Cassandra in Shirley, or maybe it was the other way around.

Well, the Cassandra he remembered.

Bradley went to check out his brother's room and it didn't seem to be as cluttered, so he decided to change that. He threw all the clothes onto David's bed, then piled the totes into a corner, and half an hour later he had his room back. From the linen closet he grabbed some sheets and made the bed, opened a window to air things out, and went back down to the foyer—or the reception hall, as Great-Grandma Sarah had called it—to grab his bags.

He glanced into the sitting room—which he'd always thought made more sense than calling it the living room, because people didn't live in there, they sat—and heard Emily's slow and even breathing. He felt sorry for her and wondered again whether his leaving had forced her to stay. Maybe he'd ask her before his return to Vancouver, if for no other reason than to appease the nagging feeling that lingered.

He had left for selfish reasons.

Staying would have been pure torture.

He headed back to his room—*his room*—and pulled his things out of his bags. When he opened the top drawer of the dresser, it was full of cut-out fabric and so were the other two drawers. He emptied the top one and stuffed all that fabric into the middle drawer to make room for his socks and boxers and t-shirts. A weird feeling came over him and made him uneasy, like he was settling in for a much longer stay than he'd planned.

I'm saying goodbye to Mom, and then I'm on a plane back to Vancouver, to Kate.

For some reason, those words didn't ring as true as he wanted. He wasn't staying. There was nothing here for him.

Nothing.

NINE

Bradley woke up to the metallic sound of something scraping the outside of the house. At first, he couldn't figure out where he was—it looked like his old room at his parents' house, but he hadn't been there in decades.

Bang!

Something hit the house. This time, he was fully awake and aware of where he was—he really was in his childhood bedroom. He kicked the thin sheet off of him—the night had been quite warm and he hadn't needed any blankets—threw his legs over the edge of the bed, and walked to the window. Just as he was about to have a look outside, the loud sound came a third time and made him jump.

He pulled the curtain aside and peeked.

His dad was down in the front yard looking up, and then Bradley noticed the ladder up against the house.

What the—?

Bradley pulled his pants over his boxers and grabbed yesterday's t-shirt that he'd flung onto the back of a chair, and headed downstairs. He peeked into the sitting room and didn't see Emily, shrugged, and continued out the front door.

He stood at the edge of the sagging porch and saw his dad up three rungs on the ladder.

"Dad!"

His father looked at him, but Bradley noticed there was no recognition in his eyes. He knew he'd been gone a long time, and that he was a middle-aged man now and not just a teenager, but he was pretty sure he hadn't changed that much.

That meant only one thing.

"Dad!" he said and walked towards the ladder, being careful not to scare him. "What are you doing?"

Henry hesitated a moment. "Going up on the roof, isn't it obvious?"

Bradley knew his dad had never cared for people who swore, so this definitely felt out of character. "Yes, I see that. But why?"

Henry looked up, then came back down to stand beside Bradley. "What's it to you?"

"Well, I don't want you to fall, for starters," he said, first looking at his dad and then at the roofline. That roof seemed to touch the sky and he wasn't comfortable letting his dad climb. If he fell, he'd break a few bones for sure, and at his age those bones probably wouldn't heal well. "And I can't think of any reason why you'd want to go up on the roof."

"It isn't a question of want," Henry said with obvious irritation in his voice. "I just have to go up there."

The two men glared at each other. Bradley could see his dad still didn't know who he was.

"It's Brad, Dad." A pause to see if that triggered his father's memory. "Your son."

"David isn't here," Henry said after a moment. "I don't know a Brad."

It felt like a kick between the legs: first, nothing much happening, and then the rush of nausea rolling into the pit of his stomach followed by a storm of numbing, breath-catching agony that reminded him of the time David had purposely hit him with a baseball in that same area when he was ten, just because he was pissed off that Bradley had eaten the last piece of chocolate cake—it had been Bradley's birthday cake, so why David thought he had dibs on it had once again been a mystery to everyone but David.

Once his breath came back, Bradley tried a different approach. "You see all those pictures in the house, the ones on the wall along the stairs? Those are pictures of me, David, and Emily."

"You're that skinny kid," Henry said after a beat. "That's you?"

"Yeah," he said. "I'm the skinny kid."

"Damn," Henry said. "I've been wondering who that was. David and Emily, I see all the time. Well, Emily. David not as much. But the other one I never see."

"I've been away," Bradley said, feeling the shame scratch the back of his throat. "So, why do you want to go on the roof?"

"Because of the horses."

Bradley looked confused. He couldn't have heard right.

"Horses?"

Henry looked up. "They wake me up every morning, those damn horses on the roof. So I've got to get them off."

"You've got to get horses off the roof?"

Henry looked at Bradley. "Something wrong with those ears?"

"I just wanted to make sure I heard you correctly." Bradley scratched the back of his neck. "How are you going to do that?"

Now it was Henry's turn to scratch the back of his neck. "I don't . . . Guess I hadn't thought of how I was going to do that."

"It's not like you can throw them off the roof."

"Don't be stupid," Henry said. "That'd kill them. I just want them off the roof, not kill them."

"That's probably best."

They both looked up for what seemed like forever. Bradley knew there weren't any horses on the roof, but how was he going to get his dad to see that? He couldn't let him go up on that ladder. That was way too high, at least twenty feet. He'd never cared for heights, so he sure wasn't going up either. While his father seemed to be thinking for the moment, probably figuring out how he was going to get those horses off the roof, Bradley surveyed the area.

Things that hadn't been apparent last night in the dark looked worse in daylight, more tired, like an old man aged and beaten by the weather. The top left corner of the sitting room window had a crack that had spider-webbed in different directions. He wondered if water was getting through and causing damage inside the house.

He'd have to look at it.

The old screen door was gone. He recalled his mother keeping the front door open in the summer so a breeze could come through that screen. They'd never had air conditioning, so leaving the front door and the kitchen door open was the only way to get a breeze, unless it was one of those dreary humid days where nothing moved. Then they just melted in the heat trapped inside the house.

Thankfully, they'd had fans in their bedrooms.

He thought of Kate's condo and how perfectly climatized it always was. He still hadn't called her to let her know he was here, and part of him knew he wasn't ready to have that conversation with her. And by that, he meant the way things had been left rather awkward between them.

He knew he'd have to call her at some point today, but for now, he had his hands full with his dad.

A quick glance at his father reassured him that his dad wasn't doing anything stupid, so Bradley continued to look up and down the street, childhood memories flooding back. All the good ones included Emily and Cassandra. Those of David were best forgotten.

The house and the bakery had been the centre of his world. That's where his mother always was if she wasn't home. He stared at the bakery across the street. It had gotten a really nice facelift and looked modern and inviting. The neighbours' houses on either side of theirs had also gotten older, but it was obvious that the owners had also maintained them. Fresh paint, new eavestroughs, modern windows, manicured front lawns and gardens.

His parents had always been so meticulous about the property, but it was obvious that Dad couldn't take care of it anymore. Why wasn't David helping? He'd have to ask him when he saw him.

That thought turned his empty stomach.

The east side of the street had remained mainly residentials with a few homes converted: a hair salon, a lawyer's office, and a physiotherapy facility.

The west side had always been commercial and the buildings lining that side of the street all appeared to be in good condition or had been newly renovated. Looked like the village had done a great job of making sure it remained rooted in its heritage but also belonged in the twenty-first century. People, by nature, were drawn to new. There was the bakery across from the house nestled between an Italian restaurant and an antique shop. There was another air salon/spa, a pub, Johnny's old gas station—minus the pumps, so it was just a garage now. Bradley couldn't see the old Brody Hardware store. He'd had a huge crush on Christine Brody back in middle school. He hadn't thought of her in years and now wondered what had happened to her.

Not that he was that curious. It was just a passing thought as he sorted out the past, and maybe figured out the future. More and more, he was beginning to think that his plan of landing, spending a few days, and hopping on a plane back to his life wasn't going to be as flawless as he'd envisioned. It had been easy to pretend the family was just fine when he'd been sheltered from what was truly going on, but now that he was home, the ugly scars were becoming noticeable.

And impossible to ignore.

It would be easy to blame Emily for not telling him, but he knew she'd only told him what was necessary. His little sister had always been the strong one, the dependable one, the last one to complain.

Bradley took a long breath and turned to look back at his dad, who was now ten rungs up the ladder. Jesus, he was just like a kid. You couldn't turn your back on him.

How had his mother handled him *and* the bakery?

അ �

Emily ran out of the bakery in a panic when she saw her dad up on the ladder and Bradley seemingly oblivious to what was going on.

"Dad!" she shouted. "Get down from there before you get hurt."

She waited for a couple of cars to go by, then dashed across the street like the worried mother she had become, inheriting a role she had not auditioned for nor really cared to get. But he was her father and until she could find the time to look into her options, she was going to do her best to keep him safe.

Still, he was becoming more and more a handful. Emily wondered if it had anything to do with Mom dying. Could her dad tell that his wife was gone and he was blocking the pain as best he could and, in the process, was hindering his mental capabilities?

Could her death have triggered his Alzheimer's to accelerate?

She had no idea if that was possible. She didn't even know if doctors would know that, since the illness was still a bit of a mystery to the medical world. Even so, when everything was settled, she'd get professional advice. And get her two brothers involved. This wasn't a burden for her alone to bear.

But it wasn't easy. She already missed her mom and was having a hard time getting used to her being gone. Just this morning, she had woken in a start, noticed that it was almost five in the morning, and as she was about to rush to the bakery to get things going, she saw the mess of books still on the floor and had to put them back on the shelves before someone—her dad—tripped over them.

Thankfully, by the time she'd walked into the bakery, Jeanine had already been there and getting things done. The other woman had told Emily to go back home, not to worry, but she had stayed because it gave her something to do, kept her mind busy, was sort of therapeutic.

It brought serenity to her chaos.

Besides, she knew that Bradley was in the house and hoped that he'd step up and look after Dad. Except that now her dad was going up the ladder for God only knew what reason and her brother was busy doing nothing but staring down the street as if expecting someone.

Was Kate coming?

Just then, she saw Bradley turn around and in a few quick steps was standing by the ladder.

"Dad, get down from there," he said.

"Got to get those horses off the roof."

"There aren't any horses on the roof," Bradley said. "Just come on down."

"No."

Emily caught up to her brother. "What's he doing? You need to keep an eye on him. He's like a kid."

"Yeah, well, it's not like I've had any warning," he snapped. "Could have told me you were leaving. I woke up to him doing this."

"It's almost ten."

"I'm still on Vancouver time."

Emily took a breath. "Sorry. I didn't think I was going to be gone so long but I got busy. Anyway, why is he on the ladder?"

"Apparently we have horses on the roof that wake him up so he wants to get them off."

"His hallucinations are getting weirder," she said. "He's seeing things that aren't there more and more."

"Jesus!"

"We need to get him down," she said. "Can you go get him?"

"You know I hate heights."

"No time to be a baby," she said. "Just get Dad down. He's not that high yet."

Minutes later the three of them were stepping into the house, Dad cursing a fuss about not being allowed to get the frigging horses off the roof and how they were just going to wake him up again tomorrow morning.

"I've got to go home and get some of my things," Emily said. They were sitting at the kitchen island and Emily had just fixed her dad breakfast: eggs, toast, and chocolate milk. "You'll need to be on him, make sure he doesn't try to go back up there."

"Where'd he get the ladder?"

"In the garage," she said. "We can lock it up. The key is on the key holder by the front door. We'll need to hide it from now on."

"How long will you be gone?"

"Couple hours." She saw the near horrified look in his eyes. "You'll be fine."

"Easy for you to say."

"It's not like I did this every day," she said. "Mom did. She knew how to take care of Dad. But she's gone and it's up to us now. Time to grow up, big brother."

"Don't act like him," he said. "I don't need you to chase me away too."

Emily didn't miss the insinuation.

"Can you keep an eye on Dad?"

"Yes," he said. "Go do what you need to do."

Emily started to leave.

"You know, Dad doesn't know who I am," Bradley said. "Is that going to stop him from listening to me?"

Emily turned to face her brother. "He hasn't seen you in a long time. He doesn't always know who I am either. His capacity to reason is deteriorating, so no, he probably won't listen to you, not because he doesn't know who you are but because he doesn't understand right and wrong." She saw Bradley struggle with what she'd just said. It wasn't easy to accept that their dad, the man who'd been the head of the family forever, acted like a child most of the times now. "We need to keep him safe because he can't do it for himself."

"Weren't you trying to convince Mom to put Dad in a home?"

Emily nodded. "We just need to get through the next few days, then we'll figure it out."

"We'll need to, Em," he said. "Seriously."

"I know," she said, and headed toward the front door. "I'll be back as soon as I can."

CR 80

Bradley got the ladder down and carried it into the garage at the back of the house, his dad in tow, complaining the whole time that they hadn't gotten the horses down so why was he putting the ladder away.

It was hard for Bradley not to smirk.

The situation was somewhat comical. How many times had his dad heard him or David or Emily whine like that when they were kids, and ignored them? Maybe being a parent wasn't all that difficult.

Bradley hooked the ladder to the wall horizontally, and noticed that the old Buick Century Station Wagon—the Boat, as they'd called it then—had been replaced by a newer Buick Encore, in a sharp Satin Steel colour. He walked over to the driver's side and sat behind the wheel.

Nice.

His parents had always owned Buicks, even in those horrible 1980s when the models had looked like deformed spacecrafts meant to be good on gas but not so good in looks. Those beasts had lacked some serious style.

Bradley got out of the car and realized his dad was missing again. He shook his head, locked the garage door, and pocketed the key.

"Dad?"

He quickly scanned the back yard and didn't see his father but he sure noticed the neglect. In the far corner where the firepit was, two dead trees; the gardens were full of weeds; the patio was being overtaken by the overgrown lawn; and what had been a beautiful deck was a mess of rotting pressure-treated wood.

More things to take care of before his return to Vancouver. At this rate, he was going to need a few months.

"Dad?"

He sort of ran to the front but his father wasn't there either, so he headed into the house. "Dad, you here?"

Bradley heard the toilet flush and then his dad came out of the powder room, minus his pants.

"Hey, look at this," his dad said.

The last thing Bradley wanted was to see his father naked. "Can you get your pants back on?"

"I need to show you something."

"I'm quite fine if you don't, Dad."

Henry stood in the doorway, making no attempt to go back in to get his pants.

"What, Dad?" Bradley said, unable to hide his discomfort. "What do you need to show me so badly that you couldn't put your pants on?"

"This," he said and pointed at his private area. "See?"

Reluctantly, Bradley quickly looked down at his father's penis and wished he hadn't. Selfishly, he sure hoped that he wasn't going to need to wipe his dad's butt any time soon.

"It looks like a penis."

"No, not that," his dad said, exasperated. "It's my balls. See how damned low they hang? That's what getting old does to your balls. Pulls them all the way down to your knees."

Bradley covered his eyes. He didn't know if he should laugh or scream. "Please go put your pants on."

Thankfully, his dad disappeared into the powder room and came back out fully clothed. Bradley shook his head and headed to the kitchen, making sure his dad followed him.

He was starving and rummaged through the fridge for some leftovers. A container with some spaghetti caught his attention, which he heated in the microwave.

He pulled a beer from the fridge and stood at the island while his dad sat on a stool.

"Want some?"

Henry nodded. Bradley plopped two equal helpings on plates, gave his dad a fork, and they ate in silence. Bradley's mind drifted and soon he was thinking of his brother. He knew David would show up at some point today, and right now, he also knew that he probably couldn't handle that reunion sober. But he had to keep an eye on his dad—

Now where has he gone?

Bradley saw that his dad's plate was already empty. He took a swig of beer, grabbed his plate, and headed out of the kitchen, shovelling spaghetti into his mouth. "Dad?" Nothing. He heard a noise upstairs and climbed as quickly as he could. When he looked into his parents' room, his dad was halfway out the window. In a panic he went to put his plate on the dresser but missed and it fell onto the hardwood floor, chipping the sturdy plate and leaving the spaghetti lying there on the floor like a bloody mound of dead worms.

"Dad, what are you doing?"

He grabbed his father and yanked him in. "What is wrong with you? Are you trying to kill yourself? Jesus, Dad, you need to stop acting like an—"

The blank stare in his father's eyes made Bradley swallow his words. He kept forgetting his dad wasn't the man he remembered.

Maybe parenting wasn't that easy after all.

Bradley pulled his dad into his arms and hugged him. "You scared me."

"I just wanted to see if I could get the horses down through the window."

Bradley let his father go and then put his hands together, as if getting ready to pray. "Dad, please. There are no horses on the roof. There is no way for them to get up there. You don't need to worry about them. Something else must be waking you up." He waited a moment. "Do you understand?"

"If Santa Claus can land reindeers on the roof, why can't there be horses on the roof that wake me up?"

Bradley took a breath and reminded himself that he was trying to reason with a failing mind that no longer understood the normal world. In his dad's new reality, horses could somehow land on the roofs of houses. And wake you up.

I need that beer . . . and many more.

"Come," he said. "Let's go back to the kitchen."

"Why? I'm not hungry."

"But I am," he said and went down on a knee to scoop up as much of the spaghetti as he could back onto his plate. He'd clean the rest later. "And you need to stay with me."

"Why?"

"So you don't fall out of second-storey windows."

"Been climbing ladders all my life," he said. "I've never fallen."

"There's always a first time."

When they got down to the bottom of the stairs, Henry headed straight out the front door.

"Dad, where're you going?" Brad left the plate on the small foyer table and followed. "Dad!"

A car came to a screeching halt.

"You almost got hit!" he shouted. It didn't seem to faze his father as he continued to cross the street. Bradley gave the woman driver an apologetic look. "He's got Alzheimer's."

She nodded. Her eyes were full of pity. She eased her car forward and Bradley waited for traffic to pass.

"Wait up."

"I need to talk to your mother," his father said. "I don't care much for you."

Bradley knew his dad wasn't speaking out of malice, but that hurt more than Bradley could have imagined, and whose fault was it that he was a stranger to his father?

Worse was the fact that he now had to tell his dad that Mom wasn't at the bakery, that she wasn't anywhere. But he didn't have the heart to tell his father that Mom was gone, that she was . . . dead.

Once the road was clear, Bradley crossed quickly and stepped into the family bakery. Everything in it was new: the flooring, the counters, the dining nook where six small round tables looked out the front window. There were pictures of all the kids on the walls, pictures of the bakery over the last hundred years, a picture of his great-grandmother, Sarah. Where had that picture come from?

He saw his father behind the counter talking to a couple of older ladies and Bradley could tell his dad was getting more and more agitated.

"Can I help you?" one of the ladies said.

Bradley realized that they had no idea who he was and he definitely didn't know any of them.

"I'm Bradley," he said. "That's my dad."

"Of course," the one that was a bit shorter but thinner than the other said. "I'm Jeanine, and this is Valery. We've been working here for fifteen years. Your mom was a wonderful friend and we're very sorry for your loss."

"Thank you."

"Your dad is looking for your—"

"I know," he said. "Unfortunately, he doesn't really know me and Emily went home to get some things. I knew he wasn't well, but I didn't think it was like this."

"A real shame," Jeanine said. "Broke your mom's heart."

Bradley waited to see if Jeanine was going to say anything else, but then she began to cry.

"I'm sorry," she said and walked away.

He stood there not knowing what to do. He didn't feel right about going behind the counter even though the bakery belonged to his family. He had no authority over anyone here, had no idea how anything worked. He just wanted to take his dad back home.

"Dad? Let's go home."

Henry glanced at Valery. "Do I have to go with him?"

Valery looked uncomfortable.

"Dad, Mom isn't here."

"Where is she?"

Bradley looked at Valery for help.

"Your dad is such a wonderful man," Valery said. "Before the big renovation, he used to help around here, fix things when they needed fixing."

"Place does look great."

"It sure does," she said. "Thanks to your brother."

"David?"

"He paid for it all," she said. "Made your mom so happy. She finally had the bakery she'd always wanted. Everything here is modern, clean. Before, we often had to cut our baking short when an oven broke down. We'd run out of baked goods to sell too early in the day and your mom worried that someday it would put the bakery out of business if people came here and always found the place empty. Now, we have fresh baked goods all day long thanks to your brother."

Bradley wasn't sure what to make of that. David didn't do anything out of the goodness of his heart. There had to be profit in it for him. There always had to be something in it for him.

Good old David.

Unless he really had changed.

"Dad, let's go home so these ladies can work. Mom isn't here."

"That's what *they* said." His voice sounded small and disappointed. "Did she go back to the house?"

Bradley wanted to tell his father that no, Mom wasn't home, Mom wasn't anywhere anymore. Mom was gone.

For good.

But he couldn't say that.

"Why don't we go see?" he said. "Let's go see."

TEN

Cassandra was driving down Main Street when she saw Bradley cross the street with Henry. Even though the family getting together today wasn't to celebrate his coming home, she couldn't suppress the excited flutter in the pit of her stomach. And her cheeks began to ache from smiling so big. She quickly glanced in the mirror to make sure Angel, who was sitting in the back with Lilly, hadn't noticed.

It was nice to see Bradley again after such a long time. She really had missed him.

She recalled the first time she'd met Bradley in the fifth grade when she and her mother had moved to Forest Creek. It had felt like the end of the world to move so far away from Ottawa (to a ten-year-old, fifteen kilometers might as well be a million) and when she had entered her new class and all the kids had turned to look at her, the one friendly smile she had seen had been Bradley's. Her new teacher, Miss Adams, who had been tall and very pretty, told her to take the empty seat beside him and as fate would have it, they'd become instant friends.

She'd had no idea that one day they'd be family.

Cassandra flicked the turn signal down for a left-hand turn, waited for a blue pickup truck to drive by, and then pulled into the long driveway. She made her way to the back.

"Is that Uncle Brad with Grandpa?" Angel said. "Kind of sucks that he only came home because Grandma died."

"It is," she said. "He had his reasons."

"Yeah, yeah, he and Dad don't get along," Angel said. "Still doesn't seem right."

"Well, it's not our place to judge."

In the rear-view mirror, Cassandra could see more words forming on her daughter's lips, but she didn't voice them. Instead, Angel looked out the back window.

"He looks nothing like Dad," Angel said. "He looks more like Grandma and Emily."

Cassandra didn't answer right away. She parked and killed the engine. She saw in her side mirror that Bradley was standing in the driveway looking their way. Angel wasn't wrong. She had never really noticed how different her husband and his brother looked, but then again, so much had happened so fast back then that it didn't surprise her now that she'd missed so much.

"That's not the only difference," she said and stepped out of the car.

ᘓ ᘔ

Bradley saw the car pull in and head toward the garage, catching only a glimpse of the driver, but he'd know that silhouette anywhere.

And it wasn't his brother's.

Which was a bit of a relief. He wasn't ready to deal with David—not yet, anyway. Besides, seeing Cassandra without David hovering all over her would be nice.

He watched Cassandra step out of the car and walk toward him. Something in him didn't feel guilty for noticing how good she looked. She had always been pretty—hot, some had said back in high school, and maybe the sizzle had fizzled out over time; hadn't it for everyone his age?—but as he watched her coming his way, he was fighting not to run to her and sweep her off her feet.

And then guilt slapped him in the face, a not-so-subtle reminder that he had a wonderful woman he loved back home. The tug of war inside his gut erupted instantaneously.

"Hey stranger," she said.

"It's been a long time."

"I wish it was under better circumstances."

"Me too."

Cassandra approached and wrapped her arms around him and Bradley hugged her back, feeling self-conscious when the hug lasted much longer than what should be appropriate.

"I'm really angry with you," she said, still in his arms. "You left me without a best friend for too many years. I should be hitting you, not hugging you."

"I'll take the hug," he said. "And I'm sorry."

They parted but remained in each other's personal space, the old familiarity between them quickly coming back. How often had they sat on the front porch, their legs touching, talking about who they liked at school, who they hated, who they thought would get pregnant before graduating high school. But that was all before she'd started to date David, when their time together had disappeared. The summer of '98 had changed to fall and winter, their friendship fading as quickly as the winter days shortened.

Even at school it had become weird between them and their conversations weren't as fluid—David had graduated the previous June, which gave Bradley and Cassandra some time to be together, but Bradley had had trouble looking past the fact that his best friend was his brother's girlfriend.

Everything had felt wrong.

But she had seemed happy, even glowing, something that he had never seen before. As hard as it was to know that he wasn't the reason for that glow, he did his best to pretend to be happy for her.

But then the cracks in her relationship with David began to show. He wasn't as attentive, he cancelled dates, and then one night in early July of 1999, a couple of weeks before her nineteenth birthday, she had come over at two in the morning because she'd found out that David was cheating on her. Bradley had wanted so much to tell her that he wasn't worth it, that she deserved better, but he'd known how much she actually loved his dumbass brother—something he could never figure out—so he had lied to her. He'd made up qualities David didn't have and probably never would, because Bradley had known that that was what her heart had needed to believe.

He could see sadness in her eyes now and an emptiness that hadn't been there when he'd left.

Maybe those innocuous lies hadn't been so innocent after all. Maybe on the long road that life is, his lies had ended up stealing her spirit. Maybe his lies were more at fault than David's unfaithfulness.

He should have stayed.

"It looks good on you, the goatee," she said. "And the earrings too. My, you sure you're the Brad I know?"

"I doubt that I am," he said. "That boy was a fool to leave."

"You'll have to make it up to me while you're here," she said, that smile he remembered and loved making a brief cameo. "I hope you're here for a bit. Your mom passing like this, Emily is going to need help and I'll tell you now, don't count on David to step up. He'll only tell you he doesn't have time, he's got ten deals in the works, and they all need his full attention."

"I'm sorry," he said.

"It's not your fault," she said. "I married him, my prince charming. Maybe if I'd listened to you . . ."

"We can't live in regret."

Her face got hard. "Oh, trust me. We can. I did. I still do." She softened. "I told you, I'm mad at you for leaving me without my best friend."

"I'm sorry," he said again.

"I was so naïve and so stupid," she said.

Bradley was about to say something but noticed a couple of teenage girls approaching, one Asian and one Caucasian. "You have to be my beautiful niece!"

There was hesitation on both their parts for a brief moment and then they hugged.

Cß ßO

Angel had a hard time believing her uncle, the one she had heard her mom talk about so much over the years, was right here holding her like her own dad never did. Somehow, for some reason, she had become invisible to her father, and although she had learned not to expect anything from him, it wasn't until this very moment that she realized how neglected and unloved it made her feel.

All because of a hug from an uncle she had just met.

Strange how a man, although family but basically a stranger to her, had just managed to make her feel like she did matter while her father made her feel like she was nothing at all.

When she pulled away, she saw a shine in her uncle's eyes that made her heart swell. She was a lovable person; she wasn't the cause of her parents' unhappiness; she could stop blaming herself.

"Hey," she said in a timid voice. "It's nice to meet you."

"Aren't you a lovely young woman," he said. "And I'm sorry that we've never met until now."

"Better late than never, right?"

"Better late than never."

"Aunt Emily says you're like a DJ at a top-forty radio station."

"I'm actually the Program Director."

"So you're not on the air?"

"Not anymore," he said. "I started as a DJ, but now I pretty much oversee the day-to-day activities of the whole station. I decide what gets to be played, but I rely on the Music Director a lot too."

"Cool," Lilly said and extended her hand. "I'm Lilly. The saddest thing is the death of the heart."

Angel noticed a peculiar look cross her uncle's face.

"She's like a walking Wikipedia of Chinese proverbs," Angel said. "It used to drive me crazy, but—"

"I'm sorry for your loss," Lilly added.

"Thank you," Bradley said. "It's definitely a sad day for the heart."

An awkward silence chilled the reunion. As happy as Angel was to meet her uncle, he was only here because Grandma Irene had died. The two emotions tugged her in opposite directions.

"Where's Grandpa?" Angel said to break the uncomfortable hush. "I thought he was with you when we drove in?"

"Ah crap," Bradley said. "I keep losing him."

"We'd better go find him," Cassandra said. "Before something happens."

"I don't know how Mom did it," Bradley said. "Dad is like a two-year-old looking for trouble."

Cassandra uttered a subdued chuckle. "Yeah, that's pretty much it."

"He's exhausting me."

"You should have been here when she was a toddler," Cassandra said.

Bradley glanced at Angel. "I'm okay, thanks. Eighteen seems like the right time to get to know her."

"Chicken."

"Okay, you two," Angel said, noticing the banter was somewhat flirtatious, which made her feel uneasy. "We need to find Grandpa."

"Yeah, before he burns down the house," Cassandra said.

"You serious?"

"He kind of almost did about a month ago," Angel said. "He'd lit all the candles in the house. Grandma loved candles."

As they headed toward the front of the house, Angel realized that she had spoken of her grandmother in the past tense for the first time. A withering sadness chilled her as the truth of that Chinese proverb began to carve her heart with surgical precision.

C3 ∞

"Irene isn't here," Henry said when Bradley entered the house. "You said she was here."

"I said let's go see if she's there."

Bradley saw the look in Cassandra's eyes and he just shrugged. He still wasn't used to his dad behaving as if he were a child and Bradley hadn't had any experience dealing with his father like this. It felt completely unnatural.

He had become the father to his father.

Bradley led his dad to the sitting room where they sat on the old couch that had belonged to his grandmother Alice.

"Dad?" he said and waited for his father to look at him. "I really need you to try and understand, okay?"

His dad stared blankly at him.

"Something happened to Mom yesterday," he said. "Remember? She was lying on the kitchen floor."

It took a few seconds but his dad started to nod.

"Mom d—" The word, full of sharp edges and unpleasant realities, wouldn't come out. He took a breath. "Mom is gone."

"Where'd she go?"

"She went to heaven," he said. That was the last thing he'd ever expect to come out of his mouth. He couldn't remember the last time he'd gone to church. Long ago, he'd stopped believing. "Mom isn't coming back."

Henry stood, full of fury. "She *has* to come back. She needs to cook my meals, wash my clothes. We need to go get her."

Bradley glanced at Cassandra, who was standing with Angel and Lilly just at the edge of the sitting room, his face pained and seemingly begging for the answer to his question: *what am I supposed to do?*

C3 &0

Cassandra moved toward Henry and put a hand gently on his arm. She had seen Irene do this a hundred times and the physical touch seemed to calm him. She was hoping for the same results.

"Henry," she said softly. "What Bradley is trying to say is that when someone goes to heaven, they can't come back and we can't go get them."

"Why not?" Henry said, his voice like a hammer. "I never said she could go."

"No one said she could go," Cassandra said, using the voice she once used when Angel was young. "But sometimes people go there unexpectedly."

"Why would she do that?" His voice sounded lost now. "I want her here, not there."

"Grandpa," Angel said and wrapped her arms around him. "We all miss her but Grandma died and she can't come back."

"She died?" he said. "Like Whiskers died last week?"

Angel pulled away from her grandfather. "Who's Whiskers?"

Cassandra glanced at Bradley.

"Dad," Bradley said, "Whiskers died thirty years ago. Emily let him out one night and a car hit him."

"So Irene got hit by a car and died too?"

"No, Mom had an aneurysm and died on the kitchen floor."

Everyone was silent for a moment, all eyes on Henry. On a deeper level, Cassandra knew exactly how Henry felt: abandoned. She'd been feeling that way for years but it was different for him—he had lost the love of his life. Then again, maybe her loss wasn't *that* different. Except her love had died long ago. A hint of envy flashed across her features. To have had what Henry and Irene had, she could only imagine and read in the romance books she devoured. Maybe those books had set unreachable expectations.

Cassandra looked at Bradley, glanced at his ring finger, bit her lower lip. Why had she seen him as only a friend? Even after—

"So, who's going to make dinner?"

An ache touched her heart. Her father-in-law, a man who had always been strong and who had never hesitated to take charge when things needed to get done, had become a small boy who worried about who was going to make his meals. There was something really sad about that.

And when she felt this way, a double whiskey was her remedy.

She looked at Bradley and shame overcame her. He had no idea what she was like now. Once he saw how low she had sunk, he'd want nothing to do with her.

Which made her want that drink even more. She knew Irene kept it in the hutch. She'd even settle for a beer even though she really didn't care for beer. Just anything with alcohol to help her climb down from the wall she could feel herself climbing. So many memories pounded the shores of her marred past at the moment, no doubt brought on by Bradley being back. She remembered all the great times they'd shared in this house, studying, talking about the future, cementing their friendship.

When she should have been cementing a relationship with him instead. So much had gone off script.

She licked her lips

Saw how Bradley looked at her.

If only he knew the lies and secrets she'd been keeping all these years. No, she couldn't ever tell him, or anyone. It was her mess to own and no one needed to know the truth.

No one.

She just needed to get through the next few days, until her mother-in-law was put to rest. Bradley would go back west and life in Ottawa would resume.

Maybe then she'd ask David for a divorce.

Not maybe.

She would.

Their marriage had been over long ago. While Angel was young, Cassandra hadn't wanted to upset her world, but like her daughter had so observantly told her yesterday, she didn't have to stay married for her sake.

Cassandra looked at Henry and envied the love he and Irene had had. She was going to miss her mother-in-law. Irene had been such a beautiful soul, a friend, a mother.

She looked at Angel. She had been a good mother to her.

Hadn't she?

"I can make you something to eat," she said and headed toward the kitchen. "We could probably all have a bite to eat."

ELEVEN

Angel watched her mother head down the hallway to the back of the house where she had spent plenty of summer days helping her grandmother bake. When she was ten, she'd stayed here several weeks and Grandma had taught her how to make chocolate chip cookies, boil an egg, grill a grilled cheese, and make Kraft Dinner. Grandma had told her that a young lady should know her way around a kitchen, not just so she could feed her family, but because she should know how to feed herself.

"One day you're going to be old enough to move out," she'd told Angel, "and you'd better know how to cook. Else you'll be a bag of bones no boy is going to want."

"Boys, yuck, Grandma," Angel had told her.

Her grandmother had chuckled. "Someday."

Now her grandmother was gone and boys her age were too immature to interest her. Maybe once she started college. Not that she was looking for anyone. All she was really looking forward to was learning all she could to help her aunt with the bakery.

"Do you mind if I talk to my uncle?" she said to Lilly.

"I'll go help your mom."

Once Lilly was out of sight, Angel watched her uncle standing in the middle of the sitting room and knew that he was remembering things from his past just by the look on his face. His eyes moved all over the room as if he was searching for something, probably a misplaced memory that might answer the questions he'd left behind.

Or maybe he was just missing Grandma.

"Uncle Bradley?"

He turned toward her. "Hey kiddo." He frowned. "I guess you're not really a kid anymore."

"I don't mind," she said. "Just glad you're here."

"I've been away too long," he said. "I . . . coming back just never seemed to be the right time, you know? So much happened, and . . ."

Angel watched him look away, like being in the house was difficult for him. She noticed that he wasn't as tall as her dad, but he definitely looked fitter. Her dad had packed on the weight these last few years. Funny how he had all those hockey trophies in his study, a reminder of his younger years when he'd been the Wayne Gretzky of his high school, but you'd never be able to tell now. It was easier to believe that her uncle would have been the jock, not her dad.

"Grandma talked about you a lot, and I could tell she missed you."

"I'll have to live with that regret now," he said. "Sometimes we make the wrong decisions. We don't think we are, but looking back . . ."

"Grandma wasn't mad at you," she said. "I think she was mad at my dad. I think she blamed him. What happened between you and him?"

"To be honest, I don't really know," he said. "We used to be best friends, and then we weren't."

"He won't even talk about you," Angel said. "It's like you don't exist."

Her uncle was looking at the pictures on the wall by the stairs. There was a picture of her dad, Uncle Bradley, and Aunt Emily when her dad was probably ten or eleven. Uncle Bradley looked like he'd been crying. Her dad had a serious frown. Only Aunt Emily seemed happy.

"I think Grandma hung that picture so we could see what we looked like in our never-ending battles, hoping we'd feel shame."

There was a tone of melancholy in the air that reminded Angel of the absence her father had left in her life. She sensed that her uncle Bradley felt the same void.

"I often think he wished I wasn't here," she said.

"I doubt that," he said. "I'm sure he loves you."

She didn't look convinced. "He has a funny way of showing it."

Bradley ran his finger through his goatee. "Your dad can be very focused. When he played hockey, he could tune out the entire world. I'm sure that's why he was so good."

"All he cares about is his work," she said. "He's never home. Sure, he makes a lot of money, but what's it good for if he can't enjoy it with his family?"

Bradley looked at her. "When he couldn't play hockey anymore, he found a new focus."

"That should have been me and my mom."

Sadness filled his eyes.

"I just want to understand him, you know?" she said. "He's my dad and I just want him to—"

Her lower lip began to quiver and then her whole body started to shake. Her uncle swept her into his arms and she cried for what seemed a lifetime. Maybe she had been waiting for this moment forever, waiting for someone who understood how she felt.

"It's hard to love someone who doesn't return the love," he said. "I still love the brother that he once was."

"That's exactly it," she said. "We love him but he doesn't love us back. It hurts."

"I know."

"Why?"

"I don't know the answer to that."

Angel pulled away and took the tissues her uncle handed to her that he'd gotten from the tissue box on the coffee table. She blew her nose.

"I must look horrendous."

"You look like a lovely young woman."

"How long are you going to stay?" she said after her composure returned. "Would be nice if you could stay a while."

"At least until Grandma's funeral," he said. "After that, I don't know."

"I'm supposed to start college Tuesday."

"You're going to love it."

"I miss Grandma."

"I miss her too," he said.

"Thanks for letting me snot up your shoulder," she said.

"Anytime," he said. "Why don't we go see what your mom made for lunch? I'm getting kind of hungry."

"I just need a minute."

Angel watched her uncle leave and then she felt it: her grandmother's absence all around her. This had been her favourite room where she'd sit and have her tea and read her books. Grandma loved to read. When Angel was younger, she'd sit beside Grandma on the small chair, cozy up to her, and Grandma would read her books. She had loved Franklin books back then and Grandma never tired of reading them. She'd have a different voice for each character.

Angel felt her world shrivel up.

First, she had broken down in front of her uncle, and now she could feel her loneliness bubbling to the top, missing her grandmother. When her mom had called her this morning to tell her about Grandma, she had shoved all her emotions deep into the crevices of her being since she was at Lilly's and didn't want to make a scene. She'd been at the kitchen table having breakfast with Lilly's parents and two brothers and the last thing she'd wanted was to spoil it for everyone.

And then her mom had come and picked them up, driven to the house so Angel could take a quick shower and grab some fresh clothes, and then back in the car to drive over to her grandparents' place.

She loved her grandma. Unfortunately, she'd been the only grandmother she'd ever known. Grandma had been so full of life, loved to laugh and never made her feel inadequate. Grandma had always been there for her.

And now she was gone.

Gone.

It wasn't fair. She knew fairness had nothing to do with it, but still, it wasn't fair. On top of that, her grandfather's illness was taking him away too. Soon, she'd have no grandparents.

She barely had a dad.

And her mom was all broken.

Uncle Bradley would leave again.

Aunt Emily was all she had.

Grandma had glued them all together, but now that she was gone, Angel could feel her family falling apart. Why couldn't her family be one of those families that loved to get together and have fun and laugh and be loud but in a good way? Instead, her family was all tense and angry and hateful.

And then it hit her again, that feeling of helplessness and hopelessness crashing through the barrier she'd erected at Lilly's, and this time her uncle wasn't there to pull her into him as raw emotions grabbed hold of her, cutting her insides until she felt like she was bleeding loneliness everywhere.

TWELVE

Bradley joined the others in the kitchen, amid the aromatic smell of homemade soup simmering on the stove. He couldn't remember the last time he'd had a home-cooked meal. He and Kate ordered takeout three or four times a week, ate out the other times, or just microwaved some frozen concoction that was supposed to be just like a homemade meal.

Not even close.

But they were both so busy all the time and worked insane hours. And, to be honest, neither was much of a cook.

"Smells wonderful," he said and grabbed a bowl from the cupboard. He ladled two big helpings and sat at the island beside his dad.

"Hey, Brad," Henry said. "How was your flight?"

Bradley nearly choked on the mouthful of soup he'd just shoved in. He stared at Cassandra.

"Enjoy the moment," she said.

"Flight wasn't too bad, Dad."

"Been gone a long time," Henry said.

"I know," he said. "I meant to come home a few times, but I could never get the time off work. You know how that goes."

"Guess they gave it to you this time."

Bradley heard the sour note in his father's voice, the accusing undertone. He thought about defending himself, but didn't want to waste the lucid moment, not knowing how long it would last.

"You remember the time you took me fishing when I was eight?"

"Over in the Jock River."

"I caught a carp and wanted to take it home and cook it but you just threw it back."

"Carp should be spelled crap," Henry said. "No one eats those damn things. You did good that day. Stayed the whole day. Didn't once whine to go home. In fact, you whined when I said it was time to go."

Bradley remembered. David had not come with them, and out in the small rowboat with his dad, he'd found peace. That year was the year David had started to torment him, and going fishing with his dad on that hot late-August day had become a memory that had stuck with him until this day.

"Too bad we never had more of those," Bradley said.

Henry slapped him on the back. "We should have spent more time together but you always had your nose in those books."

"Only because it was the only way—" He stopped himself. No point bringing up the past. It couldn't be changed, no matter how badly he wished it could. Life wasn't a Star Trek episode where you could time-travel and meet your younger self. There were so many things he'd love to tell *that* Bradley.

"He's gone," Cassandra said.

Bradley looked puzzled. "Who's gone?"

She gave a nod toward Henry and when Bradley glanced at his dad, he saw the confused glaze in his father's eyes. That's what gave it away: the lack of comprehension in the eyes.

"It was nice to talk to him."

"It was nice to see you two talk," Cassandra said. "He and David never did that much over the years. A lot of times—most times, really—it's me and Angel who come for Sunday dinner. It hurts your mom not to have her two sons here."

"Wonderful soup," Bradley said.

"I know what you're doing."

"I'm just complimenting you on the soup," he said. "Tastes just like Mom used to make."

"Your mom showed me a lot."

They stared at each other, nearly two decades of lost years between them. He noticed how worn out she looked. Not tired, but worn out, like she'd been overused. Didn't take a genius to understand how that had happened.

"I'm sorry," she said.

"For what?"

That's when they heard Angel's heart shatter like it was made of porcelain.

CB ßO

Lilly was first to run out of the kitchen and Bradley grabbed Cassandra's arm when she went to get up.

"I've got to go see what happened," Cassandra said. "Angel needs me."

Bradley shook his head. "I think she needs a friend right now."

"But—"

"Trust me," he said. "Being in this house, she probably just realized that her grandmother is gone."

"That's why she needs *me*, not Lilly."

"Give it a minute," he said.

Cassandra pulled her arm away. "No offense, Brad, but you can't just come back and think you can tell me how to care for my daughter." She stood and started to walk away.

"Cassandra!" he said and slid off the stool. "I'm not—"

She waved him off with her hand and left the kitchen. Bradley took two steps forward, then stopped. She was right. He shouldn't be trying to tell her how to care for Angel.

"So, what do I do, Dad?" he said as he took his seat again. He picked up his spoon but didn't bother to finish his soup. "It's not like I know anything about raising kids, but I remember when I was Angel's age. I didn't want either you or Mom when I was feeling like crap. What I needed was my best friend, but unfortunately, I'd lost her."

"I got an itch in the middle of my back I can't reach," Henry mumbled. "Why can't my hand reach that spot?"

Bradley moved his hand over the middle of his father's back and assessed whereabouts the itch would be, and scratched gently. It was sort of weird since he'd never shared that sort of physical connection with his dad, but he knew that it was the right thing to do. Maybe, just maybe, he could figure out this parenting thing.

And maybe he and Kate could get married and have a baby. Maybe he wasn't too old just yet.

He really should call her.

CB ED

Cassandra walked back into the kitchen, an uncomfortable look on her face. She glanced back down the hallway toward the front of the house, then joined Bradley at the island.

"Okay, so maybe you were right," she said, taking a seat across from him. "Lilly was holding her like I would and rubbing her back like I would and they were talking quietly so I decided not to get in the way."

Bradley grinned.

"Don't you dare, Bradley Knighton," she said, completely annoyed. "I see that mocking grin on your face."

"I tried to tell you."

"How would you feel if someone had just showed up and was trying to tell you what was best for the daughter you'd raised practically by yourself?"

"I'm sorry," he said.

They looked at each other, two people who had so much to tell one another, but were unsure how to go about it. It was Henry who broke the silence.

"You got any more of that soup, Irene?"

"Dad, that's not Mom, it's Cassandra."

Henry studied Cassandra. "She looks like Irene."

"You can call me whatever you want," she said as she took his bowl and refilled it. "I like a man who enjoys my cooking."

"And I like me a girl who can cook," Henry said and winked at her.

Bradley hung his head down against his chest. "The last thing I want to see is my dad flirt with my sister-in-law. Nothing good can come of that."

"When did you become such a fun-sucker?" she said.

"Fun-sucker?"

Cassandra laughed. "Angel used to throw that in David's face all the time when he wouldn't join us on a fun day because he had to work. Do you have any idea how many times I hosted her birthday parties all by myself? Well, your mom and dad and Emily always helped, but your wonderful brother was always MIA. I actually don't think he ever made it to a single one of her parties." She plastered a fake smile on her weary face. "Isn't that shameful?"

"You don't need to convince me that my brother is—" he said, but stopped.

The floorboard in the hallway had just creaked.

A throat was cleared.

Cassandra had her back to the kitchen entrance and didn't turn immediately. She tried to make eye contact with Bradley but he was looking right past her.

Instantly, all the air in the kitchen seemed to have been sucked out.

"Hello, little brother," David said, the tone of his voice as warm and welcoming as a January blizzard. "Nice to see you."

THIRTEEN

Cassandra closed her eyes and took a deep breath before she turned her head to face David, and when she saw her husband standing at the edge of the kitchen sporting that grin she had once loved, even thought it made him look cute, her insides hardened. The passage of time had a way of re-shaping reality.

Too bad he'd come so early. She'd barely had enough time to break the ice with Bradley and would have loved to catch up for a while longer. With any luck, he'd be in and out and they could all relax.

"We didn't hear you come in," she said.

"That was pretty obvious," he said while looking at Bradley. "Well, look what the cat dragged all the way from the west coast."

"Mom's *only* been dead for a whole day," Bradley said. "So kind of you to finally show up and make time to mourn her passing."

A frosty silence filled the room.

"I had deals to close," David said with an air of self-importance. "And Mom isn't going anywhere."

Cassandra could feel Bradley was about to explode and quickly glanced over, seeing his usually calm blue eyes burning. She put a hand on his arm.

"Well, aren't we *chummy*," David said.

Cassandra pulled her hand away. "Can't you two behave? For your mom's sake. It's what she would want."

"You know what our mother wants now?" David said, his tone mocking. "Is she talking to you from the grave?"

Bradley stood and moved toward his brother. "I'd hoped the years might have changed you, but I see you're still an ass." He walked past David and headed towards the sitting room.

"There he goes, running away again," David said. "I guess it's easier than taking a stand like a man."

"Really, Dave," Cassandra said. "Give it a rest. You haven't seen him in years . . . and for your information, yeah, I know what your mom would want. I actually made time for your parents."

Cassandra stood and thought of following Bradley, but she couldn't leave her father-in-law alone to fend for himself.

"Henry, you want more soup?"

Henry stared at her, glared at David, frowned, and shook his head.

"I need to go to the bathroom."

"You remember where it is?"

Henry nodded, got up, and walked out of the kitchen, passing by David without saying a word.

"Jeez, he didn't even say hello."

"I didn't hear you say hello either," Cassandra said. "He's *your* dad."

"Yeah, well . . . it's not like he understands what I tell him anyway. He looks confused all the time."

Cassandra took a couple of deep breaths.

"He's not an idiot," she said. "His memory is failing but he still understands plenty. Sounds to me like you're the one who's confused."

She noticed how uncomfortable her husband suddenly seemed. It made her feel sorry for Henry, not David. How sad that her husband had no idea how to interact with his father now that he was sick. With Irene gone, there would be nothing to hold the family together.

And this was the only family she had left.

Maybe *that* had also kept her from ending her marriage. She loved this family, had made it her own.

"If you're afraid to talk to your dad, then why did you bother coming? That's why we're all here; to take care of him, help him get through this. Help each other get through this. Your mom was such a wonderful woman, like a mother to me."

The truth of it hit Cassandra hard and the last thing she wanted to do was cry in front of her husband. If she could be proud of one thing she'd done over the years, it's that she had never cried in front of him. She gave him a fake smile and got busy clearing the dirty dishes, then poured the leftover soup into a container and put it in the fridge, and wiped down the counters.

She then left the kitchen to go see what everyone else was up to.

Cʒ ൭

When Cassandra reached the sitting room, she saw Bradley sitting in the sofa chair across from where Angel and Lilly were on the couch. Angel was under control now and gave her mom a reassuring smile.

"You okay, honey?"

Angel nodded and wiped her nose with a tissue. "Grandma's absence became real when everyone went to the kitchen and I was all alone in this room. She loved to sit in the chair Uncle Bradley is in and read or knit or just enjoy the silence of the house. That's what she told me once when I was staying overnight and I came down from my room and found her there sitting in the dark with a cup of tea in her lap."

A knowing grin spread across Cassandra's face. Irene had loved to add a splash of whiskey into her tea, which reminded her: she needed to find that bottle.

"Is Dad here?" Angel said. "I thought I heard his voice."

"Yes," Cassandra said. "He's in the kitchen."

"He walked right by me and Lilly and didn't say anything?" she said, annoyed.

Cassandra shrugged. She was done making excuses for him. She had made so many over the years and she no longer saw the point in trying. Maybe when Angel had been young, she had believed her mother, but she was too old for lies now.

The toilet in the powder room flushed and Henry came out without his pants on.

"Henry, your pants!" Cassandra said.

"Grandpa," Angel said as Lilly turned her head away. "Gross."

Bradley jumped to his feet, grabbed his dad by the arm, and walked him back to the powder room.

"Why does he do that?" Angel said.

"He's forgetting, honey."

"I thought he'd just forget, like, things that happened in the past, not putting on his pants."

"It's going to get worse."

"Seriously?"

"Unfortunately," she said. "He's going to forget who we are, where he lives. He's going to forget how to do basic things like go to the bathroom."

"Oh, I don't want to clean that up."

Cassandra wanted to agree with her daughter, but she knew none of that was going to be Henry's fault. Every day that went by, he got a little worse, and every day Cassandra felt a part of her ache a little more watching him deteriorate that way, knowing there wasn't anything that she could do.

"At some point we're going to need to place Grandpa in a home," she said. "To keep him safe, and have trained people care for him."

"First Grandma, and now Grandpa," Angel said. "I hate that they got old."

"No one can stop time," Bradley said as he returned with his dad, fully clothed. "Your mom is right. We'll need to look for a good home for Grandpa."

"What's with the *we?*" David said. He'd just joined them, a glass in hand with something that made Cassandra lick her lips. "You'll be back on that plane before the dirt hits Mom's coffin, leaving *us* to deal with Dad."

Lilly whispered something to Angel and walked out onto the porch.

"David—" Cassandra said. "Right in front of your daughter and her friend."

"Why is her friend here anyway?" he said. "Angel's a grownup now. If she doesn't want to hear any of this, she can leave too."

"I'm not leaving," Angel said.

David raised his glass to his daughter.

"Jesus, Dave," Cassandra said.

"If we're going to air out the Knighton family closet, she has a right to stay," David said and took a generous sip. "I applaud her for it."

"You're an ass," Cassandra said.

"It's fine, Mom."

Cassandra simply shook her head.

"It's okay, Cass," Bradley said.

"Well, the chumminess keeps getting better," David said and raised his glass again. "*Cass.*"

"Seriously," she said, hating the need to defend her friendship with Bradley. "Your brother and I were friends long before you and I started dating. He's always called me Cass. I actually don't remember him ever calling me by my full name."

The room went quiet. David sipped his drink, his steely eyes on her. Cassandra felt not just her husband's stare but Bradley's and Angel's too. She suddenly felt excluded, the stranger in the room. She could feel her insides melt with loneliness.

She wasn't *real* family.

Her eyes began to water. Without looking at anyone, she turned on her heels and left the room.

"The bottle's in the hutch," David called after her.

❧ ❧

Bradley watched Cassandra leave the room, then glared at his brother. He wasn't really sure what had just happened but it was obvious that David and Cassandra hated each other. This wasn't a couple going through a hard spell; this was a very unhappy and unhealthy relationship. He'd heard the insinuated undertones in Cassandra's words earlier, but to actually see this hostility out in the open, in front of Angel—thank God Lilly had had the common sense to excuse herself—made him wonder what had happened between them. He knew a lot of marriages didn't last, especially when a couple married as young as David and Cassandra had been, but he honestly hadn't expected this.

Neither Emily nor his mom had mentioned how bad things were between his brother and his wife.

"What was that all about?" Bradley said.

"Your little *Cass* tends to be overly dramatic."

"You really need to let that go," Bradley said. "That's your wife, the one you said your vows to—"

"The last thing I need is a lecture on marriage from you," David said. "If you're such an expert, why aren't you married? Oh, let me guess—"

"You'd better stop right there," Bradley said. "I'm not a little kid anymore."

"Well, goody for you."

"Why did you bother to come if all you're going to do is start trouble? We're supposed to be here for Mom."

"Hear, hear," David said, lifting his glass. "I'd drink to Mom, but I'm all empty."

"Why don't you boys show some respect?" Henry said, his voice strong. He was standing in front of the fireplace, looking at the framed wedding picture of him and his wife. "Your mother died yesterday. She loved you boys. Broke her heart the way you two have been bickering all these years. I should have smacked some sense into the two of you long ago."

"I'm sorry, Dad," Bradley said.

Henry turned around to face his sons. "I know I'm sick. My mind is going and I'm becoming a burden. So I'll say this now while I can. You boys are family and family should stick together. I don't know what stick you have up your ass, David, but it's time you pull it out. No one here is your enemy." He paused and stared at David. Then he looked at Bradley. "And you came home. Your mother would have liked that, knowing that you finally came home. You should have done that long ago. She talked about you all the time. She loved your phone calls, but when she hung up, she'd put the phone on the kitchen counter, make herself a cup of tea—and sat in that chair right there. It broke my heart to watch her sit so still, her back ramrod straight, the cup in her lap, and . . . and tears running down her face. It wasn't easy for her, to have her son so far away while the one that was close by couldn't be bothered with us."

Henry glared at both of them.

Bradley stared down at his feet, his shame too big to swallow. "She always sounded like she was happy for me."

"Mom always liked you best," David said. "She had a soft spot for you."

"All she ever wanted was for the two of you to get along," Henry said. "Instead you fought like the fate of the world depended on who won. You boys exhausted us."

"Dad?" Bradley said.

"I've said all I'm going to say," Henry said. "You're grown men now. Act like it."

Bradley wanted to say more to his dad but he saw that vacant look in his father's eyes return, the lucid moment gone.

"I need another drink," David said and left.

"Grandpa's right," Angel said once her dad was out of the room. "Grandma really missed you."

"You spent a lot of time with her?"

"Some," she said. "When I was younger. She'd take Sundays off to be with me."

"That's nice," he said, feeling both good and horrible at the same time. "I'm glad she had someone like you around."

"You seem really sad," she said.

Memories blocked his airways.

"I guess it's because of my dad that you stayed away?" she said.

"It's more complicated than that," he said.

"Everything about this family is complicated," David said once he returned with a fresh drink. "We have skeletons yet to be discovered."

Bradley eyed his brother and wondered how many drinks he'd had already.

"Instead of speaking in riddles," Bradley said, "why don't you explain yourself?"

A mocking grin spread across David's lips while his callous eyes seemed to egg Bradley on. This was the same old David. Bradley could begin to understand Cassandra's misery.

But with Angel in the room, he wasn't going there.

"I really wish you and Mom didn't fight," Angel said.

Bradley glanced at his niece, feeling like she had just stolen his thought, and then he turned towards David just in time to glimpse an unfamiliar softness in his brother's eyes that almost seemed like some sort of pained apology.

"You don't have to stay married, Dad," Angel said. "I know you don't love Mom."

David gazed into his cup. "I once did. When she was pregnant with you. I was the happiest I'd ever been. I really thought . . ."

"What?" she said.

He shrugged. "Life doesn't always turn out the way we hope."

CB ℘

Angel loved her dad, but she often hated him. Maybe not him, but his behaviour, his need to control, his need to have the upper hand. And she definitely hated the way he'd turned her mother into a lonely and broken woman who wanted nothing more than for him to still be in love with her.

He once had loved her mom but he wouldn't tell her why he'd stopped. It saddened her because she couldn't remember how they might have been when she was young. How she would have loved to remember her parents in love, happy, laughing together. All the memories she had were of them fighting, her mom yelling and being torn apart while her dad stood just feet away, cold and distant.

Why?

That question had bugged her more and more lately—the *why* of their broken lives.

Why didn't he love her mom anymore?

Why had he become so distant with his own daughter?

Why did he hate Uncle Bradley?

So many whys.

Why did he cheat on Mom?

Why couldn't he ever hug me?

Why didn't he ever say he loved me?

Why did he treat me like I didn't exist?

Why did my dad hate everyone in his family?

Why? Why? Why?

She hated that word. She hated feeling so neglected. She hated feeling unimportant. She hated that her dad didn't love her.

Her dad didn't love anyone.

At least, no one in the family.

And for that, she actually felt a part of her heart wither and die because it was really sad to think that this man who had given her life was unable to appreciate all the wonderful rewards that came from loving his family.

Like being loved back.

Life doesn't always turn out the way we expect.

What did that mean? He'd actually looked sad while saying it, like it pained him to speak those words. She had never seen her dad show vulnerability before, or if he had, she couldn't remember.

It still didn't make him less of an asshole.

CR ₿J

Cassandra found Irene's bottle of whiskey quite easily—it was right where David had said, just sitting between Irene's good china plates that they always used for Sunday dinners and special occasions like Easter and Christmas, and her crystal flutes that they never used. She grabbed a glass from the hutch, poured a generous two fingers into it, and gulped the fiery liquid in one big swallow.

It burned going down her throat and then exploded as it hit the bottom of her stomach. Good thing she'd had a bit of food earlier or she might have gotten drunk instantly.

Which was her intention. Being in the same room as David made her feel like she was lost in a house full of mirrors, every turn deceitful, the exit an illusion that couldn't be found.

Cassandra remembered walking out of that church on December 4 into a small blizzard, the storm cutting out the world in front of her, making her feel lost and lonely. It was her wedding day and what she should have felt was blissful happiness.

Instead, she was having heart palpitations and wished she could go back an hour and tell the limo driver to simply drive by and take her as far away from this place as possible, to save her from making the biggest mistake of her life.

She refilled her glass.

The signs had been there all along. When David had been a no show on her birthday, it had been Bradley she had run to, Bradley who had consoled her, Bradley who had convinced her that David would never be right for her.

And she had believed her best friend, but then she'd discovered that she was pregnant and when she'd told David, he had totally surprised her. He'd promised never to see Josée again, that he'd be faithful, that he loved her and she had just made him so happy. He was going to be a dad and couldn't wait. While the idea of becoming a mother at the age of nineteen had horrified her, David had been thrilled.

Thrilled!

She saw a side of him that day that she had never seen. He was so loving, attentive, unselfish. And then he'd surprised her once more by proposing. She hadn't expected that. All she'd wanted was to tell him she was pregnant, thinking that he should know, expecting him to drop her on the spot, but instead he'd asked her to marry him. *Marry* him. Getting married had never crossed her mind. They were too young to get married.

Cassandra had wanted to believe that he really loved her. That he'd be faithful now that he had a child coming. But there had been that little voice in her head warning her, confusing her. She was just nineteen. How could she know whether she was doing the right thing? Her thoughts were a mess, her chest full of doubts. She'd wanted desperately to talk to Bradley.

But once Bradley found out that she and David were getting married, he was gone within a week.

Things had happened so fast after that. She got caught in the whirlwind of Irene and Henry's excitement, and before she knew what was happening, it was the morning of her wedding, she was four months pregnant, and she didn't have it in her heart to disappoint her new in-laws who had always welcomed her into their home.

So, standing at the top of the church stairs, feeling the cold wrap itself around her as the snow whipped her face, she'd pushed her uneasiness down her throat and walked out into the December numbness, a new husband under her arm.

And to be honest, looking back as she downed her second glass of whiskey, those first three years of marriage had actually been really good.

CB ED

Bradley saw the internal battle going on inside of Angel and his heart went out to her. He'd only been around his niece for maybe two hours, but already he could tell that she was a strong and positive young woman who loved both her parents but was also torn by their tumultuous marriage. She didn't want to take sides, and it pained her to do so.

Not a decision he envied.

And he could see how desperately she needed to reach her dad, find out why he was the way he was. Bradley had to hold his tongue—he wanted to tell her not to bother, that it was a waste of time because no one understood David—but there was something about Angel that told him if anyone could somehow reach David, it was her. He'd seen that determination before, long ago in a young Cassandra. He remembered the way she had been proud and a bit cocky when she'd told him that it was just her and her mom, that she didn't need a dad who treated them like dirt, lied to them, didn't love them.

There was some real sad irony here that he didn't want to entertain.

His thoughts turned to Kate. He still hadn't called her, nor texted her. He had left things awkward between them and now he wasn't sure where they stood. What if she was gone when he got back, whenever that might be? He still had no idea when his mom's service was going to be, but he figured it was a few days from now. And then there was his dad to think about.

He was going to be here at least a week, possibly more. At some point, he was going to have to let Kate know, if not as his girlfriend, then as his boss. Someone was going to have to pick up the slack at the station.

His life was playing tug of war.

David cleared his throat and Bradley was pulled back to the here and now. There was some sort of silent standoff between his brother and Angel that he'd missed. Or maybe he was just in the way for them to have a tête-à-tête. But then again, his dad was sitting quietly in the chair closest to the fireplace and he couldn't leave him to fend for himself. Angel would probably step up.

David, probably not.

So many painful memories seeped through these walls. He hadn't known exactly what to expect when coming home, but *this* was starting to remind him of why he'd moved away, and by *this* he really meant David. He supposed he'd hoped that his brother had changed, but he hadn't; his ego was still too big for this house and Bradley really didn't want to get into it. This was supposed to be a day of mourning. Their mom was gone and they should all be here supporting each other, celebrating her life, sharing stories.

Instead they were jabbing each other just like before, as if time had simply waited for them to get back together before it continued, uninterrupted, like nothing had changed. But *Bradley* had changed. Or so he'd thought. But his brother always got the better of him. He would have thought that he'd be past all of that, but just being in the same room as David made all his good intensions drift through his fingers like mist.

It pissed him off that they couldn't put aside their stupid childish behaviours for the sake of saying goodbye to their mother.

He had to shoulder some of the blame. He'd run away and had left everything unresolved, including his feelings for Cassandra. As great as it had been to see her again, he knew they weren't the same two people. He'd held on to that fleeting spark for so long and now he didn't know what to do with it.

That spark might even have cost him Kate.

Bradley walked to the front window. His eyes traced the small crack he'd noticed earlier, the one that had spider-webbed into the top left corner of the outside frame. And in the corner, there was an actual spider's web.

It felt like the entire house was trapped in that web.

He pulled his phone from his back pocket and typed *Miss you*. He stared at the text, then pressed the button with the X on it and deleted his message.

He shoved his phone into his back pocket.

Trapped in a spider's web.

Bradley dragged a hand across his face. The day was only half over but he was already beat.

CR 80

Angel glanced at her uncle who was standing with his back to her, looking out the front window. Her grandfather was sitting in the chair, seemingly falling asleep. Her mom hadn't returned from wherever she'd gone to. Lilly was out on the porch and for a moment, Angel entertained joining her.

But her dad had opened up and she wanted to probe. This didn't happen often—ever?—and for some reason he'd let his guard down.

"What does that mean?" Angel said. "Did I screw up your plans? Force you to marry Mom?"

David looked at her, then glanced away. Angel noticed that her dad seemed uncomfortable. There was genuine pain crossing his face. "You were the best news I'd ever gotten. I really thought that finally my life was going to turn. It was only later that . . . things changed."

"I don't understand," Angel said. "Why was your life so horrible? Grandma and Grandpa are great. Are you blaming Uncle Brad?"

"It's more complicated than that."

"Everyone says that but no one explains," she said, the frustration reddening her cheeks. "Why don't you tell me, Dad, why it's so complicated? Like you said earlier, I'm an adult now. I can take it."

David met her eyes. "I know. But it's really not for me to tell. You should ask your—"

Just then Cassandra came into the sitting room and chased away whatever it was that David was going to say. Angel let a scream die in her throat.

"Did I interrupt something?" Cassandra said.

Angel saw her uncle turn around. He looked defeated. They made eye contact and he gave her an apologetic smile that she returned.

"You're drunk," David said to his wife.

"You're not far behind," she snapped back.

"Can the two of you just stop?" Angel said while throwing her hands in the air. "I'm so tired of your petty fighting. You don't need to stay together because of me. Get a *fucking* divorce."

No one spoke. Everyone looked away. The room shrank as decades of tension settled in like an unwanted intruder.

ଔ ଓ

The look of shock on David and Cassandra's faces was rather amusing, and Bradley had to admit that for a brief moment, he'd stopped breathing too. It wasn't every day that parents heard their child literally swear at them with such conviction and authority.

Bradley was impressed. His niece had more balls than he'd had when he was her age, and from what he remembered about Great-Grandma Sarah, Angel seemed to be a lot like her.

Which wasn't a bad thing when you were part of the Knighton family.

"Yes, your mother and I could get a divorce," David said. "Now that you're an adult and soon will be on your own, you definitely don't need us."

"Not like you did much—" Cassandra said.

"Mom, you need to let that go," Angel said. "I have. Dad was busy working. Move on."

Cassandra looked ashamed and sat at the far end of the couch.

"We should talk about selling the house," David said.

"Ah, the real reason you showed up," Bradley said. "I shouldn't be surprised."

"Dad can't stay here by himself," David said. "We have a house, Emily has a condo, and you'll be going back to Vancouver. I'm sure I can get a real nice price for this place. Prime location now that the village is growing with that new subdivision being built in the west end, so a lot more people are looking to move here."

"You want to sell Grandpa's house?" Angel said. "This is Great-Great-Grandma Sarah's house. We can't sell it, Dad. It's wrong."

Henry grunted.

"Dad," Bradley said, "we're not selling your home, so don't worry."

"Grandpa can't stay here by himself," David said, looking at his daughter. "We can't keep something just because we have some sentimental feelings for it."

"Sometimes that's the only reason why we keep something," Angel said. "I love this old house."

"Angel is right," Bradley said. "We all love this house. Not everything is a deal waiting for you to make."

"That's where you're wrong," Cassandra said, slurring slightly. "*Life* is a damn deal waiting for him to make."

David ignored his wife and eyed Bradley. "Are *you* going to look after this place?"

"We can hire a company to look after it."

"And are you going to foot the bill?"

"I'm sure the three of us will manage."

"Now you're speaking for Emily?"

"She's not going to want to sell the house either," Bradley said. "She might even want to move in. Closer to the bakery."

"Well, that's another discussion," David said.

"What did I say," Cassandra said. "Everything is a deal."

"Mom," Angel warned.

"Your father thinks he can sell anything."

Angel shook her head. "Mom, really."

Cassandra stared into her glass.

Bradley felt bad for her, but right now he needed to deal with David. "That bakery has been in the family for a hundred years too. Emily ran it with Mom and I know she'll want to keep running it."

David smirked.

"What's so funny?" Bradley said.

"A couple of years back, I put a lot of money into the bakery," David said. "Mom asked me if I could help, and I did."

"You want a medal?"

His smirk seemed to swallow his face. "No. But the bakery belongs to me now, so I can do whatever I want with it."

"What does that mean?" Bradley said. "The bakery belongs to all of us."

David shook his head slowly. "Nope. Mom signed the deed over to me. My promise to her was that as long as she ran it, we'd keep it in the family, but once she could no longer manage it, I could do with it what I wanted."

"Just like I said," Cassandra said.

Bradley gave her a dirty look before turning his attention back to his brother. "Does Emily know this? She's been working in the bakery since she was a kid. That bakery belongs to her. Why would Mom agree to this?"

David said nothing.

Bradley clenched his jaw. "You gave Mom no choice, did you? If she wanted the money to renovate, she had to sign it over. You're something else."

"It's business."

"Dirty business," Bradley said. "To your own mother. That seems low even for you, but I guess I shouldn't be surprised by what you do."

"You disappeared decades ago. You turned your back on this family and now you think you can just come back here and tell me what I can and can't do? Huh-uh, little brother. As far as I'm concerned, you don't have a say in anything that goes on here."

"David Knighton has ruled," Cassandra declared and raised her glass. A frown crossed her face. She went about refilling her empty glass.

Angel rolled her eyes.

Bradley ignored Cassandra. "It doesn't matter if I live here or across the country. I'm still part of this family and I have as much say about everything concerning this family as you do. And so does Emily. Her hard work is the reason the bakery is doing great, not your loan. You can't seriously think you're the only one who'll decide what we're going to do?"

David took a long sip of his drink. "I have a signed deed."

It made no sense to Bradley why David would do this. "If we have to, Emily and I will seek legal advice. There must be a way to stop you."

"You can try," David said. "But I'm pretty sure you'll lose."

"I start culinary arts Tuesday at Algonquin," Angel said. "You know that. I was going to join Grandma and Aunt Emily after I graduate. It's not right, Dad."

David couldn't look at Angel.

"We'll figure something out," Bradley said to his niece. "Because you're right: this isn't *right* at all."

FOURTEEN

mily pulled her compact car behind David's latest toy, a silver Audi Q5. She had no idea how much it must have cost, but she was sure that she could get three Hyundai Accents for what he'd paid, which suited her just fine. Didn't matter how much money you spent on a car, it lost its value fast, cost money to fix, and over time they all rusted. Canadian winters didn't discriminate in that regard. When roads were snowy and icy, salt took care of that and cars eventually paid for it.

Emily took a deep breath. She'd been gone long enough for the little Knighton clan to gather, and as thrilled as she had been to see Bradley again last night after being away so long, she doubted that he and David were going to kiss and make up.

She doubted they'd even shake hands.

Oh Mom, I wish you were still here.

Emily stepped out of her little car and peeked across the street at the bakery. There was a constant flow of people coming and going and she felt a sense of pride and accomplishment in the turnaround she and her mom had achieved over the last year and a half.

At least her mom had lived long enough to see the family business thrive again.

Emily turned to look at the house, and felt that as good as things were across the street, on this side an air of tension hovered over the family home like a dark cloud on a stormy summer's day. There was only one unknown: when was the outburst going to happen.

Not if.

When.

Bradley and David under the same roof after all this time would be like two bulls corralled into the same arena to determine once and for all who was the biggest alpha. Back in the day, she would have said that David was, but after last night, the Bradley that had left as barely a man had returned stronger and more assured of himself than she recalled. Bradley reminded her of her dad now, whereas before he had been more like her mom.

And David being David, he wouldn't see that, partly because he failed to notice change, and partly because he was still arrogantly cocky and believed that he was better than everyone else. She guessed he wouldn't have been so dominant when he played hockey if he hadn't been, and he wouldn't have built a successful real estate business, but there was a fine line between being self-assured and being a plain dumbass.

David teetered on that line too often.

She had to admit that she kind of relished the idea of seeing Big Brother knocked down a little, but then she also feared that he'd win again and send Bradley running back to Vancouver, this time for good.

She didn't want that.

Emily recalled when she was ten and Bradley was twelve, her parents had taken them to the drive-in in Gloucester and they'd fallen asleep in the back seat after watching *A League of Their Own*. She had woken later to see a distraught Ripley all sweaty as the alien monster's slimy mouth was inches away from her face and Emily had screamed so loud that her mother started to scream and her dad spilled his Coke and Bradley woke up and immediately wrapped his arms around her and told his parents they had to leave right now.

Right now!

That's who Bradley was to her: the brother who kept the monsters away. He'd always been there for her after each broken heart and had been the one to suggest she go to Algonquin College to study culinary arts because he knew that she'd be great at it after seeing how much she loved helping at the bakery.

Seeing him now after so much time apart only to know that he'd be gone from her life again soon made her desperate to coax him into staying. David wasn't part of her life and would never be. Besides, David had never saved her from the Alien monster.

It was selfish, but the way she saw it, she had just lost her mom, her dad would mentally be gone soon, and that left her alone. Cassandra was a good sister-in-law, but she was fighting her own demons, and Angel was on the cusp of adulthood, ready to start her life.

At thirty-five, Emily knew better than to hope for a man to sweep her off her feet any time soon. She was attractive, but too strong for all the men she'd dated so far.

And being a bakery owner in a small village of eight thousand people didn't exactly give her a lot of opportunities to meet Mr.

Right. The sensible thing might be to sell the bakery and try to get a job in a fancy shop in Ottawa or even move to Toronto, but that bakery had been in her blood for too long, and there was no way she was going to be the one to disappoint Great-Grandma Sarah.

No way in the world was she going to give up on the family bakery.

Emily grabbed two duffel bags full of clothes from the hatchback and left her laptop, ereader, and specialty foam pillow—which had cost her a pretty penny but was a big help with her neck pain—in the back seat to be retrieved later. She took a breath and headed toward the front door.

She stopped at the bottom of the porch stairs and glared at the steps she climbed daily as she and her mom would come home for a quick bite to eat at noon, but that climb was going to be different this time. This time, that climb was going to change the rest of her life. This time, her mom wasn't with her.

She walked up the steps and stopped. Lilly was sitting by herself on the old porch swing and the two looked uneasily at each other.

"It's easy to find a thousand soldiers, but hard to find a good general," Lilly said.

Emily was about to ask but suddenly she could hear the war going on inside the house.

"Thanks for the warning."

Emily stood straight and opened the front door. She could smell blood and fear in the air and without a doubt knew that David had to be at the centre of whatever was going on, and she was sure that she wasn't going to like whatever it was that he was trying to sell to the others.

Because with David, everything seemed to be a one-sided deal.

CB ∂O

The first thing Emily did was to drop her bags on the floor, take a calming breath, and join the happy family. She quickly noticed that all the adults—except her dad—had drinks in hand, so that accounted for how loudly they were talking, or in this case, nearly screaming at each other.

She made eye contact with her niece, who simply shrugged and stared back with great big eyes full of helplessness, and then she looked at her dad, who was lost to whatever reality had befallen him. That filled her heart with sadness, but she was also glad that he wasn't really witnessing the carnage that was happening right in front of him. Emily pulled a brave mask over her face even though her instincts told her to simply back out and leave.

She knew that wasn't an option.

The responsibility of mediating the family through the next few days until they buried her mother had fallen on her already tired shoulders, so she saw no point in prolonging the inevitable and jumped right into the rapid-fire conversation.

Sometimes, she hated being stuck in the middle of the sibling rivalry, but she always remembered that Alien movie and couldn't leave Bradley to face David by himself. David could be such a Neanderthal but he was her brother too, family, and family had to stick together, especially in times likes these.

"HEY!" she yelled.

To her amazement, the room fell silent instantly and they all turned slowly toward her. Her stomach tightened as she stared back at the wild eyes of the well-inebriated.

Great, she thought. *The zombies know I'm here and they look hungry.*

Like children, they all started to talk at once, each trying to get his point across to her as quickly as possible so that she would side with him or her, but all she heard was a bunch of garbled nonsense which gave her a headache.

She could use one of those drinks.

Ironically, being the baby of the family, she was going to have to be the parent and settle whatever dispute had them all frothing at the mouth. And somehow, she needed to be impartial and not be too hasty to condemn David.

Not yet, anyway.

"David wants to—"

"Brad has no say in—"

"If my darling husband wasn't—"

"I do *so* have a right—"

"No he doesn't—"

"You don't decide everything—"

Emily stood frozen, unable to move or speak, a bystander that had arrived after the accident. They were supposed to be mourning Mom's passing, but that looked like the last thing anyone was thinking of. Emily had been gone long enough to allow herself, in the privacy of her empty apartment, to grieve, to be angry, to shout, to swear, and to grieve some more until she had shed all her tears.

She knew Bradley had probably grieved quietly when he'd gone to bed last night, as was his way, and Cassandra and Angel would have grieved in their own way when they'd found out.

Which left David.

All-business David.

All-heartless David.

All-about-me David.

What exactly made him tick? There had to be something behind that exterior armour, a heart of some sort. What had turned him into such a harsh and distant man?

Why did he always seem to hate them all?

Instead of bowing to their childish behaviours, Emily crossed her arms and stood there exactly like her mother used to do to them when they were young, giving them a look that said *if you're going to behave like idiots, you don't deserve my attention.*

Eventually, the noise started to diminish, until it stopped.

"So—"

"David wants to—"

"Brad's been away too long and—"

"If David hadn't cheated on me all—"

"SHUT UP ALL OF YOU!" Angel shouted as she came to stand beside her aunt. "You're all a bunch of stupid grownups. Grandma just died and all you can do is bicker about the house and the bakery as if the decision is yours to make. It's NOT! The bakery belongs to Aunt Emily and the house still belongs to Grandpa. You're all just a bunch of morons." She stared at them all, especially her dad. "Maybe for once in your life you can think of someone besides yourself."

David opened his mouth but something made him swallow his words.

"I'm going outside to be with Lilly," she said.

"No," Emily said with an air of authority she'd never known she had. "You stay right here."

"But—" Angel said.

"I need you here because right now, I don't know what's going on and you've been here all this time, so you do." She eyed her brothers. "And I don't trust either one of them to tell me the truth."

An unnerving silence settled inside the house at 1202 Main Street in the sleepy village of Forest Creek, founded in 1822 by Scottish and Irish immigrants who had left the old world in hopes of a better life. Nearly two hundred years later, for the Knighton family, it seemed that life was anything but better as sibling was pinned against sibling, wife against husband, truth against lie.

Emily looked at her dad and tried to will him to have one of his lucid moments right now. If her brothers were going to listen to anyone, it would be Dad.

Hope fled.

Emily's eyes shifted to the wedding picture of her mom and dad on the mantel. They looked so young and happy. They'd still had their whole life ahead of them—but their time had now passed.

Emily pushed her shoulders back.

FIFTEEN

Bradley had recognized earlier this morning that Emily was no longer the shy and self-doubting baby sister he'd known growing up, but he hadn't quite noticed this self-assured and determined woman.

"Everything was fine until—"

Emily put up a hand to quiet Bradley. "Angel? You want to tell me why they're all frothing at the mouth? I was only gone a few hours."

"Dad wants to sell the house and the bakery," she said and let out a broken sigh. "And . . ."

Just then Henry walked out of the room.

"Dad, where're you going?" Emily said.

"To my room," he said with a hint of defiance. "I need to get away from the lot of you crazy people yelling and screaming. I can't hear myself think."

"Did he call us *you people?*" David said.

"Give him a break," Cassandra said and finished her drink. She refilled two fingers' worth from the bottle she was holding. "He's gone through a lot."

"You should go easy on that," David said. "You know how you get when you drink too much."

"How *I* get!" Cassandra said loudly. "Like you'd know how I get when you're never home."

A hard stare crossed David's face. "This isn't the place or time."

"Why not?" The slur to her speech was getting worse. "Seems like a fine time to hang our dirty laundry."

"Cass," Bradley said.

"Yeah, *Cass*," David mimicked.

"Real grown up," Bradley said.

"Hey, *you're* the one getting chummy with *my* wife again."

"Who apparently you've neglected for a long time."

"That's enough," Emily said, once again sounding like their mother. "The two of you are acting like five-year-olds."

"Who made you the matriarch?" David said.

"I did."

Bradley watched his brother struggle with that slap to his ego. Emily had surprised them again, but before David could regroup, Cassandra staggered over to her husband.

"You smell like her," Cassandra said, standing up close to David. "That slut you sleep with."

"You mean your best friend?" David said.

Cassandra shook her head. "She's not my best friend. She just used me to get you. You both used me. You deserve each other."

"It wasn't like that," David said. "I just . . ."

The smack of her hand across his cheek stung them all into silence. David checked his lip for blood.

"You'll live," Cassandra said.

Seemed like everyone had stopped breathing and waited to see if anything else was going to happen. They all just stared at each other, adversaries where family should stand united, distrustful when trust was needed.

The Knighton family was crumbling.

And before anyone did say something, yelling and cursing from the second floor sliced the brittle silence that had settled uncomfortably between them, pausing the battle as one by one they dashed upstairs to find out why Henry was freaking out.

CB ⅋O

Bradley was first through his parents' bedroom door and scanned the room. All he saw was his dad standing by his night table, pointing an agitated finger at the opposite corner of the room by the closet door.

"You get out!" Henry yelled. "I told you last time, I have nothing for you. I hid everything so you wouldn't steal it, so get out. GET OUT!"

The others filed into the room.

"Dad?" Bradley said and waited for his father to look at him. "Dad, there's no one there. No one is here to steal anything."

Henry glared at him. "You're in on it too. I don't know who you are but I want you out of my house. I'm calling the cops."

"Damn it Dad, there's no one here," David said.

"Don't talk to him like that," Cassandra shouted. "Can't you see he's scared?"

David ran a hand across his bald head. "This is why we need to put him in a home, so he's safe. So people who are qualified to look after people like him can take care of him."

"People like him," Cassandra said with a snort. "Listen to yourself. Just a minute ago you were offended when Henry called us *you people*, and now you label him *people like him*."

"This really isn't any of your business," David said. "He's not your dad."

"I've spent more time with him over the years than you have," Cassandra said through gritted teeth. "I have as much right to decide what happens to Henry as you do. Probably more."

"Enough!" Emily said. "Maybe the two of you should leave so that we can let Dad calm down without all this nonsense going on."

"Sorry," Cassandra said and moved back to the doorway.

"We need to—" David said.

"I don't want to hear it," Emily said sharply. "Cassandra is right. You've been MIA for way too long to decide what is best for Dad."

"You—"

"I said zip it, Dave, and I mean it."

Brother and sister were locked in a duel of glares. David was first to look away. He took a few steps back.

"Have it your way," he said.

"What do we do with Dad?" Bradley said to Emily. "He still looks like he's seen the devil."

"We need to try to calm him, make him see there is nothing to fear."

"Let me," Angel said.

Emily gave her a nod.

"Grandpa," Angel said and walked toward him. "That's Uncle Bradley. Your son. He's been away a while but he's home now and he's telling the truth. No one is in your room to steal anything from you. We won't let anyone hurt you or steal your things. Promise."

The air in the room was full of quiet tension. Angel glanced at her aunt and uncle. Emily gave her another encouraging nod.

"Remember when I was eleven," Angel said, "and you and Grandma came to my dance recital? I had a solo part and missed two steps and was so mad with myself, but you stood up when the music stopped and hollered and clapped so loud that I forgot I'd messed up. You were always there for me and we're all here for you now."

Henry looked at her a long time before recognition bubbled up in his eyes. "Pretty hard not to believe an angel."

"I love you, Grandpa," Angel said and wrapped her arms around him. "I hate it when you go away."

Henry stroked her hair. "I hate it too."

CS 8O

After the others headed back down, Bradley and Emily stayed with Henry until they were sure he was okay, that his hallucinations had passed.

The three of them were sitting on the edge of the bed, facing the antique dresser that had belonged to Great-Grandma Sarah. A frameless mirror hung above it on the wall that had last seen a fresh coat of white paint in the 1950s.

"I miss my Irene," Henry said and put a hand over his heart. "Right here."

Emily took his other hand. "We miss Mom too."

"I wish I could have come home once in a while," Bradley said.

"She talked about you all the time," Henry said. "She was so proud of you, having left home so young and having that success. She called you her radio celebrity son to everyone who would listen to her at the bakery. They were always asking her about her celebrity son and she was more than happy to tell them all about you."

Bradley felt his face heat up. "I was nothing like a celebrity. I announced songs that were played, babbled some nonsenses to fill the gaps, recited traffic reports when I did the afternoon shift."

"You and Kate turned that station around," Emily said, the pride in her voice unmistakeable. "You were nineteen when you left, still wet behind the ears, as Dad often said. But you stuck it out. And met the love of your life."

Bradley looked away.

He did love Kate, but—

Marriage and babies?

Maybe not babies, but a baby. What if he wasn't cut out to be a dad? And since being back home, he'd seen the mess Cassandra had become. Maybe if he'd stayed . . .

But she had been pregnant with David's baby. There had been no reason for him to stay. But it was hard not to feel guilty and somewhat responsible. Maybe he just liked to torture himself, run away from happiness.

Run away from things he was afraid of. Was that what he was doing again? Except this time, he had run back home instead of away.

"Kate's great."

"I thought she would have come with you."

"She wanted to come," he said. "I just didn't know how things were going to be here so I thought it best if she didn't."

"It would be nice to meet her someday."

"You will," he said.

"Before the wedding, I hope."

He smiled awkwardly, and lied. "No wedding anytime soon."

"She could still come, if she can get away," Emily said. "Mom's funeral might not happen until Friday. I still need to call the funeral home."

"We're burying Mom in the Forest Creek Cemetery, right?"

"With everyone else," she said. "She wants to be cremated. There's lots of room for all of us."

Henry let out a quiet moan. "She was a good woman."

"She was a good mom and a better friend," Emily said. "I'll really miss her at the bakery."

Bradley noticed from the reflection in the mirror that all three of them had long silver streaks running down their cheeks. His mom had not been a simple woman, at times harder than his dad. She'd helped all three kids with their homework, made sure chores were done before playtime or TV time, and hadn't put up with their nonsense.

One thing had always bothered him, though, and maybe he'd just imagined it, but he'd always felt like she'd treated David a little differently, let him get away with a little more than she had with him and Emily. He'd always been envious of that. Just because he was the oldest, she'd loved him a little more.

Which had made it hard for Bradley to tell her everything David did. So, he'd endured the bullying, and learned to resent David a little bit more as time passed.

Resentment was hard to get rid of, even after all these years. Part of him didn't want to get along with Big Brother. Bradley was still a bit jealous that David had been his mom's favourite, and her favouritism had played a big part in his running away.

That, and losing Cassandra.

"So," Emily said. "Big Brother wants to sell the house and the bakery."

Bradley let out a big sigh. "He says Mom signed over the deed for the bakery when he lent you the money."

Emily was quiet. "I see. And the house?"

"Sees an opportunity to make a buck," Bradley said. "He has a point, though. Dad can't stay here by himself."

"No, he can't," Emily said, looking at her dad. "But he won't be. I'm going to move in. Makes sense to be close to the bakery anyway."

"You can't do both, Em," he said. "Dad's only going to need more and more care."

She looked at her father. "I know. It's just hard to accept."

"It is."

They both looked at Henry. "You okay, Dad?" Bradley said.

"Your great-grandmother had only one wish when she died," Henry said. "That bakery should stay in the family for as long as there is another generation to run it."

Bradley wasn't a lawyer but if Mom had really signed over the deed to David, he didn't think a whole lot could be done if Big

Brother was set on selling the place. "Then we'd better not break Great-Grandma Sarah's wish."

SIXTEEN

Cassandra sat on the couch, her glass empty and her head spinning, the bottle calling her but she wasn't sure it was a good idea. She eyed her husband, who was pacing back and forth across the sitting room with the patience of someone who had better things to do than be here supposedly mourning the passing of his mother.

It was difficult not to despise him.

There was a long list of things he'd done to warrant her anger but the one that grated most on her nerves was the way he'd shown so little interest in Angel's life. They only had the one child, so the least he could have done was spend more time with her, be there for the special moments in her life, show her a little love.

"Did those two fall asleep?" David said after checking his watch for the hundredth time. "I'd really like to settle things."

"Why? Josée waiting for you?"

"I have a showing at six."

"Seriously?" she said. "You couldn't let someone else do it? Your mom just died yesterday."

David looked at her a very long time and she couldn't quite tell what the look on his face meant. If she had to guess, he was probably trying to figure a way to make himself appear like he was hurting, but in all the years she'd known him, she had never seen him care enough about anyone to feel any sort of loss. She often wondered what Josée saw in him, especially since the handsome and fit man he'd once been wasn't who was standing in front of her now.

Well, some men could rock baldness and David was one of those, just like Henry. Unlike his dad, who still remained fit and solid, David should be careful with his weight gain. That and the stress of chasing the next deal could easily bring on a heart attack.

She might despise him, but she didn't wish him any harm. It was a battle she'd been losing for years, loving and hating him at the same time.

She was ready to let go of both emotions.

Move on.

Start a new life.

"I'm sorry that she died," he finally said. He paused and she saw him struggle to find what he wanted to say. "But we were never really that close."

Cassandra felt her face crumble. She couldn't have heard him right. Maybe she was more drunk than she realized. Irene had always asked about David when she and Angel came over for dinner and he couldn't join them. Irene had always wanted to know if everything was all right with them—and Cassandra had always felt guilty about lying to her mother-in-law. And it had always surprised her that Irene never noticed, or if she had, she'd never said anything.

"What are you talking about?" Cassandra said. "Your mom always asked about you, wanted to make sure you were all right. She was always disappointed when you didn't show up for Sunday dinner."

There was a long pause.

"I learned from my mother."

Okay, she must be drunk after all because she couldn't figure out what David was talking about. "You learned what?"

He gave that look that she hated, the one that made her feel small, dumb, and not worth his time. What had she done to make him hate her so much? She had loved him with all of her heart and had thought that he loved her too. She remembered the night that she'd truly fallen in love with him. It was Canada Day and a bunch of them had gone downtown to take in the festivities on Parliament Hill and then watch the fireworks, and that day had been spectacular. David had made her laugh, had made her feel like she was his world, had told her he loved her.

She couldn't remember the last time he'd made her feel that way or told her he loved her, or the last time they'd kissed with passion. She really didn't know when exactly their marriage had died.

Too long ago.

Since he wasn't answering her, she poured a finger of whiskey into her glass and downed it. How many was that? Four? Five? Did it really matter?

She poured another but didn't touch it.

Her eyes wandered toward the stairs, eager for the others to join them. Being alone with David wasn't at the top of her list of fun things to do.

CЗ 80

When Angel came into the house to join her parents in the sitting room, a spear of sunshine passed through the front window as the sun moved from behind a cloud. Instantly, Cassandra's dark mood was pushed aside.

Angel had always been her sunshine, the light that made her life bearable.

"Is Lilly all right?" Cassandra said. "Guess it wasn't a good idea to bring her today."

Angel sat beside her mother. "I just wanted to have a friend with me, you know? Help me keep it together. I wasn't expecting this."

"No one did."

"And it's all my fault, I suppose," David said.

"Please, Dad," Angel said. "Put the guns away. For Grandma's sake."

He looked away.

"That was great how you got to Grandpa," Cassandra said. "I know this is hard on you."

"It sucks," Angel said. "I feel so sad seeing him like that. It's not fair."

"I know."

"I remember when I was six and he took me to the Forest Creek Fair because Dad was busy as always and you'd gotten sick. Grandma and Aunt Emily were at the bakery because the Fair was always great for business."

Cassandra ran a hand down Angel's long hair. It was so soft and gorgeous. Her hair had been like that too at that age, but over time it had gotten shorter. It now barely touched her shoulders.

"I loved the car derby. It was loud, but Grandpa would talk into his hands like he was the announcer and it made me laugh so hard. He'd come on the rides with me and scream louder than me. He'd buy me cotton candy and ice cream."

"All the important fair food groups."

Angel nodded. "Yep."

"Those were good days," Cassandra said.

Angel was silent for a moment. "And now Grandma is gone and Grandpa . . . I know I'm eighteen but I've always liked hanging out here with them. I always had a good time. They were fun."

David snorted but said nothing.

"You're still here?" Cassandra said, not hiding her annoyance. "I thought you had some big deal to close."

"It's a showing. At six. Here in town."

Cassandra eyed him suspiciously.

"Mom, Dad," Angel said. "Can the two of you just put it away? You guys have any idea how growing up in the middle of this hate has been for me?"

"Your mother—" David said.

"Oh, shut up, Dad," Angel said and immediately put a hand to her mouth.

"Well, sounding more and more like your mother every day," he said.

"Maybe if you'd been around and spent time with her," Cassandra said.

David glanced away.

"Never anything to say when I'm right," Cassandra said.

"You're drunk," he said.

"And whose fault is that?" she said. "Maybe if you'd paid attention to me like a husband should. Funny how you used to tell me I was your world. Guess I was a very tiny, small world."

He didn't say anything.

"Like Angel said earlier, we might as well get a divorce," Cassandra said and downed her glass of whiskey. It had never tasted this good. Finally, the rest of her life could begin. "I've had enough."

SEVENTEEN

Bradley and Emily made their way down the creaky century-old stairs that had made it impossible for them to sneak in late at night when they were teenagers and coming home past curfew. Growing up in a small village like Forest Creek, there wasn't much the kids could do to get in trouble except hang out in someone's back yard with a fire going and pass around beers someone had snatched from a home fridge.

And maybe smoke a little weed.

And maybe a couple or two would wander away to find a quiet space to make out. Nothing harmful.

Until someone got pregnant.

Happened quite often. But Bradley hadn't expected it to happen to Cassandra, especially after her heart was broken on her nineteenth birthday. He'd really thought that Cassandra and David were done after that night, but once his brother found out she was pregnant, the dumbass did the decent thing and married her.

How things might have been different if those two things hadn't happened. After he'd left for Vancouver, on nights he was alone and feeling sorry for himself—there were plenty of those for more years than he cared to admit—he'd wonder if things would have turned out differently if he'd told her how he really felt long before she started to date David. He'd always been afraid to ruin their friendship, but in the end, doing nothing had ruined it anyway.

Even if he'd told her he loved her, they might have tried to date only to find out they were just meant to be friends. He might have ended up going out west anyway, and meeting Kate.

He needed to call her so they could talk about marriage. And a baby.

If this day ever gave him a moment to pause and take a breath.

He felt all of the day's weariness in his neck and upper back, and his brain was trying to sort everything out, but he felt like he was losing. All he knew was that there was no way he could just dump all of it on Emily and go back to the west coast. That wouldn't be fair to her.

But it was like nothing had changed in nearly twenty years. The same craziness had carried over from the past to the present. Leaving probably had been the right move for him. Leaving again wouldn't be easy if he and Emily didn't win over David. The guilt of seeing Emily lose everything wouldn't be something that he'd be able to shrug off.

As they reached the bottom of the stairs, he wondered what other nonsense could possibly be dragged out of their dark and rancid closet of lies and secrets.

CB EO

Bradley had just stepped off the last stair when he heard Cassandra echo what Angel had said earlier. The word *divorce* reached his ears and he came to an abrupt stop. Emily ran into him and then swatted the back of his head.

"What'd you do that for?" he whispered.

"For stopping without telling me," she said quietly.

"Didn't you hear what Cassandra just said?"

"About frigging time, if you ask me," Emily whispered. "I would have kicked David's ass out the door a long time ago if I'd been her."

"They were so in love when I left," he said. "Planning their wedding and all."

Emily shook her head. "It didn't last long. Two or three years."

"So why wait until now?"

She shrugged. "Wanting Angel to grow up in a house with both parents."

"What's the point if it's an unhappy home?"

"I don't know," she said. "It's amazing she's turned out as good as she has. Unfortunately, Cassandra hasn't fared as well."

"I should never have left."

"And what could you have done to change things?"

"I was her friend."

"And David was her boyfriend, then her husband. And she was pregnant." Her eyes softened. "I figured out long ago how you really felt about her. She got pregnant, David proposed, you left. Nothing secret there."

"Did Mom and Dad know too?"

"I'm not sure," she said. "You and David got pretty good at pretending nothing was wrong. But I saw, I noticed."

He said nothing.

"Welcome home," Emily said and ruffled his hair. "I'm glad I don't have to do this alone."

He gave her a soft, apologetic smile. "I have a feeling you don't really need me. You're not the little sister I left behind."

"Maybe not," she said. "But it's still nice to have you here."

CB EO

Cassandra saw Bradley and Emily return without Henry and figured they'd managed to put him to bed so he could get some rest. The stress of losing Irene had to affect him, even if he wasn't coherent all the time. She had seen how much Henry had loved his wife, had even envied Irene for the way her husband, after more than forty years of marriage, still looked at her with the hungry eyes of a boy madly in love.

Her heart ached for that sort of affection.

What woman's wouldn't?

Her eyes followed Bradley, who seemed to be avoiding her for the moment, or maybe he was simply trying to assess the situation. He was looking at David to see what he was up against, and she understood. Her husband was sitting in the seat closest to the fireplace, his leg crossed over like someone without a care in the world, but Cassandra could see the tension oozing out of him.

That ray of sunshine that had followed Angel into the room earlier suddenly disappeared and an air of coolness elbowed itself in like an invader. The room felt a little darker, as if it had adjusted to the mood settling in.

Cassandra took a sip of whiskey, trying to pace herself now. Her head was spinning and tomorrow she knew she was going to pay for it. She was pretty sure that tomorrow she was going to pay for a whole lot more than just a hangover.

She took another sip.

Bradley finally looked at her and it saddened her to see pity in his eyes. Pity was the last thing she wanted from him. She had made mistakes. Everyone made mistakes. She was tired of apologizing for those mistakes.

Tired of paying for them, too.

What she needed right now was a friend.

Nothing more.

Just her childhood friend, the one who'd listened, the one she used to laugh with, the one she should have been in love with.

And she had been, but as a friend. And maybe she had been afraid to ruin that friendship by seeking more from it.

She didn't know. It was so long ago that she couldn't really be sure of her feelings from back then. The only feelings she was certain of right now were those she had for David.

The kind that turned your heart to stone.

So, yeah, she wanted a divorce. Not because Bradley was back, not because she thought that maybe, just maybe, they might have a chance. No, she wanted a divorce because she had finally run out of excuses for not facing the rest of her life on her own.

CB EO

Angel had never seen her mom so determined; the intensity in her eyes almost made her look crazed. She knew the alcohol was helping her mother find her gumption, but it still unsettled Angel.

And then there was her dad sitting in that posture that she'd seen too many times, like he had this, and no one was going to outdo him.

Angel could actually feel the room get colder as the tension shrank the space like a deflating balloon. Her parents were like a perfect storm, a cold front about to collide with a warm front.

And then Uncle Bradley and Aunt Emily entered the room, bringing with them an electrical charge that jolted Angel. It was almost like little fires had been lit under everyone.

She couldn't breathe.

All she wanted to do was to flee, to run out of the room, out of the house, away from whatever was going to happen.

But she wasn't a kid anymore and she really needed to be part of whatever it was that was coming. What was the worst thing that could happen? Not like she didn't know her parents were probably going to get a divorce.

CB ED

Emily stood in the wide opening where the sitting room and the front hallway merged, her eyes moving from person to person, assessing moods. She had once been a timid girl but that was before many failed relationships—with guys too weak or too controlling to deserve her love—and years of working with her mom at the bakery had turned her into a woman who could deal with anything.

And this situation needed to be dealt with.

David needed to be dealt with.

She and her oldest brother had never been close, and not by her choice. For some reason, David only saw girls as something to conquer or possess, or both, and with her being his sister, he'd seen neither the need nor desire to bother with her.

Probably because he had never seen her as a threat.

Which she hoped was going to work in her favour. With Mom dying, three things were left up in the air: the situation with Dad, the house, and the bakery.

They all knew what would need to be done with Dad. It wasn't going to be easy, but being a Knighton had never been easy.

As for the house, it belonged to her Dad now and when her mom had drawn up her will, she had also written up a power of attorney that gave Emily the authority to look after Henry's affairs should he become incapacitated. Mom had seen Dad begin to show the same signs as his father when he was about the same age. Dad's father had also had Alzheimer's, so Mom had known what was coming and she'd wanted to make sure that if anything happened to her, she'd be leaving things in order.

So if David thought that he was going to score big on the sale of the house, he was going to be greatly disappointed. No way Emily was selling Great-Grandma Sarah's house.

Which left the bakery.

Sure, he had loaned them the money, but Emily was having a hard time believing her mother would have signed over the deed to David. That just didn't sound like something her mom would do. She knew what the bakery meant to Emily. No, David had to be bluffing.

Why else would Irene have willed the bakery to Emily? It didn't make sense.

Emily eyed David.

He must be bluffing.

She knew her brother.

But he could be a very shrewd businessman.

That left her feeling uneasy.

CO ∞

Bradley had once loved Cassandra. Yes, they had been friends for a long time, since grade school, but at some point—and he couldn't exactly tell when that happened—his fondness for her friendship had stepped over that line and he had fallen madly in love with her.

He had never told her.

Like any shy and insecure introvert, he'd hoped that his actions would show her how he felt, that she would *catch his drift*, but that had never happened.

That was his fault for lacking the confidence to take a chance.

Looking at Cassandra right this moment, how vulnerable and broken she seemed, he knew they had both made the wrong decision. He would have loved her the way she would have needed to be loved, like she deserved to be loved, but it was too late for that now.

His life was different.

He loved someone else.

It didn't mean that he didn't care for Cassandra, and if he could help her, he would. He just needed to be careful not to cross that line, because it was so easy to think that nothing had changed now that he was back.

Yet, everything had changed.

Lives had been lived, lives had started, lives had ended. People had grown stronger while others had wilted, and they had all squandered the one commodity that could never be given back: time.

He definitely felt conflicted, especially after hearing Cassandra ask David for a divorce. That seemed to open doors he knew should remain closed.

But . . .

Maybe some people did forget and moved on from their first true love, and maybe if Cassandra wasn't sitting right here in the sitting room—older, yes, but still very much the way he remembered the girl that had both stolen and crushed his heart, the girl he'd never truly forgotten—he wouldn't be thinking *what if?*

And risk losing Kate.

Which he didn't want. He had every intention, once his mom was buried and all the other nonsense they still hadn't sorted out yet was dealt with, to be back on that plane and back to Kate.

She was his life.

Cassandra made eye contact with him and he felt his heart weaken. It was like his intentions had been nothing more than mist floating through his fingers.

"Are you okay?" he said.

Cassandra looked into her empty glass. "I haven't been okay in a very long time."

"You going to save the damsel in distress?" David said.

Bradley shot a glare at his brother. "That was supposed to be *your* job."

"I did marry her," David said. "But then . . . things changed. Life can sometimes lie in the worst way."

"You should know," he said. "You're the biggest fake I know."

"Not quite."

A question mark crossed Bradley's face.

"It's okay, Brad," Cassandra said. "I appreciate what you're trying to do, but I don't need saving from anyone."

"Mom—"

"It's fine, sweetie," Cassandra said. "Your Dad and I, it hasn't worked in a long time. Our conversation yesterday, I think it finally woke me up, made me see that you were all grown up, that it was okay for me to take my life back."

"I know, but you're still my parents—"

"You'll be fine," Cassandra said. "You're an adult and you'll go on to live your life soon."

"Your mom is right," David said. "Some things run their course and then it's time to move on. Speaking of which," he said as he turned to look at Emily, "we need to talk about selling the house and the bakery."

Emily crossed her arms and put on a grin that resembled the same one David had become infamous for. She didn't say anything, just stared at him.

A flash of hesitation pulled David's brow into a frown. "The bakery belongs to me and Dad can't stay in the house by himself."

She continued to stare at him until he started to squirm in his seat. Then she spoke in a no-nonsense tone. "You had better produce that deed you keep bragging Mom signed over to you. As for the house, I have power of attorney over Dad and I'm definitely not selling it."

CR 80

Emily really hoped that David was bluffing about the deed, but her brother wasn't one to bluff. That sparked anger to rise into the back of her throat. What had her mom been thinking? And why hadn't she told Emily? That bothered Emily more than the fact that David may now own the bakery. She hadn't thought there had been secrets between her and her mom, but it turned out that she'd been wrong.

What was the point in drawing up the will? Well, Mom had known that if Dad died before her, the power of attorney for her dad would be void and then the house would become a tug of war between her and David. The will clearly stated that the house belonged to Emily if Henry was also deceased.

But the bakery couldn't be willed to Emily if it now belonged to David. And that really made Emily's stomach churn. She had worked her entire adult life in the bakery, and to think that her brother could simply sell it darkened her thoughts where her mother was concerned.

She wondered what David would have said to convince their mother to sign the deed over to him. The fact that he was already talking about selling while Mom hadn't even been buried yet told Emily that it held zero sentimental value to him, and all he saw were dollar signs to fatten his pockets.

Like he needed more.

Without the bakery, she'd be out of a job, but not just a job, a love. She loved that place and the people who worked for her. Her anger rose as she realized that those ladies would also be out of work. Jeanine had been there fifteen years.

Oh, Mom!

Emily hadn't wanted to take the loan from David, but they'd needed quite a lot of money and mortgaging her condo hadn't been an option. Her Mom hadn't been willing to remortgage the house either, which had left them with one choice.

It was too late for regrets. Besides, the place had totally turned around and was booming. Why would her brother want to sell it now? It was Great-Grandma Sarah's legacy. How could he sell that?

Emily needed to find a way to convince David to keep it.

CG EO

Bradley saw a crack in Emily's confidence and began to worry that David might actually have the deed to the bakery. He shouldn't be surprised. He guessed his brother had learned something over the years from losing so often at Monopoly. But this wasn't a game. That bakery was like a family heirloom.

You kept those, no matter what.

Bradley glanced at his niece and saw her fidget on the couch. He could feel it too. Something was coming. It had gotten too quiet in the house. Through the open window, shrieking voices from kids running on the walkway drifted in, followed by a few cars that sounded loud and angry.

Outside noise typical of a Saturday afternoon.

Except, it wasn't.

Bradley looked at the clock on the mantel: 4:13. He was so glad that Kate wasn't here. This wasn't the Knightons' best performance. Movement from the corner of his eyes drew his attention and he turned toward Cassandra just as she spilled some whiskey on her lap. He really wanted to tell her that she should ease off on the drinking, but he knew it wasn't really his place. Besides, his beer was on the coffee table so he'd look like a hypocrite—although he definitely hadn't drunk as much as she had.

He was trying not to judge.

But she was a mess.

Had being married to David really caused this?

ᛒ ᛒ

Emily noticed Bradley staring at Cassandra and even she had to admit that she had never seen her sister-in-law this bad. But she had no time right now for Cassandra. She was having her own battle with David.

How could she get him to change his mind?

"Why do you need to sell the bakery?" Emily said to David. "It's turned around. It's making some really good money."

"When I invested in the bakery, that's exactly what it was—an investment," he said, the cockiness in his tone coming across like a condescending slap. "That bakery belongs to me now and I can sell it for *really* good money."

"That bakery has been in the family for a century," Emily said, doing her best to ignore David's patronizing tone. "You can fill your pockets from the profits for *years*, so why sell it for a one-time gain?"

David struggled to find a rebuttal. "It's the perfect time to sell it now. Books look good, the place looks like new."

"You don't think I can run it on my own?"

David sipped his drink. "When Mom asked for the money, the bakery had been in the red for a while."

"We were running a business with equipment that was new when Grandma Alice took it over back in the 1950s. All our profits went into repairs. We knew we couldn't keep going that way, which is why we asked for the loan. That's all it was supposed to be."

"I saw it as an investment," David said.

"You used us."

"Used you?" he said. "I couldn't have known Mom was going to die suddenly, just two years after I invested in the bakery. I figured if you two weren't able to turn it around, then I'd step in and sell it, but I promised Mom if it turned around that I'd leave you two to run it for as long as Mom could do it."

"Without regards to me."

"Sorry, little sister, but the bakery belonged to Mom. Maybe you should have thought of becoming half owner."

Emily bit back a retort. She hated that what David had just said would have made a world of difference, but it was something she had never thought about because she had never seen a need for it. It was Mom's bakery, which she had expected to inherit eventually.

And now she was going to lose it.

C8 80

Angel felt bad for her aunt. She knew how much her aunt loved the bakery, and now that her dad was going to sell it, there wasn't much point in her choice of college program. He was ruining Aunt Emily's life *and* hers.

It pained her to hate her dad so much right now, but he'd left her no choice. He didn't care about anyone. A good man would see how much he was hurting them all, but her dad wasn't good.

"Why are you doing this?" Angel said. "What is wrong with you? This is our family."

"This doesn't concern you," David said and barely looked at her. "This is between me and them and what is rightfully mine."

"STOP IT!" Angel yelled. "Why do you hate everyone? You hate Uncle Brad. You hate Aunt Emily. You hate Mom. And you hate me. What have any of us done to you to hate us so much? Huh? What have we done?"

"You're wasting your time, honey," Cassandra said, slurring her words badly. "Your dad sees everyone as some competition that he needs to crush. He did it to me and to your Uncle Brad."

"Do tell," David said, egging her on. "Tell them your little secret."

Cassandra frowned, bit her lower lip, then looked away from her husband.

"No?" David said. "Want me to?"

"Leave Mom alone," Angel said. "You've been nothing but mean to her for years. I never said anything before because I was too young and too scared, but you need to stop. She loves you."

"Is that right?" David said and stared at his wife. "You love me?"

"What is wrong with you?" Bradley said. "When I left here, Cassandra was such a loving and happy woman. She loved you."

"And that really pissed you off, am I right?" David said. "Isn't that why you ran off? Because she chose me over you?"

Angel stared at her uncle.

"I'd hoped coming home," Bradley said, "that things might be different, but it looks like I was dead wrong. You'll never change."

"Not everything is as it seems," David said.

"Enlighten me."

But David didn't. Suddenly, David had nothing to say.

"Not like you to give up the spotlight," Bradly said.

"It's not my spotlight," David said. "It's hers."

Bradley turned toward Cassandra. "Cass?"

She looked up at him and his legs nearly gave out. The sadness in her eyes melted her face. What had happened to the sweet outgoing girl he had known?

"I'm so sorry," she said.

"Mom, this isn't your fault," Angel said.

"I should have told you both a long time ago," she said, unable to look at them. "But I thought I was doing the right thing. Brad, you were gone and Angel was just a baby."

"Cass, what are you talking about?"

"Mom?"

Cassandra hung her head against her chest. "I made a horrible mistake. I ruined everything and I blamed David for it all." She covered her face in her hands.

"Mom?"

"Cass?"

Cassandra pulled her head up, took in a deep breath, looked at Angel, then at Bradley. "Angel isn't David's daughter."

EIGHTEEN

The air in the room was gone and no one could breathe. It was like they'd all arrived at the scene of a fatal car accident and were trying to figure out what had happened, who was hurt, and where the hell the first responders were.

Where was the help?

They needed help in the worst way.

Cassandra recoiled, folding into herself, hoping to disappear. She had just dropped the H-bomb on them and the looks of shock, anger, and blame shrivelled her heart into a tiny wilted flower.

What had she done?

Instead of David looking shocked, he looked triumphant.

"How long have you known?" Cassandra said.

The look on his face was answer enough. To think that she was the only one who had noticed the signs when Angel was young had been foolish. It made sense now, his distance to Angel, and hate for her. No wonder he'd run to Josée.

"I never had proof," David said. "Just suspicions that I kept hoping were wrong."

When she had found out she was pregnant and David had proposed, she had seen their life together as a road full of possibilities. Yes, on her wedding day she had been full of doubts, but it had passed. Her life had been changing so fast and it had frightened her. But David had been just like the David who had come to her field hockey games and cheered her on. Once again, he had been the boy she had fallen in love with.

Then Angel was born and she had never seen him so happy.

When she'd begun to doubt who Angel's father was, and especially by the time she actually found out the truth, it was too late to change anything. Her life had become a lie, a lie to hide the truth. Convincing herself that David hadn't figured it out was also another lie she'd wanted to believe. Angel was left-handed, unlike David. She had auburn hair, unlike David. She was kind, empathetic, quietly strong.

Cassandra looked away, ashamed for what she had just done. She wasn't going to blame the alcohol for her lack of judgement. This mess was on her, all of it. She owned it.

And loathed it.

"I'm sorry," she said in a tiny voice. "I wasn't thinking."

"What are you talking about?" Bradley said.

"What do you mean Dad isn't my father?" Angel said, looking like her mom had just plunged a knife into her heart. "Mom?"

"How long have you known this?" Bradley said.

"Mom! How long have you known this?"

"Cassie? This is . . . I don't know what this means," Bradley said. "What does it mean? Who's Angel's father?"

Angel stood and faced her mom, who was still looking down. She screamed, "Mom, who's my dad?"

Cassandra couldn't meet her daughter's eyes—her beautiful daughter who reminded her a lot of herself, and a lot more of her real father. She was a beautiful soul, bubbly when happy, withdrawn when sad.

Of course, David would have noticed all these differences. She had wanted to believe that he wouldn't see. Hoped that he hadn't noticed since he'd paid so little attention to them. But that hadn't always been true. He had started to withdraw not long after her own suspicions had started. Until then, he had been a wonderful father and husband.

Oh God, could it be true? Had she ruined his life too?

No wonder he'd grown to resent her. She had trapped him. Not knowingly. She really had thought that he was the only one who could have gotten her pregnant. But once she had realized the truth . . . keeping the secret to herself all these years had been the right thing to do. If no one knew, no one got hurt. Except that secret had been like a cancer inside of her, killing her slowly.

She poured the last of the whiskey into her glass and gulped it down with a shaking hand. She needed another bottle. Maybe even two. She hadn't seen another in the hutch. She couldn't remember where her mother-in-law kept the booze. There had to be more, a backup bottle.

Somewhere.

"Mom, answer me," Angel said, her voice strained with hysteria. "My whole life has been a lie. You've just told me my whole life has been one big *fucking* lie, so answer me."

Cassandra raised her head slowly, her mascara running down her face, phlegm streaming from her nose to her upper lip, her eyes an ocean of regret.

Angel kneeled in front of her and took her hand. "Mom, please," she said with the broken voice of a child. "Who's my father?"

Slowly, Cassandra turned her head toward the boy she had once made love to in a moment when her heart had needed mending, and she had never understood how beautiful that moment had really been until she had stared at the DNA results years later.

She had believed her life had ended that day, but she couldn't have been more wrong. Her life had ended just now.

CB ♂

Angel let go of her mother's hands and was barely able to get her legs to support her. There was an aftertaste in the back of her mouth that tasted like yesterday's dinner. Her breath came fast and shallow.

"Uncle Brad is my dad?"

She stared at her uncle. How could he be her dad? He'd been living in Vancouver since . . . She couldn't remember what her mom had told her. He had left long ago.

Because he loved my mom.

She bit her lower lip, glared at her mother, then shifted her eyes to her uncle again.

No, her dad.

This family was . . .

The man she had called *Dad* her whole life was actually her uncle and her uncle was her dad.

Effing bonkers. All of it.

What the hell had her mom been doing? Thinking? Jesus! The profanities exploded inside her head in murder-scene violence.

"You've lied to me my whole life!" Angel screamed and slapped her mother across the face. "Ohmygod!"

A hand shot to cover her mouth and she took a step back, not believing she had just hit her mother. This couldn't be happening to her. She loved her mother. She had always felt she could trust her, depend on her, that no matter what, her mom was there for her.

"I never expected you to hurt me more than Dad—" She paused, looked at David, and his face blurred instantly. Two rivers of phlegm ran from her nose. "Is *that* why you've hated me all this time?"

She didn't wait for an answer.

"I've got to get out of here," she said and ran out of the room and out the front door, her feet unable to carry her away fast enough from the family she knew nothing about.

⊂⊃ ⊂⊃

Bradley watched his daughter—*daughter*—run past him, and felt completely powerless. As much as he wanted to help her make sense of what had just happened, what had just happened made no sense to him either.

Angel was his daughter, not his niece. He had missed his daughter's birth, her first smile, her first crawl, her first steps, her first day at school. He had missed it all.

He turned to Cassandra and for the first time in his life, he yelled at her. "Are you *kidding me*?"

"I'm so sorry," was all Cassandra could say over and over.

Bradley turned his back to the mother of his child, because right now he couldn't look at her. What kind of person kept a secret like that? No wonder she was so broken.

"Did you know?" he asked his sister.

"No," she said. "I had noticed that Angel didn't have much of David's features, but she looked like a Knighton to me."

"And you?" he said to his brother. "How long have you known Angel wasn't your daughter?"

"I just found out too," David said.

"But you suspected. Isn't that what you said earlier?"

David nodded. "I kept hoping I was wrong."

"Is that why you stayed married?"

He looked at his empty glass and put it on the side table. "I think so."

"You think so?

"What do you want from me?" David said. "For four years I thought Angel was my daughter and then I started to wonder. And while I was wondering, I became a shitty father. There. Is that what you wanted to hear?"

Bradley didn't answer. He couldn't imagine what his brother had gone through, living with that unknown. "Strange that you didn't bother to find out. It would have been easy to get your own DNA test done."

"Maybe I didn't want to."

Bradley ran a hand across his face. He grabbed his phone and called Kate, but it went to voicemail. He ended the call without leaving a message. How was he going to tell her he had a daughter? What was he supposed to do now? He couldn't go back to Vancouver.

"I was just nineteen," Cassandra said. "I never thought that our one time . . ."

Bradley turned abruptly. "You should have made sure."

Cassandra got up and staggered past Bradley but he grabbed her arm. "Where are you going? You're in no condition . . ."

"Let go of my arm," she said. "You're hurting me."

He let go and Cassandra wasted no time to step outside.

"What a mess," Bradley said. "Does anyone remember that we're all supposed to be grieving for mom?"

David and Emily remained silent. Bradley just paced like a caged animal, mumbling profanities under his breath. He was so angry with Cassandra. And he was worried about Angel, but he knew that Lilly was with her.

"You should go make sure Cassandra is okay," Emily said. "I know what she did was pretty awful, but she's drunk—"

"I know," Bradley said. "I just can't believe this."

"We'll figure things out later," Emily said. "Let's just make sure everyone is all right."

"For what it's worth," David said, "I totally adored Angel when she was a baby."

Bradley eyed his brother but didn't have anything to say right now. David had been there for all of Angel's firsts. He shoved his anger back into the darkness of his thoughts and stepped out onto the porch, expecting to find Cassandra sitting on the old swing, but she wasn't there.

NINETEEN

A ngel and Lilly were sitting quietly under a hundred-year-old oak tree, their friendship not needing words to fill the void. Angel's tears had finally dried up but her thoughts were a mess inside of her head, the expressions on her face chasing each other: confusion, anger, sadness. An endless loop of *my life sucks right now*.

She looked up at the mammoth tree that cast a shadow across the small memorial park. She remembered coming here often with her grandmother, Grandma Irene always making sure to bring snacks for them and some peanuts for the squirrels. The little brave souls would come right up to Angel and snatch their prize from her hand.

The park had been created long ago, probably even before her grandmother was born, to commemorate the fallen soldiers of Forest Creek who had died during the Great War.

"My family has owned that bakery since World War One," Angel said. "And now my dad—well, David—wants to sell it. We're as much a part of Forest Creek as the names of the soldiers on that plaque. My Great-Great-Grandmother Sarah started that bakery."

When Angel had come running out of the house, she'd just kept going, needing to get away from the lie that had been her life. She'd heard Lilly call after her but she couldn't face her friend. The farce that had played out inside the house had destroyed everything she'd known, including who she was.

She had slapped her mother.

Tears filled her eyes and she couldn't really see properly, but she didn't care. And she didn't care that she'd hit her mom. Her mom deserved it. Her hand still stung.

She had never hit her mom before. She shouldn't have done that. Just for a moment, anger had consumed her with such ferocity that it had possessed her. Her mom would recover from the slap.

Angel wasn't sure how *she* was going to recover from the lie.

Once Lilly had caught up to her at the park, Angel had told her everything, and then her grief had been too much to hold back.

"That's a long time," Lilly said. "Your Great-Great-Grandmother must have been exceptional because women didn't really have businesses way back then."

"I never thought of that," Angel said. "Grandma Irene used to talk about Great-Great-Grandmother Sarah like she was both afraid of and in awe of her. I know she got married when she was seventeen, lost a couple of babies, and still ran the bakery. My Great-Grandma Alice was the youngest. She was the only girl, so she ran the bakery with Triple-G Sarah."

"That's funny."

Angel didn't smile. "Grandma Irene told me that one when I was young. I had trouble saying all those words together."

"You're lucky to have so much history here," Lilly said. "Me and my brothers are first generation."

"Maybe your Triple-G kids will talk about you someday."

"Maybe."

Angel fell quiet again. She pushed the cuticle on her right thumb with the nail from her left thumb. When she was done, she moved on to her right index finger. Traffic went by on Main Street in an endless flow of Saturday shoppers. In an hour, everything would be closed and then the streets would be deserted, everyone relegated to cooking inch-thick steaks or massive burger patties on backyard barbeques, cold beers in hand, parties winding down or just getting started.

"I always wondered why my Uncle Bradley never came back," she said. "I guess he was in love with my mom but she was in love with David." She sighed. "Feels weird to be calling my dad by his first name."

"Except he's not your dad."

"He's not my biological dad," she said. "But he sort of is my dad, isn't he? People adopt kids all the time and those people are those kids' parents."

"That's different."

"I don't want different," Angel said. "I want normal."

"Sorry, kid," Lilly said and pretended to hit Angel in the jaw. "Normal is not in your picture."

Angel half-laughed. "That was lame."

"I know."

A boy of maybe eleven walking a Collie looked at them while his dog did his business. He then bagged the goodies and walked away as if he didn't have a care in the world.

"Were we that carefree not that long ago?" Angel said.

"I think so," Lilly said. "And then we grew up."

"I remember when I was twelve, how I couldn't wait to be sixteen. And now that's come and gone and I don't know what I was expecting."

"I think all kids want to be older and all old people want to be young."

"At least now I know why my dad—David—didn't like me much."

"I'm sorry."

"Not your fault," she said. "I'm so pissed off at my mom right now."

Lilly didn't say anything.

"I mean, what right did she have to hide this from me? She had none. It wasn't her secret to hide. I should have been told so I could choose what to do. David should have been told. Bradley should have been told. We never got that choice. It's not right."

She grabbed a small branch and used it to dig into the hard ground. It snapped. She threw the broken piece as far as she could. A bird was singing above their heads but no matter how far back Angel craned her neck, she couldn't see it. Two women, maybe her mom's age, jogged by and Angel caught snippets of conversation that meant nothing to her.

"My life sucks."

"It will get better."

"Right now, it doesn't seem possible," Angel said. "I don't really know who I am."

"Technically," Lilly said, "you're a Knighton either way."

A half-pained half-sneer crossed Angel's face. "I hate you."

"In hardship, we see true friendship."

They grinned at each other, the way friends do when they connect on a deeper level. Angel got what Lilly was telling her, but it still hurt to find out that her life was a big lie. She had no idea how difficult of a choice it must have been for her mom, but right now she didn't care. She was angry with her mother and she didn't know if she was going to be able to forgive her.

"All these years, I thought I'd done something wrong to cause David not to love me," Angel said. "But it was my mom's fault. She lied to us."

Angel threw the other half of the stick away. It landed about three feet from the other broken piece. A squirrel came out from the bushes, stood on its hind legs, sniffed the air, then scurried away to the left into a thick hedge of cedars.

"Remember Gabby?" Lilly said.

"From work?" Angel said. "She quit two months ago."

"That's because she got pregnant and her mom kicked her out so she went to live with her dad in Toronto," Lilly said. "One night, I was working with her and she kept rushing to the bathroom, so when I asked her what was up, she told me. She was out of her mind. She was on the pill, she said, so how could she have gotten pregnant? Her boyfriend dumped her as soon as he found out."

Angel looked at Lilly for a long moment. "But my mom slept with both of them, so how could she be so sure that I was *David's* baby?"

Lilly shook her head. "Maybe she was afraid neither would want her if she found out who the father was. Or maybe she just never thought you could be Bradley's."

"That seems obvious now," Angel said. "I'd probably be freaking out if I found out I was pregnant . . . but—"

Angel lost herself in thought, trying to see her mom at her age, caught in a love triangle. Is that what it had been for her? Had she loved both of them? What had made her choose David? Had Bradley done something to make her go with his brother? Bradley seemed nice. Maybe he had been different back then. Maybe David had been the nice one. Thinking of her mom that way wasn't easy.

None of this was easy.

When Angel was younger, she had never understood why her mom would yell at her dad to stop cheating on her. Her mom would tell him that she loved him and she didn't understand why he was doing that to her. Angel only learned later what cheating meant for a couple and then she was angry with her dad. Mom was beautiful, she was funny, she took care of them. Angel could never see what there was not to love.

She understood now. David had figured out that he was a stand-in dad, so he'd never quite invested himself in the role, probably wondering when it would all come crumbling down, the lie they were living.

Waiting for the lie to be exposed and set him free.

Angel wondered why he'd waited so long. Maybe part of him had hoped that he was wrong. She could kind of understand that. Didn't make it right how he'd treated her, ignored her. *She* hadn't known about the lie. *She* hadn't told it.

Her mother's secret.

Exposed.

Finally.

Maybe that was a good thing. Her mother had finally set them all free, free to choose what came next.

Angel screamed, loud, and long, and she felt Lilly wrap her arms around her and rock her like her mom used to do when she'd had a nightmare.

"It's okay," Lilly said. "It's going to be okay."

"N-no . . . it's not . . . it's not okay . . . I . . ." She swallowed her pain. "I'm just angry with them."

"And you have the right to be."

"But I'm also relieved that I finally know the truth. No more wondering what I've done wrong, no more wondering why my dad doesn't seem to care. No more wondering why my mom is so broken. It all makes sense now. Well, most of it."

Angel looked at the memorial plaque. She couldn't read it from where they were, but she knew some of the names. Jack O'Brien's name was on that plaque. He had been Great-Great-Grandma Sarah's younger brother. He had been just eighteen and had volunteered to go fight the Germans and had never come back home. His body was somewhere in Europe, or whatever was left of it after a century.

"I always wanted a brother or sister," Angel said. "Now I know why they never had another baby."

"Siblings are overrated," Lilly said with a smile.

"It might have made us a real family," she said and fell silent. "I don't know how I can forgive my mom."

Lilly looked pensive and then a smile crossed her face. "All things are difficult at the start."

"I don't think you've ever said anything truer."

"She's your mom."

Angel suddenly felt her heart beat heavily. "God! I hope so."

Lilly touched her arm. "You'll be okay."

Minutes passed in silence. The sun played hide and seek with big white fluffy clouds and a late-summer cicada performed one last time. Angel's thoughts bounced around from her mother and the pain she had caused everyone to the void her grandmother's passing had left in her heart to the layers of frustration she felt at the possibility of losing the family business.

"I don't want David to sell the bakery," she said. "Aunt Emily loves that bakery and so do I. It's the reason I'm taking the same college program she took. Without Grandma, she'll really need me now. He can't sell it. Can he?"

Lilly shrugged. "I don't know."

TWENTY

assandra ran out of the house and had no idea where she was going. All she knew was that she needed to get away from the carnage she had caused. She shouldn't have been surprised that the revelation hadn't shocked David. In fact, she couldn't believe that she'd been foolish enough to think that he wouldn't have noticed. It explained the way their lives had turned out . . . but it didn't explain why he hadn't called her out on it long ago.

It didn't matter now.

The two people she had wanted to protect were the two people she had hurt the most. Especially Angel. She didn't know how she was going to face her daughter again after what she had done. She wouldn't be surprised if Angel never wanted to see her again.

And that would break her heart.

Cassandra crossed Main Street in a blur of intoxicated anger and shame, and staggered down the sidewalk until she cut across a side street and headed past Smallbrook Street toward Cedar Street. During those many mini-breakups with David, she had often found her way to St. John's Quiet Garden where its natural isolation and beauty had provided exactly the escape she'd needed to ease her through her pain and doubts.

Today, she didn't think the garden would do any of those things for her, but she didn't know where else to go hide and regret what she had just done.

Her mother would be so disappointed that the daughter she had raised to be strong and independent had turned out to be anything but. Part of Cassandra's reasoning, at least the lie she liked to tell herself, was that she had grown up in a home without a father, and she hadn't wanted Angel to grow up that way too.

She'd also thought that Bradley had wanted nothing to do with her, and telling him he had a daughter wouldn't have brought him back home. Why else would he have moved as far away from her as he could?

It had been best to keep the secret to herself.

But it was out now and she had to figure out what to do next. She knew that Bradley and Angel would want an explanation, but she really didn't have much more to offer than she'd thought she was doing the right thing. She had married David and she had tried to make their marriage work, but now she knew that he couldn't keep loving her once he'd realized that Angel was probably not his. One more sign she should have noticed, but didn't.

Cassandra leaned over and threw up on someone's front lawn.

"Sorry," she whispered once she was done. She walked away, tears of shame running down her burning cheeks. "I'm such a failure, Mom."

A boy and a girl rode by on bikes and she saw them look at her with disgust and maybe even with a little bit of panic in their eyes. Why wouldn't they? She must look like some crazed drunken woman that was best avoided.

Her heart sank even more at the thought that that had been her and Bradley once, best friends who had had no idea that the wrong love was going to ruin everything between them someday.

Why couldn't they have stayed twelve forever?

She turned down Cedar Street and made her way into St. John's Quiet Garden, stepping back in time to the worst and best night of her life.

Her nineteenth birthday.

CB EO

Bradley stood on the porch like he had done so many times in the past, reminiscing about his last day here when he'd finally realized Cassandra would never be his. On that late summer day of 1999, he'd had no idea where he was going, how he was going to get there, what he would do, but he'd finally made the decision to leave Forest Creek, not because he really wanted to, but because he couldn't bear to see Cassandra with his brother.

And now . . .

Cassandra had really messed up. He was really struggling to understand what had just happened, but more so, what Cassandra had been thinking. Then it hit him that he himself had to shoulder some of the blame. He had known she was pregnant before he left, *and* he had known what had happened on the night of her nineteenth birthday.

He could have asked her to make sure the baby was David's. Instead, he'd accepted that it was his brother's and he'd run off to the west coast, blocking everything out that reminded him of what he'd lost.

As angry as he was with her, he'd failed too.

David never knew, obviously, that Cassandra had cheated on him until years later.

What a mess they were.

Poor Angel. He was glad she had her friend with her. Not that he could bring Angel any sort of comfort. In fact, he wouldn't fault her for not wanting any of them near her right now.

He had to find Cassandra.

She had run off pretty drunk and Bradley hoped she didn't get hit by a car. He was pretty sure he knew where he'd find her and she would have crossed Main Street to get there. Luckily, Forest Creek was still very small and the traffic wasn't anything like in Stittsville or Barrhaven.

Bradley made his way across the street towards the back of the bakery. There was an empty lot behind the building because that land actually belonged to them, so no one had been able to build a house on that piece of property. As he walked through the knee-high grass and weeds, Bradley realized why David was so keen on selling the bakery.

It stood on a really nice chunk of land that would probably fetch a lot of money.

One problem at a time.

He reached the end of the vacant lot and turned down Smallbrook Street, cut across Church to Cedar, and made his way toward St. John's Quiet Garden, known back in the day as Make-out Heaven. As Bradley walked through the garden, memories elbowed one another—teenagers drinking behind those trees, couples making out behind bushes here and there, a group of boys making fools of themselves trying to get the attention of a group of girls.

It was also the perfect place to mend a broken heart.

He'd come here a lot to be alone, especially when Cassandra was over and he couldn't stand to watch her and David together. He had loved her company when they'd been best friends, but once she and David had started their on-and-off relationship, she had stopped coming over to spend time with him. Even if she had wanted to, David would simply *possess* her and give Bradley that fake smile that said *she's mine.*

So Bradley would leave the house and wind up in the Broken Heart Garden, as he'd liked to think of it. Sometimes, he'd see a bunch of guys from school hanging out and join them; other times, he just went to the far end of the garden and sat by the little creek that snaked through the park. Beyond the creek, a wall of trees stood old and tall, the entry to a forest that went on forever.

He was glad to see the forest hadn't been chopped down.

Bradley shoved his hands in the pockets of his jeans as he walked towards the girl who had haunted him ever since their one night together.

The night of her nineteenth birthday.

CB EO

Bradley heard footsteps behind him and felt anger rise in the back of his throat. He wasn't in the mood to talk to one of the guys right now, he just wanted to be alone. He was so tired of seeing his girl with his brother.

Why had she picked David over him?

He just didn't get it. All these years that he and Cassandra had been friends, all the times she had told him how annoying and self-centred she thought David was, and now she was just like all the other girls, talking about David all the time and how great he was. He heard this all day long at school. So what if the guy could play hockey and be like the best player on the team? He was still a jerk who thought he could get whatever he wanted.

Whoever he wanted.

Cassandra wasn't even David's type. He liked the loose girls in tight jeans who wore too much makeup and shoved their tongues down his throat. Cassandra barely wore makeup, kept her long hair in a ponytail most of the time, and dressed in pants that were just a tad loose.

All that changed, of course, once David started to pay attention to her, and before long, she was no longer coming over to hang out with Bradley; she was only ever here to be with David.

"I just want to be left alo—" he said and turned, the words dying. "Why aren't you with David? It's your birthday."

"Can I sit?" she said in a trembling voice. "I really need you right now. Please."

With his left hand he motioned for her to sit beside him. They didn't say anything for several minutes, and he hoped his silence would make her leave.

"You hate me."

Bradley inhaled deeply and let it out noisily. Even though it was nine, the July sun had just set and it wouldn't be dark until nearly ten. The night was hot and sticky, and in the far distance, he could hear kids playing and the drone of a lawnmower.

"I don't hate you."

They sat in silence for a few more minutes, Bradley not knowing what to do with his hands. He wanted to touch her so badly, lace his fingers with hers, press his lips against hers—all the things his brother got to do. It should have been him. Cassandra was *his* friend.

And he'd fallen in love with her long ago, but he hadn't known how to tell her, afraid that if he did, it would ruin their friendship.

Too late for that.

"I just don't understand why."

"I don't either," she said and he heard the truth in her words. "He's nothing like you."

Bradley bit back his words.

Cassandra ran both hands through her long hair, letting it fall back over her bare shoulders. She was wearing a spaghetti-string top and short shorts, with flip-flops on her feet. Her toenails were painted pink.

Bradley bit his lower lip and looked away. He didn't like looking at her because . . . well, it got the wrong ideas running through his head, ideas that would leave him frustrated and longing for her even more.

He loved the way she smelled, like vanilla with a hint of peppermint. Probably the soap she used to wash up. None of this was helping him and he started to get up, but she grabbed his hand and he stayed.

"He's got this way of making me feel special," she said, "that's different from the way you make me feel."

"Wonderful," he said sardonically. "What every guy wants to hear about his brother."

"He started to show up at my field hockey games," she said. "You never did."

"You always played at the same time I had English class," he said. "Besides, David's done with school and he couldn't figure out what to do, so he did nothing this past year. So, yeah, he had time to go to your games."

"I know," she said. "I didn't mean it that way." She paused and he felt her looking at him, but he refused to look at her. "He started to cheer for me so loudly that it was all everyone could hear, and, you know, it got me playing even better."

"Great."

"I guess part of me wished it was you cheering for me like that."

"I couldn't cut class."

"I know," she said. "And then when I came over to your house, I started to see David differently, like the cheerleader at my games, and I started to notice other things."

"Like what a butt-hole he is."

Cassandra looked off in the distance. "Well, no."

A wall of silence went up. Bradley wanted to leave, but he was also curious. As much as he wanted to hate her right now, his other feelings wouldn't let him.

"He started to show up at my locker."

"Yeah, I sort of noticed since our lockers are together," he said. "He shouldn't have been in the school at all, but all the teachers loved him too, so no one said anything."

"He always knew when you weren't going to be there, so he'd come and talk to me, and I saw a side of him that reminded me of you: kind and attentive and funny."

"He can be deceptively charming when he wants something."

"Yes, he can."

"But the real David isn't that charming." He turned in time to see her wipe a runaway tear. "I'm sorry. I didn't mean to be a jerk. I just . . . think he's going to break your heart in the end."

"I know," she said, her voice thick with sorrow. "But I can't help it. I keep going back to him like he's a drug I can't do without. I hate myself for it. I hate that I'm hurting you. I hate that I love your dumbass brother."

Bradley felt the tip of the knife penetrate the skin in front of his heart, and slowly, inch by inch, slice through until his heart stopped beating. Hearing the girl he loved tell him that she loved his brother was the worst feeling in the world.

He had just died.

"So why are you here?" he said. "To totally hurt me?"

She shook her head and her shoulders began to shake, and then the dam broke.

"He's been cheating on me with Josée."

"Your best friend?"

"Not anymore," she said. "I've heard the rumours. It's a small town. He didn't show tonight. He was supposed to pick me up at six and we were going up to Kanata for dinner and a movie. I started to walk over to your place and I saw them as he drove by with your dad's truck and . . ."

She lost it then.

Bradley reached out and held her. She cried into his neck and he felt wetness from her tears against his skin. He inhaled her scent and hated himself for thinking this could be the best thing to happen—for her and David to break up, because maybe then he could have her.

"Here," he said and put something in her hand.

She pulled away and looked at what he'd given her.

"Birthday present," he said.

She let the chain unroll slowly. It was a small pendant in the shape of a C. "You shouldn't have."

"I'm not sure why I bought it," he said. "When I saw it, I knew I wanted you to have it."

"It's beautiful," she said. "Help me put it on."

He did. "Looks great."

Suddenly her lips were on his mouth and her tongue pushed through his lips and he had no idea what to make of this and his emotions took over.

He kissed her back, hungry and desperate, his hands exploring parts of her he'd dreamed of but never imagined he'd ever get to touch. It was nearly dark now and when Cassandra started to undo his pants, he realized that she wasn't the same girl he had known, that she wasn't innocent or shy or afraid to take what she wanted.

A bit of David had rubbed off on her.

He was about to pull away but suddenly she straddled his hips and as the last of the light faded away on this hot summer night, he and Cassandra shared a moment that belonged to them and them only. Once it was over, he felt tears escape the corners of his eyes. He could barely make out her face now in the darkness that had settled all around them, but he didn't need to. He knew how beautiful she looked. And then he felt her lips on his again and they kissed like the lovers that they were at this very moment. Not a word was said, no promises that this was the beginning of something, no lies of a future together.

Just now.

C03 80

Bradley stood a few feet away, trying to decide how he was going to do this. A huge part of him wanted to go nuclear on Cassandra for what she had done, but the sensible part of him figured she had probably paid that debt many times over. Still, just yelling at her would make him feel better.

For a minute or two.

And accomplish nothing.

He sat down beside her but said nothing. The spot looked familiar, perhaps a little aged, like them. She had been the one to come find him that night. Felt like their lives had come full circle.

He watched her from the corner of his eye play with the rings on her left hand.

"I was remembering the last time we were here," she finally said.

"We're not teenagers anymore."

"No, we're not."

They stared ahead, neither saying more. Bradley was fighting the feelings he'd had for her back then with how he felt right now.

"That was," he said, "not exactly what I'd expected to find out when I came home for Mom's funeral."

"I can't tell you how sorry I am," she said. "I made so many mistakes, liked to blame David for them, and believed protecting my secret was the right thing to do."

He said nothing.

"But I was wrong," she said. "I've lied enough, but it's time I learn to live in the truth, if that makes sense?"

He remained silent. She continued to turn her rings.

"I honestly never even considered that Angel could be yours when I first realized I was pregnant," she said. "It was just the one time."

"Still."

"I know." She pulled the rings off her finger and held them in her hand. "I've lived the punishment for my mistakes a thousand lifetimes, trust me. Oh Brad, I messed up so bad."

"Yeah, you did."

"I'm afraid I might have lost Angel," she said. "I have never seen her so hurt. What I did was worse than David ignoring her all these years."

Bradley looked at her. "I know she's hurting. I'd guess a lot more than I am. Even though I feel cheated right now, she has to grasp that she isn't who she thought she was. That would be difficult for anyone. She's going to need some time."

"I love her so much," Cassandra said. "All these years, she's been my world, and I really thought I was protecting her. What was I *thinking*?"

He couldn't answer that. All he knew was that they would have to get past this somehow, all of them, David and Emily too. For the first time in a long time, his stance toward his brother softened a bit.

But he was still David. It was best to remain cautious. Bradley didn't think this was going to change his brother's mind at all about selling the bakery. It might make him *more* determined, give him *another* wrong he feels needs to be righted.

"I don't need these anymore," she said and tossed her rings into the creek. "Reminds me too much of everything I destroyed."

"You could have sold those," he said, trying to lighten the mood.

"I wouldn't want another woman to wear them," she said. "Bad karma."

He nodded. Time passed by in silence. It wasn't entirely uncomfortable. It was needed.

"That night," she said, and couldn't continue. He waited. "I came looking for you because I really needed you. Not just physically, but emotionally."

They looked at each other, an ocean of hurt scattered across years of lost possibilities buried in lies and denial. A golden retriever ran up to them, barked a couple of times, which startled them, and returned to his owner, who apologised.

"I know," he said when stranger and dog had moved on.

"He called me the next day but I told my mom to tell him I wasn't feeling well. He called every day and my mom told him the same thing every time. I couldn't get the image out of my head, seeing him and Josée in your dad's truck. Finally, he decided to come over and I was going to break up with him, but he promised me that nothing had happened between him and Josée. She'd been having trouble with her car and had needed a ride to get to work in Barrhaven, so he'd driven her and when he came back, I was gone."

"Did he get lost coming back?" Bradley said.

Cassandra offered him a sad smile. "Before I could ask him that, he started to promise me he'd make it up to me for missing my birthday, and like I told you before, I just couldn't say no to him."

Bradley looked away.

"And then when I realized I was pregnant and told him," she said, "I had never seen him so happy."

"So what happened?"

"I think maybe it was when Angel turned three, or maybe it was four," she said. "I don't quite remember. But that's when he started to shut me out."

"Do you think he suspected about Angel?"

She shrugged. "I always thought he was her dad. I mean, you and I had that one night. I didn't think I was ovulating, but I was such a mess. I think I forgot to take my pill for a few days. Anyway, when Angel was around three, I started to notice things like she used her left hand a lot, her hair colour, her eyes. So I had both their DNA tested."

"And you never told him?"

"I couldn't," she said. "I had to think about Angel. He was her father."

"But she was young enough that she would have been fine if you'd left him then."

A pained expression crossed her face. "I think I was afraid of being alone, of failing in her eyes. She was all I had and I didn't want to lose her too."

He nodded.

"You were gone," she said. "I had it in my head that you must hate me, especially as the years passed and you never came back. I had driven you away. Depriving Angel of the father she knew seemed worse than keeping a secret."

"But he ignored her, is what I keep hearing."

"He worked crazy hours to provide for us," she said. "That's what I told her. Most of it was true. We can't complain in that respect. We have way more than we need."

"I never hated you," he said. "I stayed away because I couldn't get you out of my head. I should have told you how I felt long before that night."

"You're not to blame," she said. "I loved having you as my best friend and I didn't want to lose that. Until that night, I actually hadn't realized that you meant more to me than just being my friend. Which is why I tried to break up with David, but, well, we know that didn't happen. When he's nice, he's so addictive. I know it's hard for you to believe. I loved you both, but I was so *sure* he was the father."

"So, what happens now?"

She pursed her lips and pulled something on a chain from her shirt. She rubbed it between her fingers.

Bradley realized it was the pendant he'd given her. Seeing her still wearing it while she had tossed her wedding rings into the creek jumbled his feelings.

Cassandra and Kate.

How could he even be thinking this? Cassandra had, for lack of a better way of looking at it, stolen a part of his life that he couldn't ever get back. His feelings for her should be dead. Kate was everything he wanted now.

"I have a daughter I need to make amends with," she said. "After that, I have no idea."

"*We* have a daughter," he said.

A cringe crossed her face. "Yes. We. But she doesn't hate *you* right now."

"No, I guess she doesn't."

He felt a spark of anger ignite in him, but it didn't last. Staying angry with Cassandra wouldn't give him back the years he'd lost. What he needed to figure out now was where his life stood.

Bradley had come here to bury his mother and instead had found out that he had a daughter. He hadn't planned on staying, but now he wasn't sure he could leave again.

TWENTY-ONE

Emily stood at the edge of the sitting room, alone with David, pondering her next move. She knew he wasn't about to let go of his plan to sell the bakery, so she had to find a way to make him see that that wasn't in his best interest. The family business was thriving again and she was confident that she could keep it going that way for years.

She knew the bakery sat on a big piece of land, and maybe they could sell some of it, but Great-Grandma Sarah had founded that business in an era when women didn't do such things and it killed Emily to think that everything her great-grandmother had accomplished would be for nothing.

But right now, she was tired, and a duel with David wasn't really what she wanted to take on.

"Why don't you just go?" she said. "Everyone is gone and I'm sure you're not waiting for any of them to return. Besides, I need to call the funeral home and plan Mom's service."

"I'm meeting someone," he said.

"You can't be serious," she said, losing her composure. "You've got someone coming to see the house? I told you, the house isn't yours to sell."

"Not the house," he said, looking at his watch, "the bakery. I have a client coming at six."

"Get out," she said, shaking her head. "Mom died yesterday and you already have a client? You can wait for him in your car if you want, but right now I don't want you here."

David stood, put his glass on the coffee table, and walked past Emily without uttering a word.

"I don't understand why you're so dead set on doing this," she said as he stepped onto the porch and held the door open for a second, "and I'm sure Mom hadn't expected you to do this either. She trusted you with that deed."

David walked away, the door closed, and Emily was left alone with her anger. She couldn't let him do this. It wasn't right. If only her mom had talked to her about it, maybe the two of them could have come up with a better alternative. As angry as she was with her mother, she was more disappointed that her mom hadn't trusted her with this part of the renovation plan.

Emily needed to warn Jeanine, so she phoned her and told her to expect a visit from David. After she hung up, she walked up to the front window and peeked at the bakery across the street. She could feel her heartbeat against her chest and her face get warmer. There had to be a way to stop David.

"What's all the arguing for?" Henry said.

Emily screamed. "Jesus, Dad! I didn't hear you coming down the stairs."

"What were you and David talking about?"

Emily was tired of standing and flopped onto the sofa chair, her head resting against the back cushion, her eyes staring blankly at the ceiling. A day—that's all it had been since her mom had died and left this mess behind.

A damned long day.

"How did you sleep?"

Henry made his way to the couch and sat on the edge, his back straight, his hands together between his knees. "Okay, I guess." He ran a hand over his bald head. "I keep seeing things that aren't real."

Emily sat up. "Yes."

"I'm becoming unpredictable."

"Unfortunately." She couldn't look at him. "It's not your fault, Dad. But the disease seems to be progressing more quickly lately. I have no idea how long we have until . . ."

"You have to put me in a home."

She could feel the hands of guilt around her throat. "I'm sorry."

"Brad is here?"

"Yes, he came home for Mom's funeral."

"When did she die?"

"Just yesterday, Dad."

"One day."

"One lousy day."

She watched her father. It was so nice to be able to talk to him, but not knowing how long it would last, she pressed on. Maybe he'd have answers for her.

"David wants to sell the house and bakery."

Henry frowned. "Did he say why?"

She shook her head. "He won't say, other than that Mom gave him the bakery for the loan he gave us. Seems strange that Mom wouldn't have mentioned this to me. Why would she do that? If David does really have the signed deed, I don't think we can stop him. But I have power of attorney for the house, in case you're not able to manage."

"Your mother and I thought it was best to give it to you," he said. "I guess she didn't tell me about the deed either, or I've forgotten if she did."

"So that's what we were arguing over . . . amongst other things."

"Where is everyone?"

Emily had an edge to her laugh. "Dad, it's been one crazy day."

"I have something for you," he said and headed up the stairs.

"Dad?"

"Hang on."

"Will this day never end?" she mumbled to herself. "I just want to run away. Maybe Brad can stay and I'll move to Vancouver. Worked for him."

"Who you talking to?" Henry said when he returned.

"No one," she said and let out a sigh that was full of hysterical tension. It would be so much easier to just let David have his way. She could find a job somewhere. But the bakery wasn't just a business, it was her life. "What's that in your hand?"

"Your mother made me swear that I'd give this to you before I couldn't remember where I'd put it," he said and handed her an envelope. "It was just in my sock drawer but I figure I'd better give it to you now."

Emily reluctantly took it. Stared at it. Flipped it back and forth. Ripped it open.

"Do you know what it's about?"

"No," he said. "Or I forgot."

Emily unfolded the papers and began to read the letter her mom had left. The words told a tale that stole her breath. Family secrets she had never known inked on 8 by 11 sheets of white paper held between trembling fingers. The words both enlightened and infuriated her, exposed her mother in ways she couldn't have ever fathomed.

They had all lived a lie.

Emily glared at her dad but couldn't quite find the strength to be mad at him as he sat there, an almost childlike glow on his time-aged face. The one person she was most angry with was her mom—not just because of these secrets she had chosen to keep hidden all these years, but also for not being here to explain why she had kept the truth from them.

She grabbed her phone and texted Bradley.

She heard a buzz.

His phone was on the side table, by the fireplace.

"We have to find Brad," she said to her dad. "He needs to read this."

"Who?"

Emily started to laugh one of those maddening laughs that comes when you'd rather scream. This had been the worst day possible, and this letter didn't help. If nothing else, maybe she finally understood her brother David's motives.

TWENTY-TWO

Bradley and Cassandra sat quietly staring at the creek, looking like a couple just enjoying a beautiful early-September Saturday afternoon by the brook instead of two people trying to piece together truths and lies that had completely disrupted their lives. Bradley still couldn't believe Cassandra had just tossed her rings into the muddy water, but he understood the symbolic significance of her need to cleanse herself of everything in her past that reminded her of the mistakes she had made.

There was no one else to blame.

Had it been a burden to her? He couldn't begin to understand how horrible it had to have been for her to keep that secret for so long, and he could see that it had cost her more than a marriage. She wasn't the same person he had known. She had paid dearly for her mistakes.

He knew he would need to forgive her, because staying angry with her would only drain him emotionally. Of course what she had done was horrible, but it wasn't unforgiveable. A person always had the power to choose to give forgiveness or not. Forgiving opened the door to move on and rebuild.

And that's what he wanted.

He and Cassandra had a daughter and he wanted to get to know her. Angel didn't need him and Cassandra to hate each other. She'd already grown up with parents like that.

"What are you thinking?" she said.

"How can I leave again?" he said. "I have a daughter."

"I'm sorry," she said.

He turned to her and waited until she looked at him. "We need to decide right now how we're going to push past this. I know you're sorry, and I still have anger inside of me, but neither will change what happened, so, I propose that this is the last time you tell me you're sorry, and I'll do whatever I need to do to let go of my anger and forgive you."

She put her hand on her pendant. "That would mean the world to me, to know that you don't hate me."

"I don't hate you," he said.

"Thank you," she said in a voice that sounded tired and worn. "You shouldn't give up your life out west with Kate. Angel is old enough to go visit you, and you could come visit too."

"That's one choice," he said. "But it would feel like being a weekend dad. Angel and I would never really get to know each other."

"I'm sor—" she started to say but stopped. "It's going to be hard not to keep apologizing."

"I know."

"Maybe you and Kate could move here?"

He shook his head. "This place is so not Kate. Maybe *I* could fall back into my old life, but I can't ask her to give up everything she's worked for her whole life."

"Could you really?"

He shrugged. He thought of the conversation he and Kate had had just yesterday morning and he didn't know that he could go back to Vancouver and marry her knowing what he had back home—and he wasn't thinking of Cassandra.

He was thinking of Angel.

And he didn't want to run off on her. She had just learned that her dad wasn't her dad, that her uncle wasn't her uncle, and that her mom had lied to her for eighteen years. His desire to stay was very simple in nature. He had a daughter and he really wanted her in his life. Maybe they'd never be true father and daughter, but if he ran off again, he *knew* that they never would.

Staying would give them both the chance to find out.

And Cassandra?

All these years, he'd been unable to truly let her go, and to lie to himself that he didn't have any feelings for her now just because of what she had done would be hypocritical. Justifiable, but hypocritical. But was he *in love* with her? Neither of them was the person from 1999. The Cassandra from back then, that's the one he still loved.

That girl wasn't here.

Maybe now he could finally move on.

He just couldn't see how he'd be able to keep Kate if he stayed here. He'd always thought that Cassandra was the one that kept him from truly committing to someone else, but now it was his want to be a father that was pulling him back home.

He closed his eyes.

Was he really ready to say goodbye to Kate, to his job that he loved, to the life on the west coast that he had grown accustomed to?

"I don't know," he said. "But Angel seems pretty amazing and . . . I have a daughter. A *daughter*. I never saw myself as a father, but now I kind of like the idea. I don't know what sort of relationship I can have with her, if any at all, but I feel like I need to find out."

"You'd be giving up a lot."

"I know," he said, "but I'd also be gaining a lot."

C3 &0

Angel and Lilly were heading back toward the house, Angel still a little numb from the truth she had just learned, thankful that her friend was there to help her get through this. She had no idea what she would say to her mom when she saw her, or how to act around Bradley—or David, for that matter—but she'd figure it out.

She hoped.

A lot of questions had been answered when her mom revealed her secret, and it didn't make things easier to accept, but maybe now, knowing the truth, she could get on with her life. If David actually did sell the bakery, her college plans would need to change. Working with Aunt Emily appealed to her, but working in another bakery didn't. It wouldn't be the same.

With Grandma Irene dying, nothing *was* the same.

"What's your da—" Lilly said and caught herself. "What's David doing?"

Across the street, David shook hands with a man who was short and stocky, they exchanged a few words, and then they both entered the bakery.

"I don't know," Angel said. "But we're going to find out."

They waited for a line of cars to go by, and then crossed the road. Angel felt like a spy, which was both thrilling and scary. Not scary in the sort of way that she could get killed, but scary because she was afraid of what she might find out. She was old enough to figure out what was going on, which wasn't all that hard to guess since David had said he wanted to sell the family business.

And that short man had looked like a baker.

"Hurry," she said to Lilly. "I want to catch him and stop him before it's too late."

"How do you plan to do that?"

"I don't know," Angel said and started to run. "Keep up."

Angel reached the bakery first and burst through the door. Several pairs of eyes turned her way: David, the short man, Jeanine, Suzie, and Valery.

"What's going on?" she said.

"Listen, Angel," David said and took a step toward her, "I need to show Mr. Brasseau the bakery so you'll need to leave. In fact, Jeanine was just about to lock the front door since it's past six and we're closed."

"I know that," she said. "I've worked here plenty of times. And this is a family bakery and I have as much right to be here as you do. At least I'm not trying to sell it from under other people's nose."

David seemed a little embarrassed by what she had just said. *Good*, she thought.

"Angel," he said, trying to hide his annoyance, "I really need you to leave."

Lilly came in and stood by Angel.

"I need both of you to leave. Now!"

"I don't think you get to tell me anything, *Dave*," Angel said. She hoped her fear hadn't come through in her tone. She had never done anything like this before and she was scared. "Does Aunt Emily know about this?"

"Go home, Angel." David turned to his client. "Let me show you the back. I'm sure you want to see what we've got."

Angel, helpless, watched David walk away from her and was about to say something when she saw Jeanine shake her head and move toward her.

"Emily called me and filled me in," Jeanine said. "Just because he's showing the bakery doesn't mean this man is going to buy it. This could take weeks or more anyway, so don't worry."

"But I love this place," Angel said. "You all love this place."

"We do," Jeanine said. "I have faith in your grandmother. Things will be all right."

It took a second for Angel to grasp what Jeanine was talking about. "I wish she was here, because then this wouldn't be happening."

"Your grandmother *is* this place," Jeanine said. "Go home and try not to worry."

CB ᘓ

When Emily came out of the house with Henry in tow, she breathed a sigh of relief that Angel and Lilly were crossing the street. Trying to find everyone while keeping an eye on her dad wouldn't have been easy.

"Aunt Emily, David is showing the bakery to someone who wants to buy it," Angel said in a panic. "We can't let him."

"I know, sweetheart," Emily said. "But I'm not sure we can stop him if he's really set on selling it. Let's not worry about it right now. What I need from you is to go find your mom and Uncle Bradley."

Angel gave her a queer look.

"Your dad?"

"I have no idea what to call either one right now," Angel said, exasperated. "So Lilly and I figured we just call them by their names until I can make sense of this."

"Good plan," Emily said. "So, can you find your mom and Brad for me?"

"They're not here?"

"Your mom took off just after you did and then Brad went looking for her. My guess would be to check out the old Make-out Garden."

Angel and Lilly giggled.

"And we thought *our* generation had come up with the name," Angel said.

"That name probably existed in the days of your Great-Great-Grandma Sarah. Wouldn't surprise me if that's where she and Great-Great-Grandpa—"

"No need to say any more," Angel said and waved her hands in a cut-off gesture. "And if Mom and Brad aren't there?"

Emily thought it over. "Maybe the Jock River Bridge. Brad and I used to hang out there when we were young. He liked to fish and I just liked to get away from David."

"Fish?"

Emily gave a quick shrug. "Don't think he ever caught any. I just think he wanted to get away from David too, and it gave him a reason to stay out all day."

"Okay," Angel said and turned to go, but then stopped. "Did you try to text him?"

"His phone is on the coffee table," Emily said. "And your mom's purse is on the floor in front of the couch with her phone in it."

"How did you guys ever get along without cell phones?"

Emily smiled. "We went looking with our two legs, just like you're going to do."

She watched Angel and Lilly go.

"I'm going to call the funeral home," Emily said.

"Who died?" Henry said.

Emily's shoulders sagged. "Come on, Dad," she said and guided her father into the house. "Hungry?"

"I'd love one of those buttery brownie things you make, Irene," he said. "Always knew you were going to be a good wife."

Emily didn't bother to correct him.

ଓ ଅ

Bradley got to his feet, offered his hand to Cassandra, and pulled her up. They stood inches apart, close enough that he smelled the whiskey on her breath. Her lips, full and inviting, had always been a weakness for him.

He turned his head.

They started to walk back across the garden toward Cedar Street, and when Cassandra staggered a bit, he grabbed her arm.

"You okay?"

"Still a bit drunk," she said. "I really went to town."

He said nothing.

"What am I going to tell Angel?" Cassandra said. "She must hate me."

"I don't think she hates you," he said. "She just found out that her life isn't exactly what she's known. I think she'll be fine once you two talk."

"I never knew you were such an expert with kids," she said.

"Kids, no," he said. "I'm just winging it, but she's not really a kid anymore."

"I guess not," Cassandra said. "One day, I was changing her diapers, and the next she's off to Algonquin."

"You should be proud," he said. "You raised a wonderful girl."

Cassandra looked down and tucked her hair behind her right ear. Bradley took her arm gently and waited until she looked at him.

"I mean it," he said. "You did a great job."

A tear ran down her cheek. "I wish you'd been here."

"We can't change that," he said. "But I'm here right now. I can be part of her life . . ."

He didn't say more because there wasn't anything more to say. There were so many questions, uncertainties, and decisions left up in the air. The longer he stayed, the more difficult it would be to leave and to start believing in a future that was completely the opposite of what it was yesterday.

CR ED

Angel and Lilly rounded the corner onto Cedar Street and stopped abruptly. Angel felt her body tense and her jaw started to ache she was clenching it so tight. She couldn't look at her mother.

"You okay?" Lilly said.

"I don't know," Angel said. "What am I supposed to say to her?"

Lilly was quiet.

"Please, not one of your grandmother's proverbs right now."

"You can't ignore her forever, since you live with her."

Angel noticed her mom looking at her and her legs wanted to go the opposite way, back to the house. Lilly could stay behind and tell her mom and Bradley that Aunt Emily was waiting to talk to them. She didn't have to talk to her mom right now. She didn't want to.

It had seemed easier back in the park to forgive her mother.

And what about Bradley? He was her biological dad. What did that mean to her? Part of her had liked it better when he was her uncle. Now it would be all weird.

The only good thing she could see from all of this was that she now knew why David had acted the way he had. Felt like a big letdown compensation prize.

"Can you tell them my aunt is looking for them?"

"No," Lilly said and grabbed her arm. "I'm the outsider here."

Angel's face filled with desperation. "Please. You know my mom."

"Even a dragon struggles to control a snake in its native haunt."

"Really?" Angel said. "You just called my mom a snake."

Lilly gave a non-committal shrug.

"Fine," Angel said. "Let me confront Voldemort."

Lilly laughed.

"What's so funny?" Bradley said when he and Cassandra caught up to them.

"Nothing," Angel said, leaving no room for further questions on that subject.

Bradley nodded. "You okay?"

Angel noticed her mother stand back a bit and avoid eye contact. "I'm okay," she said in a tone that disagreed. Then she looked at Bradley. She couldn't quite think of him as her dad yet. Maybe eventually. "What about you?"

Bradley stroked his goatee. "*Surprised* is kind of putting it mildly."

"Yeah," Angel said. "I'm pretty much pissed off at her."

Bradley glanced at Cassandra, then back at Angel. "I think you two need to talk."

"Aunt Emily is looking for you," Angel said. "She needs to tell you something."

"She didn't say what?"

"No," Angel said and turned around. "We should go."

"Why don't you hang back with your mom and Lilly and I will head out?"

"Lilly doesn't—"

"I'll just stay out on the porch," Lilly said.

Angel glared at her mom, who still couldn't look at her. This was going to be fun. A trip to the dentist would be better than talking to her mom about why she had withheld this tiny bit of information about who her dad was for the last eighteen years.

"Just give her a chance," Bradley whispered in her ear. "She's hurting too. We don't need to make her pay for it again."

Angel looked at him. "Maybe I want to."

"Just talk to her," he said and walked away.

Lilly glanced at Angel, who gave her the *go ahead, I'll be fine* nod.

Once Bradley and Lilly were far enough ahead that Angel felt pretty sure she wouldn't be heard, she turned toward her mom. "Brad says you're hurting? Good. Because you broke me into a million pieces. All these years, I believed in you, that you loved me, but you were just lying to me."

Cassandra actually took a step back and her eyes were drowning. She couldn't look at Angel.

"I have always and will always love you," she said in a tiny voice. "I never meant to hurt you, honey."

"You mean you never meant for me to find out," Angel shouted. "But I did, and now I don't know if I can ever trust you."

"I'm so sorry."

Sorry? What did that mean? People said sorry all the time. It was as insincere and flat as saying *how is it going*? It was like a tiny tap on the shoulder, barely felt, afraid to be noticed. What her mother had done required more than a tiny little *sorry*. It required a big fucking apology that didn't end, that made her feel like she had just won the damned lottery.

"I made bad decisions," Cassandra said. "Except, I didn't think I was when I made them. I really believed that I was protecting you."

Angel counted to ten before she spoke. "But you didn't."

Cassandra took a step forward and Angel matched it with one backward. Angel didn't want to let her mom off the hook. Not yet. This wasn't a boo-boo on the knee that could be made all better with a kiss and a Band-Aid. No. Her heart had been ripped out of her chest and trampled. It was going to take a miracle to put her back together.

"I know that now."

"You cheated on David with Brad," Angel said, running both hands through her hair. "And you never questioned who my father might be?"

"It was just the one time," she said. "David had forgotten my birthday and I went looking for my best friend because I felt so small and insignificant, and I didn't *think*. I was confused. I was just nineteen and I'd seen David with my best friend and I thought it was over and things happened with Brad . . . David made me feel alive and wild and carefree, and I thought it was what I wanted. I was always the good girl, the sensible girl, that girl that couldn't fall for the bad boy. But I did. Maybe because no one, including Brad, thought that I would. And maybe if I hadn't gotten pregnant, my relationship with David would have run its course, but that's not what happened, and by the time I realized who you were, I freaked out and made a snap decision to keep that secret to myself. Except it made me afraid and I

252 | François Houle

pushed David away, or he pulled away because at some point, he
started to figure it out too, it looks like. It all went bad after that,
but neither of us seemed willing to walk away. I should have. But
I was too afraid. I didn't know who I was anymore. I didn't think
I could give you the life I wanted you to have."

Angel wiped tears from her cheeks. "But David could."

Cassandra's eyes filled with shame.

"You used him."

Cassandra started to shake her head but stopped. "I suppose
I did, yes. Like I said, I made a lot of bad decisions."

"Which hurt a lot of people."

"You the most," Cassandra said and reached out to touch Angel, but she moved back. "I deserve that."

"I just can't forgive you right now," Angel said. "I just can't."

"I understand."

They stood three feet apart but between them was a lifetime
of lies that Angel couldn't see past. It wasn't like this could be
swept under the rug and they could go back to normal, whatever
normal had been for them. Her mother had totally shattered Angel's trust, more so than David ever had. David had just been
distant, uninvolved in her life, but he had never hurt her like this.
Sure, Angel would have loved to have been close to him when he
had been her dad, but it was hard to blame him now. She understood now how it felt not to be able to look past her mom's
deception. She didn't absolve him completely—he was an adult
and could have handled the situation better—but she understood.

What her mom had done, she didn't *want* to understand, because if she did, she'd have to forgive her. And right this moment, she was still too hot to forgive.

"I'm sorry I hit you," Angel said.

Cassandra's eyes filled with love. "I would have done the same thing."

"Don't do that."

"Do what?"

"That," Angel said. "Being nice, understanding, loving. I can't get hurt by you again."

"I know."

Angel wiped more tears from her face. "How can I trust that you don't have any more secrets you're hiding?"

"I don't," Cassandra said. "You know everything."

Angel wanted to believe her mom, but she was afraid. She stared at her mother, studied her like some alien whose language couldn't be understood, like every word that came out of its mouth was gibberish. Hard to believe something you can't understand. Hard to believe someone who had just destroyed everything you'd believed.

Hard to trust again.

That was the worst.

For her to trust again, she would have to make herself vulnerable and she didn't want to do that. But the alternative was to live at arms-length from her mom, like two adversaries walking wide circles around each other, day after day, night after night. She didn't want that either.

Angel wanted the lie to have never existed.

But she couldn't have that either.

She started to feel like the world was too small around her. She couldn't breathe. Invisible hands formed around her throat and were cutting out her oxygen intake. Her lungs were gasping for air, her chest felt like it was going to cave in, her head was spinning.

"Angel, what's—"

CB ED

Cassandra watched her daughter become overly distressed and the mom in her kicked in. She was no longer hiding behind her fear, the wrongs she had done pushed aside like week-old leftovers, and she stepped forward just in time to catch Angel as she started to fall.

It had been years since Angel's last panic attack. They had been frequent when the fights between Cassandra and David had been regular, but in time those had died off with Cassandra's hopes of salvaging her marriage—something else she had blamed David for, but once again, something born from her own lies.

Cassandra thought her daughter's dead weight was going to pull her down with her, but all that athletic training from years of playing field hockey and volleyball came back out of retirement and she was able to ease Angel onto the road. Not the best place to pass out, but at least she had prevented her daughter from smacking her head on the asphalt.

She sat on the road and put Angel's head in her lap and ran her hand through her daughter's beautiful long auburn hair. A flood of guilt tried to drown her, but she held her head above it all, tired of feeling sorry for herself, tired of hiding in the mess she had created, tired of blaming her husband.

The only thing that mattered was right here with her.

"Hey sweetie," she said when Angel started to open her eyes. "You're okay. You passed out."

"Where are we?"

"On the side of the road."

Angel moved her head and looked around. "Oh!"

"It's okay," Cassandra said and helped her daughter sit up. "But you gave me a scare."

Angel gave her mom a sorry sort of smile. "Thanks for catching me."

They both got to their feet. Cassandra wanted to say something but everything that came to mind felt trite. Her hands kept wanting to touch Angel, bring her comfort and safety, but that right had been rescinded. At least for now. She hoped it wouldn't be forever.

"You're welcome."

A moment passed between them where they made eye contact and a private conversation seemed to occur instantly, the sort of understanding that could only happen between a mother and daughter who had just gone through hell and made it out alive— wounded, shaken, but still in one piece.

"I love you," Cassandra said.

"I know."

TWENTY-THREE

Emily had just finished making arrangements with the funeral director when she heard the front door open and close. Her chin fell against her chest and she took a breath to calm down, then she put the phone on the counter and rushed toward the front door. Her annoyance and fatigue climbed on top of each other and left her with very little energy.

"Dad?" She waited a beat. "Dad?"

She wasn't surprised. A sudden shot of adrenaline kicked in and she burst through the front door, jumped off the porch—her knees reminded her that she wasn't ten anymore and should really use the stairs next time—and she stopped by the street. She looked up and down but didn't see him.

"Crap!"

She ran to the back of the house but the back yard was empty. She stood with her hands on her hips, indecisive. She entered the house through the back door and sprinted up the stairs, hoping he was in his bedroom.

Her dad was not there. She checked all the bedrooms and the bathroom and she couldn't find him. She hurried down the stairs and nearly lost her balance. Luckily, her hand found the railing and stopped her from a bad fall. She crashed through the front door in full panic.

She had just lost her dad.

"Where would he go?" she muttered under her breath. "Dad, where are you going? I don't have time for this today. Jesus, where is everyone? I can't do this alone."

To her left, the rest of Main Street led to the Jock River Bridge—which had been completely redone just last year—and out of town. To her right was Franktown Road, which split Forest Creek down the middle, with the older homes on the south side and the newer development on the north side. It was a busy street during the day, but now that it was after six and all the shops were closed, traffic would be lighter. Still, the thought of her dad crossing Franktown Road and getting hit by a car made blood rush to her head.

She started to run up the street.

Emily had never been a good runner. It required a lot of effort. She'd always envied joggers who seemed to float just above the pavement and didn't seem to struggle to breathe. By the time she reached the corner of Main Street and Franktown Road, she had a stitch burning a hole in her left side and her lungs were tight and gasping for air.

She stood at the corner with her hands on her knees, panting like a dog on a sweltering day. She had no idea why she hadn't jumped in her car; probably thought she might miss him if she drove by too fast.

Didn't matter now.

To her left, the road led out of town and there was nothing there to draw her dad. To the right, there was a small plaza with a grocery store, a Tim Hortons, and a few other shops. And the cemetery.

Maybe, she thought.

Emily had nothing else to go on. The cemetery was where all the generations were buried—the Knightons, the MacDonalds, the O'Briens. Her mom was going to be buried there on Friday. Maybe her dad thought his wife was already there and he'd gone to visit.

She couldn't run anymore so she walked as fast as the stitch in her side allowed. She couldn't see him ahead of her and she was beginning to doubt her instinct. What if he'd gone down to the Jock River Bridge after all? He and Bradley used to go fishing there. She stopped, turned around, took a few steps, turned around again. Which way? She rubbed her forehead as if trying to pull the answer from her brain. Nothing came.

"Keep going," she said to herself just as a young teenage girl walked by and gave Emily a weird and somewhat cautious look. "Sorry. I'm looking for my dad. You didn't happen to see an old man walking that way?"

"I just came from Cranberry Street," she said. "I didn't see anyone."

"Thank you," Emily said and headed east again. She passed Cranberry Street, then Kingsley Street, and still didn't see her father. "Where *are* you?"

CB &

Bradley left Lilly out on the porch—she was going to call her mom—and he walked into the house, expecting to find his sister, but after calling her a couple of times and getting no answer, he went looking. He wondered what it was she wanted to talk to him about but guessed it must have something to do with David. Between Cassandra's bombshell and David's determination to sell the bakery, Bradley felt exhausted.

And he still hadn't been able to talk to Kate. What was he going to tell her now? He had no idea what he was planning to do, so maybe it was a good thing he hadn't reached her yet. There was a bit of irony in the fact that just a little over twenty-four hours ago she had brought up her desire to maybe have a baby with him, and he had basically balked at the idea, and here he was, a father after all.

Granted, Angel wasn't a baby and didn't really need him. In fact, she might not even want him in her life. As much as he wanted to be in hers, he realized that she might not feel the same. Being her uncle was one thing, but being her dad might not be as enticing to her.

They would need to talk.

He wondered how Cassandra and Angel were getting along, whether they had managed to resolve anything. He hoped so. Not that he expected Angel to let her mom off easy, but he'd seen how close they were before all of this and he didn't want to think about their relationship being completely ruined. Changed, for sure, but hopefully not irreversibly damaged.

He heard voices out front.

"Emily and Dad aren't here," Bradley said when he stepped out onto the porch and saw Angel and Cassandra. "Her car is still in the driveway." He pointed toward it.

"Maybe she took Grandpa with her to go stop David," Angel said. "Since we took too long to get back."

"Possible," Bradley said. "But her phone is on the kitchen counter."

"That's a bit odd," Cassandra said.

"I agree," Bradley said. "I'd say she left in a hurry and simply forgot it or didn't have time to get it."

"You think something happened to your dad?" Cassandra said.

"What could have happened to Grandpa?" Angel said, her voice rising.

"I don't know, honey."

"She would have taken the car if that were the case," Bradley said. "Maybe he just left the house without telling her and she's gone after him."

"They can't be far then," Cassandra said.

"We should split up and go look for them," Bradley said. "I'll get my phone."

"Me too," Cassandra said.

After they had retrieved their phones, they all congregated on the front lawn. Although he knew he really had nothing to do with everything that was happening, Bradley couldn't shake the feeling that he was the cause of this crazy day. It was like his coming home had set in motion a sequence of events that just seemed to be getting worse.

"Angel and Lilly, you two go down to the bridge, look around, and if you don't find Grandpa, text your mom. We're going to head up to Franktown Road." He looked at the driveway and saw Cassandra's car blocked by David's and Emily's cars. "Guess we're on foot too."

"Where are you going?" Angel said.

Bradley shook his head. "No idea. Text us and maybe we'll know then. Hopefully you find him by the bridge. He used to love going there and sit by the river."

"He took me there often," Angel said. "And talked about you and him fishing."

That made Bradley smile.

"Grandpa missed you a lot," Angel said.

"It was hard not to come back," he said and looked away, hoping they wouldn't see the guilt in his eyes. So much had happened while he hid on the west coast. "Guess it was a mistake."

"What was?" Angel said. "Not coming back sooner or coming back at all?"

"We should get going," he said, looking at Angel. "The sooner we find them, the sooner we can find out what Emily wants to tell us."

Bradley and Cassandra watched Angel and Lilly as they began to run south through what was once the downtown core of Forest Creek, where all the shops were. It had once been a vibrant stretch of road when his parents were young, but it had become run down over the years. By the time he'd run away, everything had looked old and dated. The bakery had been no exception, but after it had been renovated, several other businesses did the same. Business was slowly returning to Main Street.

"You're liking this," Cassandra said.

"Liking what?" he said.

"Being a dad," she said. "I see it on your face."

"It's that obvious?"

She nodded.

"I'm not hating it." They started to walk up toward Frank-town Road, picking up the pace until they reached the intersection. "I just don't know how she feels about it."

"I don't think she does either," Cassandra said. "I didn't make it easy on you both."

"How was your conversation?"

"Hopeful."

That's exactly how he felt about the entire situation. And confused. He had no idea what the future held now, what he was going to tell Kate. With each passing minute he felt more and more like staying. Ideally, he'd be able to convince her to give up their life in Vancouver and move to Forest Creek. He didn't think that had any chance of happening, which left him the difficult decision of choosing between his daughter and the woman he loved.

And then there was Cassandra.

He hadn't totally left her off the hook, but it was also hard not to think of the history they shared . . . and the child they had conceived. For a second, he wished he didn't know about Angel.

But it passed.

Once they reached Franktown Road, they headed east, toward the new plaza and the old cemetery, crossing streets that hadn't changed in decades. Bradley did notice that where there once had been a gas station, it was now just a lot with Amish built sheds for sale. The old service bays had been turned into an antique store.

"That's good," he said. "Maybe we can all be hopeful that everything will somehow work out."

"Yeah, and I'm Mother Teresa."

They stopped, stared at each other, and started to laugh. Hopeful. Maybe not everything could be worked out, but Bradley felt that some of them could be.

"I needed that," Cassandra said. "I think I'm beginning to live again. That secret . . . it was like being buried alive for the last eighteen years. And I finally dug myself out." She glanced at Bradley. "If only I could have done that without hurting you and Angel."

"Can't undo it now."

"No, it can't."

Bradley put a hand on her arm to stop her. "I know I can't really speak for Angel, but I really believe that we'll be fine. The shock of it all will fade, and then we'll have two choices: accept or keep blaming you. My money is that she'll accept. She doesn't strike me as the sort of person who'll hold a grudge."

"She's not." Cassandra hesitated. "You?"

They started walking again, passing by an updated version of the old MacEwen gas station on the opposite side of the road. Bradley was looking straight ahead when he spoke. "I'd be lying if I said I didn't hold grudges, because I've been holding onto one for half my life. Maybe it's time that I let go of that one."

"You didn't exactly answer my question."

Bradley glanced at her as they kept walking. "I did play a role in all of this. I could have stopped us that night, but I didn't. I wanted you so much, had for a long time. My mistake was to never question you when you became pregnant. That was a mistake made by a nineteen-year-old boy who wasn't thinking very straight. Every day, I waited for you to tell me it was over with you and David, and the more days passed that I didn't hear those words, the more depressed and angry I became. The only thing I thought about once I heard that you were getting married was to get as far away from you and him as I could. So, if there is a grudge to be held about what happened, it's a grudge against my-self."

"You're being too easy on me."

They stopped in front of the cemetery. "Probably. I just don't see the point in punishing you any more than you already pun-ished yourself."

"I just hope you're not trying to be my white knight."

That drew a tired smile out of him. "I'm not that pure."

They were staring at each other when Cassandra's phone buzzed. She looked at the text from Angel and then showed it to Bradley.

No sign of Grandpa at the bridge. What now?

"Tell her—" Bradley started to say, but stopped. He looked past Cassandra's shoulders. "Tell her we found them."

CB EO

Emily stood at the far end of the cemetery where the family plots were—she hadn't been here in a long time and couldn't believe how many of her ancestors were buried here, starting with her Great-Grandma Sarah's parents, who had died in 1939 and 1944, neither yet seventy. She had found her dad right here, thank God, and when she'd been about to scold him like he used to do to her and her brothers, she'd realized that she'd be wasting her time. The look on his face, that was the look of a man who was com-pletely heartbroken.

Her anger choked itself out of existence.

"She's not here," he said. "I looked at all the headstones and didn't see her name. Why isn't she here?"

"Mom is still at the funeral home," Emily said. She couldn't bear to tell him that she was actually in a freezer somewhere. Now that she'd made the arrangements, they were going to cremate her body. It saved space in the cemetery and would allow a few more generations to be buried with the rest of the family. "She'll be buried here Friday after the service."

"Oh," Henry simply said. "Is that far away?"

"Today is Saturday, so it's almost a week away."

Henry frowned. "How many days is that?"

"Six days, Dad. We're going to bury Mom in six days."

"I see," he said and fell silent. The whistle of a train approaching cut through the air, but they'd both been hearing trains rush by the village their whole lives, so neither reacted. A few birds took off from the trees lining the edge of the cemetery, but other than that, once the train had gone by, it was utterly quiet where they stood.

"Dad, we should go."

"I miss your mother," Henry said and Emily knew how he felt. "But she could be a hard woman. I thought maybe eventually she would accept what her mother had bestowed on us, and she did up to a point. She just never crossed the line she'd drawn for herself."

Emily touched the letter she had folded and stashed in her back pocket. Another exposed family secret that answered a lot of questions, but she wasn't convinced it was going to solve anything. It certainly made her see her dad differently; her vision of him was a bit muddy now. And the fact that she had never noticed her mother act weirdly all these years either showed that her mom had been a master of deception, or that Emily had paid little attention to what was happening around her while growing up.

A bit of both, probably.

"We should go home," she said. "The others will be wondering where we went."

"You need to understand," he said, looking at her. "She loved all three of you, she really did."

"I read the letter, Dad," Emily said. "Mom explained it all. Don't worry."

Henry looked relieved.

"I'll have to show the others," she said. "They all need to know."

"Yes, yes, you should," he said. "Everyone needs to know."

She didn't believe that the letter would help in any way, but she hoped that she was wrong. Her fear was that her mom had kept this from them for too long, that the damage she had caused was irreparable, and that the person this affected the most was most likely to disbelieve it.

"Especially David," she said.

TWENTY-FOUR

Bradley saw his dad and sister standing way back in the cemetery, Emily saying something to their father that Bradley couldn't hear. Tension he hadn't realized he'd been holding in his neck and shoulders evaporated when he saw them. The need to make decisions about his dad was becoming more and more pressing. Unfortunately, too many other things seemed more urgent at the moment.

"What are they doing way out here?" Cassandra said. "They could have driven."

"I'm pretty sure Dad just took off on Em and she just went after him," he said and headed their way, Cassandra following. "Maybe Dad just needed to see where Mom was going to be buried."

"Or he thought your mom was already here."

"Possible." He saw Emily look his way and he gave a quick wave. "I'm going to stay."

Bradley felt a pull on his arm as Cassandra came to an abrupt stop. "Here, in Forest Creek?"

"Yes," he said, turning to look at her. "It makes the most sense."

270 | François Houle

"And your job? And Kate?"

"I can find another job," he said. Then sadness filled his eyes. "I can try to convince her."

"Try?"

"We're both adults," he said. "We never had expectations." *Until yesterday*, he thought, but didn't say. "Everything will work out. Trust me."

"Bradley," she said and took a step back. "Are you sure you want to do this?"

He shifted his eyes toward his dad and sister, he thought about his broken relationship with David, but mostly, it was Angel that trumped everything else. "I have a daughter."

"You do, and I get your need to get to know her, but throwing away your relationship—"

"Maybe it's not the right relationship."

"What?" she said.

He looked at her, and he saw Cassandra as he'd always seen her. She had been the reason of all his failed relationships. Maybe if he was having such a hard time committing to Kate, that meant he shouldn't be with her after all. If he was thinking this way, had he forgiven Cassandra already? Was he jumping the gun? The past day was just one big whirlwind of confusion. Admittedly, he knew he had feelings for both Kate and Cassandra.

Cassandra was here.

He didn't think Kate would ever give up her executive life for small-town boredom.

And he shared a history with Cassandra. Sure, they both knew they'd made mistakes, but maybe a future together could still be possible. So many questions and doubts to figure out were giving him a headache.

"You need to really think about this," she said.

It's all he'd been doing since boarding that plane yesterday. It's the reason he'd come alone. Obviously, finding out he had a daughter and that Cassandra had deceived them all for years had made him question his feelings for her, and initially, he'd felt that there was no way he could still love her after that, but that had been instant gut reaction, the shock of finding out the truth. Forgiving someone really did open doors to possibilities.

The idea of providing Angel a home life with loving parents also pulled him. Sure, she was an adult, but even adult children loved to go home to visit their parents.

Of course, that hadn't been the case for him, but things would be different for Angel. He was sure she was going to come around and forgive her mother, and if he stayed, they'd be able to build their own father-daughter relationship.

"I have been." His eyes softened. "Do you see us together?"

"What?" she said and stepped back. "I can't have you hurt Kate. I'd never be able to be happy, and Brad, I really need to find happiness. I just won't be part of hurting her. Don't you love her?"

Bradley felt trapped in the impossible situation he was in. He totally got what Cassandra was saying. "I love you both, but I can't have you both. You're the mother of my child. How could I possibly turn my back on you this time? I can't. I just can't. And yes, I'll probably hurt Kate, and I hate to do that, trust me. She's an incredible woman." He held his breath for a second. "I honestly don't know why she's with me. She could have any man."

Cassandra stepped up and slapped him in the chest. "You dumbass. She sees the same thing I see."

"A dumbass?"

"No," Cassandra said. "We see a genuinely good guy with a good heart."

"Oh," he said as if it was the last thing he'd expected to hear. "I . . . I . . ."

"You have no idea how in demand guys like you are," she said. "You dumbass."

"I get it," he said. "Dumbass guys with good hearts are in short supply."

She shook her head and laughed softly.

"Maybe I should start a new dating agency called Dumbass with a Good Heart."

"You're an idiot."

"Make up your mind," he said. "Am I a dumbass or an idiot? I need to make sure my slogan is just right."

Cassandra let out an exasperated sigh. "Please, don't make any rash decisions."

"That doesn't answer my question."

"After what I did to everyone, including Dave, why would you want to be with me?"

"Because I've never forgotten my first true love."

Cassandra's eyes filled with sadness. "I wouldn't deserve you. Stay with Kate. You'll be happier."

Bradley moved in and wrapped his arms around her and found her lips and, like the teenagers they'd once been, they kissed as if this was their very first kiss.

CR ♄

Emily led her dad toward the kissing couple, feeling like she was watching a beautiful sunrise after a stormy day. As weird as it was to be in favour of watching adultery being committed right in front of her eyes, she knew they should have been together long ago.

"Who's that?" Henry said.

"That would be Brad and Cassandra."

"And do I know them?"

"Yes, you do," Emily said. "He's your son. And Cassandra is . . . his new girlfriend. I think. Or is that his old girl friend who's finally become his girlfriend?"

"I don't understand," Henry said.

"I don't either," she said. "And it doesn't matter. We'll just wait until the two lovebirds pull their beaks apart from one another."

"They have beaks?"

Emily shifted her eyes toward her father. "It's just a figure of speech."

"Oh," he said. "Maybe we should just leave them be and go."

"I need to talk to them."

"Why?"

"I need to tell them about Mom's letter," Emily said. "The one you gave me earlier."

"I gave you a letter?"

Emily was sort of getting why parents could get exasperated with their kids when they asked a million questions. No wonder parents looked beat up all the time.

"You did," she said. "And unfortunately, I think it's going to be a bit of a Debbie Downer for them."

"Who's Debbie Downer?" Henry said. "She's not my daughter, is she?"

"Not that I know," Emily said. "I'm your only daughter."

Henry eyed her. "How old are you?"

"I'm thirty-five, Dad."

"How old am I?"

"You're seventy-one," she said. "Old enough to be my dad."

"Oh," he said. "And that boy is my son and he's kissing his girlfriend."

"That's what it looks like to me."

"Yeah, me too." He looked pensive. "Do *I* have a girlfriend to kiss?"

Emily hesitated a moment "You did. But she died."

"Oh," he said. "Did I like her?"

Emily put an arm around her father's waist, and kissed his cheek. "You liked her for about forty years," she said. *Give or take a few months*, she thought, patting her back pocket with her other hand. *Give or take.*

"Then I'm sorry she died."

"Me too, Dad," she said. "Me too."

CB EO

Bradley pulled away from Cassandra and saw something in the corner of his eye. He turned his head slowly, a touch of redness in his cheeks.

"Really?" he said. "You couldn't give us a little privacy?"

"You chose to do that in the middle of a cemetery for everyone to see."

Bradley looked around. "Don't see too many other people here."

"There's like three hundred people below your feet."

"And I'm sure not a single one is going to tell."

"Probably not," Emily said. "But I'm all ears, if the two of you care to tell me what is going on."

Bradley and Cassandra looked at each other with the same unknowing expression on their faces. A car pulled up in the small parking lot and three people spilled out of it. They made their way to the other side of the cemetery.

"I decided to stay," he said.

Emily shifted her gaze from Cassandra to Bradley. "I see." She paused. "It's not my business, but what about Kate?"

"I'll need to tell her everything," he said. "I'll call her tonight."

"Breaking up over the phone," Emily said. "Never sat very well with me. It's even worse now, with texting."

Bradley scratched the back of his neck. "I don't have much of a choice. I'm not going to drag this out until I can fly back to Vancouver. I owe her the courtesy of letting her know ASAP."

"You do," Emily said.

"What were you and Dad doing?" he said. "Why didn't you drive? You could have left a note."

"Are you going to let me answer?" Emily said. "Or just keep firing questions at me?"

"Sorry."

"I was on the phone with the funeral director—everything is set for Friday—when I heard the front door open and close."

Emily glared at her father. "Dad here decided to go for a stroll without me."

"Was he—?"

"Lucid?" Emily said. "I don't know. Anyway, by the time I got out front, I couldn't see him. I panicked and started running after him. I think he made his way along the back streets because I didn't see him until I got here."

"How'd you know he'd be here?"

"I didn't," she said. "I just hoped I'd find him if I kept walking." She paused. "I was really scared. Maybe we can make some calls this week and figure out what to do."

"I know," Bradley said. "One reason why I'm staying."

Emily looked at the two of them. "That's not enough to stay. Once Dad is safe somewhere, you could go back."

"Well, there's Angel . . . and Cassandra."

Cassandra gave an apologetic shrug.

"You're both old enough to make that decision," Emily said.

An uncomfortable silence settled between them and all they heard were the birds singing from their hiding place in the trees and traffic rushing by on Franktown Road. Yes, they were old enough, and all his logic told him it was the right decision, but he knew that no matter what he did, he'd always have some doubts.

"What did you want to tell us?" Bradley said.

Emily stared at Cassandra. "And you thought *you* dropped a bombshell."

"What's going on?" Bradley said.

"Let's go home," Emily said. "And get everyone together."

Cß ഓ

They were all sitting around the kitchen island, the five of them. Emily had tried to put her dad to bed but he'd insisted that he was fine, he didn't need a nap. Besides, he was hungry and wanted to eat.

Emily had ordered a couple of large pizzas but they hadn't arrived yet, so she cut up some cheese and filled a bowl with Breton crackers to tide them over. She poured four shots of whiskey—none for her dad—and she saw Angel give her an uncertain stare.

Lilly had decided to remain out front.

"It's okay," Emily said. "Once you all hear what Grandma left behind, we're all going to need this."

"Mom?"

"I'll trust your aunt Emily on this," Cassandra said. "You're eighteen and you can just go across to Gatineau and drink anyway."

"Uncle Brad—Dad—what have you done with Mom?"

"Nothing," he said. "She's just the way I remember her."

"Well, that's not who she's been."

Emily cleared her throat. She had phoned David but he hadn't picked up, so she'd decided to go ahead with Mom's letter and fill him in later. The worst part was that all of this could have been averted if their dad hadn't done what he'd done. And if their mother could have forgiven him.

Instead, all three kids had paid for their parents' mistake one way or another, with David getting the worst of it. And Emily figured he must have known. It had to be the reason why he hated them so much.

Had to be.

After reading the letter earlier, Emily had started to feel sorry for David, started to understand him a bit better. She still didn't agree with selling the bakery. That wouldn't solve anything. At best, it was a temporary fix that would make him feel better but wouldn't last.

David needed closure.

They all needed closure.

She wasn't sure the letter would bring them that, though. There was no way to get more from their mom; the words on the paper were all they had.

And with their father's condition, the chance of getting more from him was slipping away quickly.

Emily pulled the letter from her back pocket, unfolded it on the cold granite countertop, and pushed it toward Bradley.

"What's this?"

Emily took her shot glass and downed it. "A letter from Mom."

"Where did it come from?"

"Dad remembered it earlier today, after you'd gone, and gave it to me."

"I get the feeling we're not going to like it."

Emily stared long and hard at her brother, the middle child, the one who had been a buffer between her and David. She had been too young to remember David ever being nice, so reading her mom's words earlier had been a surprise. She had felt both confused and angry. She believed her mom had many regrets, but none she'd been strong enough to undo, and Emily wasn't sure that asking for forgiveness from the grave was going to bring the Knighton family back together.

"Read it," she said. "Out loud."

TWENTY-FIVE

When Bradley finished reading the letter, he put the papers on the counter and pulled his hand away quickly, as if its toxicity might burn him. No one said a word, and barely a breath was heard. They all had that zombie apocalypse glaze in their eyes.

"Drink up," Emily said.

They all did.

"That's horrible," Angel said and grimaced.

"The letter or the whiskey?" Bradley said.

"Yes," she said. "I didn't care for either."

"I agree about the letter," Bradley said and motioned to Emily to refill his shot glass. "But I can use another one of those."

He downed it.

Cassandra remained quiet.

"Mom and Dad weren't who we knew," Emily said. "Not entirely, anyway."

"What does it mean?" Angel said.

Bradley and Emily eyed each other as if a silent conversation was going on between them. Bradley reached for the bottle of whiskey and filled both their glasses, but when he went to fill Cassandra's, she put her hand over her glass.

He didn't press.

He and his sister kicked back the whiskey.

"We need to talk to David," Bradley said. "I have no idea how he's going to react. I doubt it's the absolution he's looking for."

"It might be the truth that he's always known, the proof that justifies his actions," Emily said. "The proof that he feels gives him the right to sell the bakery."

"What if it doesn't?" Angel said. "Now that we all know, what if, I don't know, maybe he can't hate us anymore because the secret is out?"

"Maybe," Emily said. "But I don't think you should get your hopes up, honey. If he knows, then David has held onto this secret for a long time."

Bradley recalled a specific day, a Saturday morning, when he and David had been playing Monopoly in David's room like they did most Saturday mornings, and at one-point David had gone to the bathroom. When he'd come back, he'd started to yell at Bradley, called him a little shit, and told him to get out and never come back in his room.

"I'm sure he knows," Bradley said, and told the others what had happened that morning. "Mom and Dad didn't argue often, but every once in a while, we heard them in their room. They never yelled or screamed. It was always low voices, but you could always tell when Mom had an edge and Dad was trying to soothe her. The bathroom was beside their room, so maybe that day they were loud enough and David heard something through the wall."

"Like what?" Angel said.

Bradley shrugged. "He never said and the few times he was nice to me after that were few and far between. Eventually, we just stayed clear of each other."

"I'm sorry," Cassandra said. "I made things worse."

Angel reached for her mom's hand. "You didn't know. No one did."

Cassandra squeezed her hand. "I just—"

"Angel is right," Emily said. "What matters is now. He needs to read the letter."

"Probably won't change a thing," Bradley said.

"We have to try," Emily said. "You just told us he wasn't always like this, that you and he were close."

Another memory pulled itself from Bradley's hiding place where he had shoved everything about David, good and bad. He and David had gone tobogganing over by the Jock River Bridge. That had been the winter before his brother turned, when Bradley had been six and David seven. There was a steep embankment down to the river that made for a great slide in the winter, and once the river froze, they could toboggan without fear of going through the ice. Not that the river was very deep, nor wide. All the kids went there, and had been for generations.

Except that day, it had been just him and David, and although it had been snowing for more than a day, it hadn't been all that cold, and the ice had still been thin.

He and David went up and down several times, having a blast in the powdery snow. About an hour in, Bradley heard some cracking when his toboggan slid over the river.

He ignored it and went back up as David slid by him.

"David, watch," he shouted from the top of the hill. "I'm gonna fly over that bump."

"It's pretty big," David shouted back. "You might be scared."

He shook his head. "I'm brave, like you."

Bradley saw his brother smile at the compliment, and then he slid down the hill at break-neck speed, hit the bump, and flew like a bird. At one point the toboggan went one way and Bradley the other, and when he landed hard on the ice, he heard David cheer. Bradley pretended that he was all right and smiled at David, who was on his way back up the hill.

And then Bradley heard the ice crack again.

Louder this time.

And something under him moved.

Quickly, he stood, but the thin ice couldn't even handle his light weight. More cracking followed and suddenly he slid into the icy water, clinging desperately to the ice around the hole.

It felt like the river was trying to swallow him.

"DAVID!" he screamed. "David, help me."

Then the ice around the hole began to crack too and Bradley felt himself sliding further into the cold river, his arms by now too tired to hang on. He screamed and screamed and then water spilled into his mouth and he couldn't breathe and he was scared and everything was dark and cold and he started to cry and he probably peed himself but he was too wet to tell and he wanted to just go home, home where it was warm and safe, where he and David could play Monopoly like they always did on Saturday morning and why hadn't they done that today instead of going tobogganing, and he wanted to see his baby sister Emily because he liked playing tea with her and even if he didn't care to play with her Barbies, he did anyway, and so did David, because she had no sisters to play with.

And just as his head completely submerged, he felt hands grab his wrists and yank him out of the water, and then his brother was dragging him away to safety and Bradley held on to David and cried and cried and cried while David told him that he was all right, that as long as he was his big brother, nothing bad would ever happen to him.

"He saved my life once," Bradley said.

Everyone stared at him and waited.

"He pulled me out of the Jock River when we were kids and I'd fallen in. It was winter and the water was so cold." He told them what had happened. "He saved me that day. I never understood how he'd managed to pull me out. He was bigger than me, I guess he got that from Dad, and he'd do push-ups all the time because he said it made his slapshot harder—he was so into Gretzky and wanted to be even better than the Great One, as he said all the time—but still."

"Like the mother who lifts a car off her child," Angel said.

Bradley looked at Angel and nodded. "But he was only seven. He saved me and I'd blocked it out. I'd been so scared and blocked it out. I don't think I ever went tobogganing there ever again."

"You didn't," Emily said. "Whenever I asked you, you always told me you didn't care for tobogganing."

"If he hadn't been there that day, I might not be here today."

No one breathed.

Cʒ ɞɔ

The letter. It lay on the countertop like a blemish, another dirty Knighton secret. Bradley stared at it but couldn't touch it again, afraid that it might swallow him whole like the river almost had on that winter day. All their lives, he and Emily had never known the harshness of their mother's heart.

But David had.

Thinking that this letter from beyond the grave could put everything right again was a lie his mother had told herself because she'd been too much of a coward to do it while she was alive, and this tainted the way Bradley had known his mom. To him and Emily, she had been a loving and caring woman who had always seemed to put them ahead of herself. She had loved her children unconditionally.

Except, she hadn't.

Anger towards his mother boiled inside of Bradley.

And for the first time in forever, sympathy for David pushed itself to stand at the forefront in Bradley's thoughts. He felt certain now that his brother had heard something on that Saturday morning, and to continue to feel animosity toward David because of his loathsome behaviour of the last thirty plus years seemed unwarranted now.

How horrible that must have been for him, to discover that he wasn't who he'd thought he was. But even worse, to discover that he wasn't really wanted. He was an obligation, like a chore that needed to be done. If only Bradley had known, he would have told his brother—that same brother who had saved him from drowning just the winter before—that he loved him, *loved* him like the *brother* that he was. Because to Bradley, David had always been his brother.

He hadn't known anything different.

Why hadn't their parents told them all? Told them, instead of hiding a secret that tried to pretend mistakes hadn't been made? They had chosen to lie instead of facing the truth, and in so choosing, they had condemned a little boy to live believing that he wasn't worthy of love, that he meant less than the others, that he was a damned *obligation*.

No wonder David was so angry.

If their mother was here, Bradley knew that he'd have gone ballistic on her. What she had done was inexcusable. She had been a grown woman and should have been able to look past the blemish that she saw as unforgivable, because loving a child, any child, wasn't something that one should ever be ashamed of, no matter how that child came to be your responsibility.

છ ∞

Angel loved her grandmother. She had spent so many days and nights here with her grandparents, and Grandma Irene had always showed her so much patience, care, and of course, unconditional love. Her grandmother had never known that David wasn't Angel's father, so how could Grandma have loved her, being David's daughter as far as she knew, but she hadn't been able to love David?

Not that Angel was forgiving David for the way he'd treated her. Seemed to her that he had done the same thing Grandma Irene had done to him. Had it been some sort of revenge?

Had it been something else?

Maybe it wasn't *her* David had been angry with, but her mom. For lying.

She certainly knew how that felt.

Even earlier today, she had seen loving pain in his eyes when he'd looked at her, even if his words were harsh, and she had seen that before, many times in the past. His body language and words would keep her at a distance, but his eyes often had seemed to contradict that. Could it be that he'd wanted to love her as his daughter, but couldn't climb the wall of lies that surrounded his life?

Her mom.

Her grandmother.

The letter, as long as it was, couldn't tell everything. The only reason that Angel saw for her grandmother to write it was because, in the end, she understood that what she had done had been wrong and, in her own way, she was asking for forgiveness.

Why couldn't she have done this while she was still alive? It was possible she had planned to but her sudden death had changed that. But she had written the letter without knowing that she would die soon, so her secret could have stayed hidden for years. It was hard to make sense of it.

This whole day was one gigantic mess, and she felt sorry for bringing Lilly. All she'd wanted was to have her best friend with her to help her get through the mourning of her grandmother's passing, and instead her family had decided to empty the family coffin that had been full of lies and secrets.

Angel grabbed her phone and texted Lilly.

CB EO

Cassandra had seen glimpses of the David who had saved Bradley, who had played with him. That's who had come to her field hockey games and been her biggest fan. That's the David she had fallen in love with. She now saw how her actions had mirrored Irene's in alienating him, and she definitely understood how that could have turned anyone bitter. But no matter how much she beat herself up, it wouldn't change anything. All she could concentrate on was what lay ahead. Maybe she and David could agree to end their marriage amicably. Maybe he could have a life with Josée. God knows after what she had just found out, the guy deserved a break.

And she needed to free herself of blaming him. She was the one who had deceived him, trapping them both in a lifelong lie. It was time that she moved on as well, whether that might be possible with Bradley or not, she didn't know. Too much was happening today to make sense of anything. She wasn't sure she deserved him. They had gotten carried away earlier in the cemetery, of all places, and she didn't like the idea of being the reason for his breakup with Kate.

She had made so many mistakes already, and didn't want to make another.

The one thing she was sure of was that she was done drinking tonight—and maybe forever—and she had the beginning of a wicked headache.

And she was starving.

CB ♂

Emily thought she'd known everything about her mother, but it looked like she'd barely known her. First, there was the secret behind the loan David had given them, which could potentially cost Emily the one thing she loved the most: the bakery. To her, it wasn't just a business, it was an heirloom passed on to her by a great-grandmother she loved and admired.

Second, there was the will that her mother had thought could right the wrong she had done, but if she had signed the deed of the bakery over to David, nothing in the will could change that.

And third, that letter showed how desperate her mother had been to try to explain why things had been so messed up for so long. It certainly made her—made them all, she figured—understand David, finally. The first time she'd read it after her dad had given her the letter, not everything had sunk in. In fact, she'd been somewhat numb.

Now she got it.

And yes, she felt bad for David.

A lot.

But she kept coming back to her mom signing over the bakery deed and she couldn't get past that. David was going to sell the bakery Great-Grandma Sarah had built, and Emily couldn't stop him because of her mother.

"What a mess," she said. "This letter won't help us. It's Mom trying to cover up a lie with another lie. That's how David is going to see this, I'm sure of it. This family is suffocating in decades of lies."

Emily poured herself another shot of whiskey and didn't offer anyone else any. She kicked it back, poured another, and kicked that back too.

"Take it easy," Bradley said. "We need to be sober."

"Because we're going to sound a whole lot more legit if we are?" she said. "This letter isn't going to solve anything and you know it. David will not suddenly want to hug and make up."

"Kiss and make up," Angel said.

"I know, sweetheart," Emily said. "I just thought it was even less likely that he'd want to do that."

"Right."

"It's obvious David already knows some of this," Bradley said, touching the letter, his earlier fear gone. "Maybe all of it. But now we know too, and we can talk to him."

"You think he'll listen?" Emily said. "This isn't a bloody nose that you can wipe clean. He's had over thirty years to stew on this."

"All we can do is talk with him," Bradley said. "I know the bakery is important, but he's our brother, Em. No matter how Mom felt, David is our brother. And now we know why he's been hurting all these years."

"I didn't help," Cassandra said in a small voice.

"No, you didn't," Emily said with a sharpness that made everyone recoil. "Sorry. I'm just . . . I'm just tired of waiting. It's after seven. How long can he be there showing the place?"

"Maybe he just left," Angel said.

Emily shook her head. "My car is behind his. He's got no way of leaving except to come in and ask me to move it, so if he's still showing his client the place, then that client must be really interested. And I don't like that."

Bradley took Emily into his arms.

"I love that place, Brad," she said into his shoulder, frustration and heartache bleeding into every word. "And I'll be damned if I lose it just because Mom lied to us our whole lives. I'm so angry with her right now. She's lucky she's not here."

"Hey, hey, little sister," Bradley said. "It will work out. I believe that. It will."

"I just . . . I just . . . can't—"

The doorbell rang. Everyone stared at each other.

"Could be the pizza," Angel said.

"About time," Cassandra said and slid off her stool. "We could all use a little food."

TWENTY-SIX

When Cassandra opened the front door, instant guilt coloured her face and her throat felt like she had just swallowed sand. It shouldn't have surprised her that this day had just gotten more interesting, and a bit more awkward as well. She was looking at two people standing on the porch: a young man of maybe seventeen with a Sens baseball cap on backwards the way kids liked to wear them, holding a couple of large pizza boxes, and a very attractive woman of about forty. At her feet stood a small suitcase.

"How much?" she said to the boy.

"Fifty-three seventy-nine," the boy said.

Cassandra gave him sixty and waited until he was gone to turn to the woman. She was striking and wore confidence like a tailored suit. Cassandra tried not to show her intimidation and was quite sure she was failing.

"You must be Kate," Cassandra finally said, doing her best to sound casual and friendly. "Please, come in."

Kate smiled and grabbed her suitcase. "And you must be the ghost I've been competing with."

C8 80

Cassandra showed Kate into the sitting room and told her to just wait, that she'd be right back. When she got to the kitchen, she plopped the pizzas onto the counter and was about to tell Bradley that Kate was here, but he was still busy trying to get Emily off the ledge so she went back to the sitting room. Leaving Kate alone would have been rude and rudeness was something her mother had never tolerated.

The other reason Cassandra decided to go back and talk to Kate was to find out why she had said what she'd said about her being *the ghost*. That seemed too good to gloss over, and there was something else Cassandra couldn't deny.

She liked Kate instantly.

That didn't make much sense because, after all, they were both after the same man, and looking at this gorgeous woman dressed in form-fitting jeans and a button-down white blouse that showed off her toned arms, Cassandra could see why Bradley was with Kate.

What Cassandra couldn't understand was why he'd want to give Kate up. Right now, she looked way older than Kate, although she was sure the woman was probably a bit older. Cassandra stood in the entry between the sitting room and hallway, studying Kate, who was standing in front of the unlit fireplace, her back to Cassandra, looking at the framed family photos on the mantle. There was the one with Irene and Henry on their wedding day, one with her and David on their wedding day—that one would be gone soon, most likely—and one with Emily and Bradley about two months before he would leave.

Funny how there aren't any recent pictures of anyone, Cassandra thought.

As if the past held all the good times.

More like all the lies and secrets.

Cassandra cleared her throat and Kate turned, that self-assurance making Cassandra feel envious. She had lost her confidence long ago somewhere in the shame of her past. Again, she couldn't figure out why Bradley would want to let Kate go. The woman was stunning, successful, and probably had her shit together, while Cassandra was looking haggard, was a complete failure, and definitely *didn't* have her shit together.

Well, she was a mother, and maybe not the greatest mother, but she'd done her best. That was something she'd always cherished, and suddenly she realized that Kate had absolutely no idea that Bradley was a father.

"It's a lovely home," Kate said. "I've always loved older homes, especially early nineteen-hundred homes. They had a lot more character than today's cookie-cutter boxes built in a hurry by fly-by-night builders trying to make a quick buck."

"Although you've got to agree that today's insulation works a bit better than newspaper in the wall."

"There is that," Kate said.

Cassandra moved into the sitting room and was about to take one of the sofa chairs when she motioned to Kate to have a seat first.

"Thanks," Kate said and sat. "I guess Bradley isn't here?"

"He's here," Cassandra said. "But he and Emily are a bit preoccupied. We've had one very long day."

"I bet," Kate said. "Not easy when a parent passes away. Not that I've experienced it, as both my parents are alive, but I've had friends who have lost a parent."

Cassandra was about to tell her it wasn't that, but then decided that if Bradley wanted to tell Kate what's been going on, then that was his choice.

"Emily was close to her mother," Kate said. "Must be difficult for her."

"It is," Cassandra said. "They were best friends, really, and business partners with the bakery."

"Bradley told me." Kate looked down at her hands. "I shouldn't have said that, earlier."

Cassandra was surprised to see Kate a little nervous. Then again, this wasn't her playground. "I admit, I'm a bit curious."

"I've known Brad three years now and we started to see each other outside of work a couple years ago, or thereabout. Two adults—"

"Having a little fun."

"Are you sure you want to hear this?"

Cassandra nodded.

Kate fiddled with the ring she wore on her right thumb. She also had a ring on the index finger of each hand. She then tucked her hair behind her left ear and Cassandra was surprised to see a row of earrings running up her ear. She counted seven. Not typical of a woman Kate's age, but maybe she'd had them since she was young.

She was the last person to judge another after what she had done. They were just earrings, but Cassandra felt they added to Kate's attractiveness. She looked at her own clothes and realized she'd been wearing these blue jeans and this t-shirt for the past ten years. Her hairstyle dated back to the turn of the century.

That's what happened when you tucked yourself away in the misery of your existence and stopped living.

"Yeah, two adults having fun," Kate said and pulled Cassandra from her thoughts. "At my age, you've given up the idea of settling down. I moved around a lot. I go wherever a station needs to be turned around. It's not always a glamourous job, especially when I have to let people go. I hate that part. It's heartbreaking. So anyway, that's how I met Brad and I saw potential in him not as a DJ, but as a Program Director. And he's aced it."

"And?"

"And for once I didn't want to leave again," she said. "So, I changed position when I got the chance, and sort of settled."

Cassandra took a moment to take it all in. Earlier, after Bradley had kissed her and ignited something in her that had long been extinguished, she had started to believe that maybe, just maybe, something might be there for them. But she could see how much Kate cared for him, loved him, and Cassandra knew that nothing about her and Bradley would ever be right. And there was something else about Kate that Cassandra couldn't quite figure out.

"Is there a powder room I can use?"

"Across the hall, first door on the right."

"Thank you."

While Kate was gone, Cassandra sat with her left leg crossed over her right, visualizing Kate sitting across from her, a glow in her eyes as she spoke about Bradley. Cassandra didn't think she had that same sort of glow. Only a woman completely—

Suddenly, it hit her.

Kate returned from the powder room and took the same seat. Cassandra watched her for a minute, and then remembered her mother. It was rude to stare and not say anything.

"How long?" she said.

"How long what?" Kate said.

Cassandra gave her a knowing smile.

"I guess a mother would know," Kate said and stood up. She paced in front of the fireplace. "Ten weeks."

"Brad doesn't know."

Kate shook her head. "I was trying to tell him yesterday morning, before Emily called with the . . . news. We never got around to it."

"Guess it wasn't planned."

"No," Kate said. "It wasn't something we ever talked about. At my age, the pill doesn't always work."

"At any age," Cassandra said. "You want it?"

Kate appeared to be chewing the inside of her cheek. "I really do. I'm forty. I'm not going to get many more opportunities. And . . . and I really love Brad. I've always been all about my career until I met him. He's made me realize that I was missing something."

"But you're not sure he loves you as much . . ."

"As you," Kate finished.

"Which is what you meant by me being *the ghost*."

"I'm sorry," Kate said. "It just came out. I didn't mean to offend you."

"You didn't," Cassandra said.

"It isn't because he spoke of you often," she said. "He never mentioned you at all to me. But I've always felt that there was something holding him back."

"Like a ghost."

Kate nodded. "When I saw you, I figured you must be the one he let get away and still wanted. I said what I said almost out of relief knowing it wasn't just my imagination, that you actually existed."

"It's so much more complicated than that," Cassandra said with a long sigh. "In fact, I'm his sister-in-law."

Kate's eyes shifted to the mantel. "That's you in the picture."

"I married Brad's brother David."

"And Bradley's been pining for you since?"

"Oh," Cassandra said. "You've stepped into a theatre and the movie is nearing the end. You have no idea what's going on."

Kate sat down again.

"Sorry," Cassandra said. "It's a very long story and actually we just learned how it started right before you arrived."

"I don't understand."

"I know," Cassandra said. "I was once Brad's best friend, until I married his brother."

Kate played with the ring on her thumb.

"Which is why he moved to Vancouver," Cassandra said. "I never quite realized that Brad was in love with me until he'd moved away. Like I said, we were best friends."

"Oh," Kate said and rubbed her hands on her thighs. "He loved you but you saw him as just a friend."

"Until it was too late."

Kate stood again. "But he still loves you." She faced Cassandra. "And do you love him? Is that why he didn't want me to come? Maybe coming here was a mistake after all. I should leave."

Cassandra got to her feet. "Stay."

"I don't want to be the fool here."

"The only fool here is me," Cassandra said. "I passed him up long ago. You have a baby coming."

"I'm quite capable of raising my baby alone," Kate said with an air of assertiveness. "I didn't get to where I am by being incompetent."

"I have no doubt that you could," Cassandra said. "But a child is better off with two loving parents."

"But that's the problem," Kate said. "Brad is still in love with you and he didn't want me to come with him because he wanted to see if there was still something between the two of you. Although if you're married to his brother, I don't see why he'd expect that."

"That's the part of the story you've missed," Cassandra said. "My husband and I are getting a divorce."

Kate's features hardened. "And you say I have nothing to worry about?"

"You have a baby coming," Cassandra said. "I couldn't live with myself if you and Brad didn't raise that baby together."

‹૩ ૪›

Angel was beginning to wonder what her mom was doing, so she took a bite of pizza and went looking for her. She thought she could hear voices and wondered if David had come back.

"Mom?" Angel said making her way to the sitting room. "Who are you talking t—"

Angel's eyes spotted the unknown woman, who seemed a bit distressed, sitting on her grandmother's couch. The woman was absolutely beautiful and she offered Angel a non-threatening soft smile that looked sort of sad. Angel returned her own quick smile and then gave her mom the look, the one that said *who is that?*

"Angel, this is Uncle Brad's girlfriend Kate."

"You mean—"

"From Vancouver, yes," Cassandra said, giving Angel her own look that seemed to say *play along.*

"Oh, right, Uncle Bradley's girlfriend," Angel said and turned to Kate. "My grandmother did mention you but I guess I'm surprised to see you. And things have been crazy here so I'm just a little scatterbrained today."

"You don't have to explain," Kate said, regaining her composure. "You're all going through a lot, which is why I thought I should be here with Brad. I know he didn't want me to meet you all under these trying circumstances, and I'm sorry if I'm intruding."

"No, no," Cassandra said. "It's fine."

"I'm sure he'll be surprised to see you," Angel said and saw her mom glower at her. "I mean, glad to see you."

Kate pulled her lips into a tight line. The conversation had trailed off and the three women avoided looking at each other. The room was getting dark and Cassandra turned on one of the lights.

"Well, the pizza is getting cold, so I'm going to go back," Angel said. "You want me to tell—?"

"Not yet," Cassandra said.

Angel returned to the kitchen and loaded a slice of pizza on a plate.

"Is that for your mom?"

"It's for Lilly," Angel said.

"She's still out front?"

Angel nodded. "Would you want to be in here if you were her?"

"Guess not."

"She's waiting for her mom to come and get her," Angel said. "Since it looks like we're going to be here a while and there's no point in her waiting for me and mom to drive her back."

"Tell her we apologize," Bradley said.

"I have," Angel said. "More times than I can count."

"Is your mom coming?" Bradley said. "What is she doing?"

"Give her a minute."

Bradley cocked an ear. "What's going on? Is David out there?"

"No, no," Angel said. "He's not. It's nothing."

Bradley got off his stool and marched out of the kitchen before Angel could stop him. "Dad, stay here."

"Who's out there?" Emily said.

Angel looked worried. "Uncle Bradley's girlfriend, Kate."

"Uncle Bradley?"

"Better than saying my dad's girlfriend is having a conversation with my mom.," she said. "I'm going out front to be with Lilly until her mom comes."

"What a mess."

"That's an understatement, Aunt Emily," Angel said and left.

TWENTY-SEVEN

B radley stopped just before he reached the sitting room because one of the voices he was hearing sounded familiar. And it wasn't his brother's voice. The last thing he'd expected was to find Kate in his childhood home. Then again, it didn't surprise him that she was here.

He should have known that she would come.

It made him smile.

And broke his heart.

Bradley took a breath and stepped into view. The two women he loved were sitting side by side on the couch, Cassandra holding Kate's hands. He could see that Kate had been crying, which wasn't something she did.

He'd seen her shed tears maybe once, and that had been after having to let go five people at the station when he'd first met her. Everyone had heard that the ice woman was coming to clean house, and he'd been surprised when she had called him into her office—he'd expected to be let go as well and was so nervous— and had told him she was going to make him Program Director. When he'd asked about Paul Brennan, the current Program Director, that's when her eyes had gotten moist.

So, to see her here sitting side by side with Cassandra, teary-eyed . . . he didn't know what to think.

"Guess who's here?" Cassandra said, turning to him. "Bet you weren't expecting this nice surprise."

Bradley shifted from foot to foot, trying to figure out what would be appropriate to say. Nothing came to mind—a big void of nothingness.

"It's okay, Brad," Kate said. "I know who Cassandra is."

He wasn't sure whether that was good or bad.

"I had to come," Kate said. "I didn't like the way things hung in the air when you left, and I thought I should be with you, help you get through this."

"I . . . I just needed some time."

"You needed to find out if you and Cassandra still had a chance."

"It's not that," he said.

"Please don't lie," she said. "Like I said, I know who she is to you."

Bradley rubbed his goatee.

"I really just needed to come home, bury Mom, try to fix my relationship with my brother. I didn't really know how I would react to seeing David and Cassandra together after so many years. I had no idea their marriage had turned the way it had."

"It's been bad for a long time," Cassandra said. "We should have divorced long ago."

"I'm sorry," Kate said to Cassandra.

"Thank you," Cassandra said. "I should leave you two together."

She stood and started to walk away, and as she passed by Bradley, their past slammed into him. She was the girl he'd fallen in love with probably as far back as that first day of school when she'd taken the empty seat beside him. Together, they had done homework in his room, her lying on her stomach on his bed and him sitting on the floor with his back against the wall under his window. They'd heard David come home and slam his bedroom door, and heard him cursing at whatever evil inhabited his room. They had ridden their bikes up Main Street to Tony's chip wagon after school to share a large bag of Tony's yummy greasy home fries. He had eaten dinner at her place—her mom had made a delicious beef macaroni dish that his mom had never done—as often as she'd eaten dinner at his house.

When they'd started high school, they had both been bummed out to find out that the only class they had together was boring history, but in grade ten they'd been lucky enough to share six of eight classes.

And in grade eleven, they had gone to see a movie—something they had done so often—and when he'd taken her home, they had sat in the car chatting, but something had changed; he'd become nervous, and he'd seen her wring her hands together. The evening had started as two best friends going to the movies, and by the end a weirdness had settled between them.

So he'd walked her to the front door, said goodnight, and driven home knowing that their friendship would never be the same again.

Looking back, maybe that weirdness had pushed her into David's arms.

"She's nice," Kate said and made her way toward him. "I can see why you still have feelings for her."

Pain walked across his face. "I didn't so much move away to pursue a dream, I ran away to escape."

"And now that you're back?"

He turned his head to look out the front window. The last of the day was being chased away quickly. It had seemed easier earlier to believe in staying and seeing if anything came between him and Cassandra. He'd told himself he wanted to stay for Angel, and that was true. But now . . . he felt like a cheating bastard. He had kissed Cassandra the way he'd wanted to kiss her that night after the movie, oblivious that his action was actually wrong. He was in a relationship, married or not, and it was wrong to have kissed Cassandra.

Kate didn't need that.

"I kissed her earlier," he said.

The words stood between them like a referee before he blows his whistle to signal the fight has begun. Kate crossed her arms while Bradley looked down in shame.

"I see."

Two words that said more than an outright tirade ever could; two words that broke his heart because he knew how much he had hurt Kate; two words that felt like the end of the best thing that had ever happened to him.

Bradley swore under his breath and stepped out onto the front porch. He saw Angel and Lilly sitting on the steps.

"Hey," Angel said.

"Hey," he said and filled his lungs with warm muggy late-summer air. He walked to the far left of the porch where the swing waited in a sad state of disrepair. Time hadn't been kind to it and it looked old and rusty. He couldn't believe Lilly had been sitting on it earlier. His two hundred pounds would probably make it scream if he were to sit in it. Instead, he stood with his hands on the railing, which needed a new coat of paint and probably should be replaced entirely as most of the spindles were rotted. It saddened him to see the house in such need of repair.

"Does Kate know about me?"

"I'm not sure."

"What are you going to do?"

He shook his head. "No idea."

Kate came outside and he felt her approaching cautiously. She was taller than Cassandra, but the top of her head still didn't reach much higher than halfway up his neck. They stood in silence while Angel and Lilly walked away toward the road.

"I'm sorry," he said.

Kate didn't say anything. A couple more minutes went by. Traffic on Main Street was light now. A young couple walked by, the man pushing a stroller while the woman held a little girl's hand.

"Did I make the trip for nothing?"

Bradley couldn't look at her. His eyes followed the couple as they made their way south, toward the Jock River Bridge. Then he spotted Angel and Lilly over by the hedges that had given them privacy from the neighbour on the right for as long as he could remember.

His daughter.

How was he going to tell Kate?

Did it matter if they were going to break up anyway?

Had she made the trip for nothing?

He couldn't answer that.

Didn't want to.

He was making a mess of a good thing.

A blind man would see that.

The breeze caressed his face with Kate's perfume. He'd always loved the way she smelled, like some sort of spring rose with a hint of mango. He was probably way off, but that's how she smelled to him, and standing right here beside her now, he didn't know how he was going to be able to give her up.

That day in the office when Kate had told him she was promoting him, he'd thought she was crazy. He'd been a DJ since graduating from college and had never cared much for Paul's job. He'd liked being on the air, spinning tunes and talking to no one and everyone. He'd especially loved the overnight shift because that's when the really interesting listeners phoned in. They talked about everything, from broken relationships to some feeling guilty about shoplifting but also loving the thrill, to did he know where they could buy drugs, to what should they do about being pregnant and too afraid to tell their parents. The night owls had been a very eclectic bunch.

He'd told Kate she was crazy to give him that job and she had laughed. He had given her at least a dozen reasons why he was the wrong guy, most importantly that Paul had been doing this job for longer than Bradley had been alive, and that's where the problem was, she'd said. Paul was a wonderful man, but the radio station needed to target the youth market, something that Paul had long left behind.

Bradley had told her that he wasn't exactly a kid himself and she had told him that she didn't want a kid right out of college, she wanted a guy who had paid his dues, understood the radio business, and who could relate to the audience. She had been listening to his overnight show for some time, ever since deciding that he might just be her guy, and he had impressed her.

Little did he figure that months later they'd be sleeping together, or that yesterday she'd be proposing to him.

That had come out of nowhere. Even if he hadn't decided to stay here, he didn't want to get married to Kate. He loved her, but he didn't need to get married.

It didn't matter now anyway.

He had cheated on her. She was probably going to tell him it was over. The reality of their ending relationship didn't give him any sort of closure and left him feeling empty.

With Kate, he knew exactly what to expect. They had a great life back on the west coast. The summers were warm and the winters were nowhere near as arctic as those in Ottawa, and they both loved to go skiing up in Whistler. Of course, Camp Fortune wasn't far away from Ottawa, and Mont-Tremblant was maybe two hours away, but they paled compared to the Rockies.

"You met Angel?" he said.

"Your niece? Yes, she seems nice."

Bradley finally looked at Kate and he could still see a bit of redness in the white of her eyes and some puffiness under the eyelids. He wanted to pull her into his arms but felt he had lost that privilege.

"She's not my niece," he said. "I found out earlier that she's actually my daughter."

TWENTY-EIGHT

For a moment, Bradley thought Kate had simply disappeared, that the body standing beside him was a trick of the mind, and any second now, she'd be gone. Minutes passed in silence, the only sound he could hear was his frantic heartbeat, steeped in the fear of losing everything he cared about.

"That must have been quite a shock," she said.

"To say the least," he said. "I was pretty pissed off with Cassandra, actually. That was some secret to keep to herself for years."

Kate touched her belly for barely a second. "So, you're a dad? How do you feel about that?"

"I feel like I need to stay here and get to know her."

"And see if you and Cassandra still have a thing?"

Kate had never needed to yell to make her words be felt. She knew how to make you feel pain while having a very casual conversation. Not that he didn't deserve her scorn.

"It's not like that," he said.

She turned to face him. "Then how is it?"

Bradley couldn't meet her gaze, so instead he followed a bee that was going from lavender bush to lavender bush along the bottom of the porch. When it was done, it flew across the lawn which looked dry and hard, with many bald spots. Nothing a yard or two of good topsoil and overseeding couldn't fix. Perfect fall project.

Looked like his list was going to be fairly long. He didn't mind. Good therapeutic work to clear the air and help him get accustomed to living back home. Maybe he'd try to get his dad to help. He had no idea if that was possible with his condition, but he'd find out.

He looked at the bakery. He had never really cared to work there, but maybe once the craziness was over, he could help Emily for a while, until he found something.

And if David didn't sell it.

"I never saw myself as the father sort," he said. "I guess that's why I freaked out yesterday with our talk of marriage and babies. But this is different. And she's not a baby, she's really an adult."

Kate continued to stare at him.

"I didn't mean to hurt you," he said. "I had every intention of coming here, burying Mom, maybe fixing my relationship with David, satisfying myself that my feelings for Cassandra were in the past, and flying back to you. I don't know that I would have said yes to marrying you, but I definitely expected to return to you. I love you."

"But you kissed your ghost."

He winced. "I'm sorry."

She turned to face forward. "So where does that really leave us? What do you plan to do?"

"I didn't expect to find out I had a daughter," he said. "I just can't pretend she doesn't exist and return to Vancouver and carry on as if my life hasn't changed."

"I can understand that," she said. "The kissing, not so much."

Shame took over his features.

"Do you still love her?"

"It's complicated."

"Love isn't supposed to be easy," Kate said. "It's messy and difficult and full of twists and turns and surprises. That's why we do what we do for love."

"I'm not sure what you're telling me."

"I think your heart has always remained here, at home, and it was waiting for you to come back."

He looked at her. "So, that's it. We're over?"

"You're staying here," Kate said and looked away. "I have my career in Vancouver."

Bradley caught something in her eyes that he'd never seen before—something like sadness suffocating happiness. He could sense that she wasn't being totally honest with him, but did he deserve more?

The front door opened and Henry stepped out onto the porch. His dad looked at them.

"I heard your girlfriend is here," Henry said. "Is that her?"

Bradley felt slightly irritated by the interruption, but there was nothing he could do about it.

"Kate, this is my dad, Henry. Dad, this is Kate."

Kate extended her hand and took a step forward while Henry did the same.

"It's about time he brought a nice girl home," Henry said.

"How are you feeling, Dad?"

"Fine," he said with a voice that didn't waver.

"I'm sorry for your loss," Kate said.

"My Irene, she was a wonderful woman," Henry said. "We met when we were kids. Dated after high school."

"Sounds wonderful."

"It was," he said. "Not that we didn't have our problems. Married this long, road's bound to be rough at times. The two of you remember that. Nothing is perfect. Got to take the good with the bad. Sometimes, there seems to be more bad than good, and leaving might seem like the easier choice, but easy isn't always the better choice. Got to learn to forgive. We all make mistakes."

"We know, Dad," Bradley said, thinking of the letter. Mom might have forgiven, but she never quite forgot. Bringing that up wouldn't really gain him anything, and right now, he and Kate had their own issues to resolve. He wasn't sure she was ready to forgive his kissing faux pas with Cassandra. It wouldn't change anything since, like she had said, he was staying and she had a career back home. "We know."

Henry stayed out, shoved his hands in the pockets of his pants. He swayed back and forth on his feet, going from the ball of his feet to the heel, and back again.

"Waiting for anyone?" Bradley said.

"Your brother," Henry said. "I hear he's at the bakery trying to sell it to someone. I can't let him do that. I have a feeling he tricked your mother into signing that deed over. That's not right."

Bradley noticed the tone of authority in his dad's voice. Maybe his father telling David that he couldn't sell the bakery was what his brother would listen to. The letter from his mom explained a lot, and there might be some truth to what his dad had just said, but convincing David once his mind was made up had always been futile.

Still, if he had tricked their mother, then maybe . . .

"You all talk like I'm not there," Henry said, "and I know I have that Alzheimer thing going on, but there isn't anything wrong with my ears. I just don't always make sense of what's happening or remember things. It's like my brain is full up and there's no more room for anything. But I can still tell right from wrong."

"It might be wrong," Bradley said, "but I doubt David will change his mind."

Henry turned toward him. "I was talking about you."

"Not following, Dad."

"That granddaughter of mine," Henry said and looked at Bradley. "She's your daughter."

"Yeah," he said.

"And Kate here, you told her?"

"Well, if I hadn't, you just did."

"I guess I did." Henry turned to Kate. "Hope I didn't ruin something for you?"

"Bradley told me before you came out," she said.

"Don't mean the two of you can't be together," he said. "She's a big girl. She can come and visit you two in Vancouver."

"Yes, she could," Kate said and glanced at Bradley. "It's lovely out there. I'm sure she'd enjoy it."

Bradley stayed quiet.

"So why is it you want to stay here?" Henry said.

"It's complicated, Dad."

"Of course it's complicated. That's why it's worth saving. Sometimes we make mistakes. You don't just throw it away at the first sign of trouble."

Bradley gave Kate an apologetic shrug.

"You find out you have a daughter and now you think you and Cassandra can be together," Henry said. "I love Cassie, like a daughter. But she's not right for you. Maybe she could have been once, but not anymore. You can't live in the past, son."

"Dad—"

"Well, it's about time," Henry said, no longer looking at Bradley. Instead, he looked in the direction of the bakery. "Your brother just shook hands with that man. He's crossing the road. I'd better let your sister know he's coming back."

Henry slipped back into the house.

"I'm not sure he meant any of that," Bradley said.

"I'm pretty sure he did," Kate said. "But I can't force you to come back with me."

Bradley rubbed his goatee.

David walked up the steps. "Who's this?"

"None of your business."

"Whatever," David said and slowed down long enough to push the front door open and walk into the house.

"I've got to get in there," Bradley said. "I need to know what is going on."

"I know," Kate said. "I'll call an Uber."

Bradley bit his lower lip, caught movement from the corner of his eye and turned in time to see Angel hug Lilly and make her way toward him.

"I hate leaving things like this," he said. "You can't stay the night? We could talk more after."

Kate hesitated. She was about to say something, but the words died before she could voice them.

"Coming?" Angel said as she walked by.

"Yeah."

"Go," Kate said.

"I'm sorry."

"I know."

TWENTY-NINE

Bradley had expected to hear shouting when he stepped into the house but it was awfully quiet. That was strange. What was going on? Why weren't Emily and David yelling at each other? If David had sold the bakery, Emily should be going nuts right now.

Was it possible he hadn't sold it?

Could his dad have talked to David already?

Didn't seem likely.

Angel looked at him and he could see in her eyes that she was as confused as he was. He shrugged and followed her.

But then stopped and glanced back at the front door.

"What is it?" Angel said.

What had Kate wanted to tell him? He'd seen it on her face that she'd been about to tell him something, but then had decided not to. Part of him wanted to go back out and find closure, but he felt pulled by the family drama. And then there was what his dad had said, about Cassie being all wrong for him.

Could his father be right?

If only Kate would stay the night so they could talk, maybe they'd figure out a way to make it work. Of course, she'd have to forgive him.

Damn it! Nothing felt right anymore.

"Dad?"

He turned toward Angel and knew he had to stay. The rest, he hoped, would work out for the best. "Let's go see what's going on."

 (3 80)

Bradley stepped into the kitchen and stood there for a second, observing Emily and David on opposite sides of the island. His dad was sitting on a stool beside his sister, and Cassandra was at the far end, her back to the back door. The silence felt superficial and ready to be shattered.

"What's going on?" he said

David shot him a dirty look and then glared at Emily again. His sister's stare didn't waver away from David. The situation could have been comical if it hadn't been so toxic.

"I asked Emily to move her car so I can leave," David said in a tone that was as calm as an approaching storm. "I'm done here and want to go."

"What happened with the bakery?" Bradley said.

"That's what I said when he asked me to move my car," Emily said. "But he won't say."

"I think we deserve to know," Bradley said.

"Why would you think that?" David said. "That bakery would have belonged to my mother, so it belongs to me now and I don't owe anyone any explanations."

"The bakery isn't yours to sell, son," Henry said, his voice strong and chilling. "It belongs to this family. You tricked your mother into signing that deed to you."

"Irene wasn't my mother."

Everyone stopped and stared at David.

The kitchen became uncomfortably quiet. Bradley could hear the breeze flow through the open window above the sink, carrying the soothing sounds of birds singing somewhere in the back yard. In the distance, car tires squealed against the road and boisterous laughter intruded, unwelcomed.

"Mom left a letter explaining everything," Bradley said and moved toward the island. He grabbed the papers that held his mother's words. "We know Mom wasn't your mother."

"Goodie for you," David said.

Bradley held his brother's glare. Maybe when they'd been kids, he wouldn't have lasted more than a second trying to stare David down, but he wasn't a kid anymore. David didn't scare him anymore.

"Read it," Bradley said and held the letter out to David. "*Read it.*"

"I don't need to read those lies," David said between his teeth. "I've lived it since I was eight. I know the story pretty well."

"You could have told us," Emily said, her voice going softer. "You're our brother."

"Half-brother," David said.

"Since we never knew, it really wasn't an issue with us," Bradley said. "And still isn't. Come one, Dave, this has gone on long enough."

"You're trying to trick me into not selling the bakery. Like I said, it belongs to me. Your mother gave it back to me because she knew it belonged to me."

"Gave it back to you?" Bradley said. "Is Dad right? Did you make Mom feel guilty and trick her into signing the deed over so you'd loan her the money? Was this your plan all along, to step in and sell it under her nose to hurt her back? Well, she's gone now. The only people you're hurting are those that never knew the truth. If we had, we would have told you that you were our brother. We wouldn't have alienated you the way you did us."

"Easy for you to say now," David said.

"Come on, man. We're family. That bakery belongs to all of us," Bradley said. "Emily loves that place. It's doing well."

"I've got a great offer for it, from Louis Brasseau."

"The short chubby kid from school?" Bradley said. "Didn't his dad work at the bakery before they moved away?"

"Denis Brasseau," Henry said. "He'd wanted to buy the bakery from your mother. Said he could make it better. Eventually, your mother told him that the bakery would never be for sale and if he wanted one of his own, that he should open one or see if there was one to buy somewhere in Ottawa."

"And now his son conveniently showed up to buy it," Bradley said. "Yeah, that's not happening."

"That's really not your decision," David said.

"Don't do this," Angel said. "We all love that bakery. Great-Great-Grandma Sarah started it when women weren't expected to be businesswomen. She left us her legacy."

David's face softened for a second when he looked at Angel, but turned quickly. "I'm probably going to take his offer."

"So you haven't accepted it?" Emily said.

David seemed angry with himself. "It's a little lower than I want."

"Just read the letter," Bradley said. "Mom wrote it for you."

David reached for the letter and ripped it in two before tossing it back to Bradley.

"That's what I think of those lies."

"They're not lies," Bradley said, picking up the torn papers. "It's Mom explaining everything. It's Mom finally telling the truth. It's Mom apologizing."

"Like I said," David said, "she's not my mother. I don't care what she has to say."

"Grandma loved you," Angel said. "It's Aunt Margaret she was angry with. And Grandpa."

"I was a damn obligation her sister left behind."

"That's what happened that Saturday we were playing Monopoly in your room?" Bradley said. "You'd gone to the bathroom and came back fuming. I'd never seen you so angry. You kicked the Monopoly board and yelled at me to get out of your room."

"Kind of hard to hear who you thought was your mother say that she isn't, that I'm some obligation her mother dumped on her, and if Dad could have kept his—" David stopped. "In his pants, she wouldn't be stuck raising his son." David looked at them all one by one, and then glared at his dad. "*His* son. But not hers."

"That didn't make you any less our brother," Bradley said.

"Of course it did," David shot back. "It makes me half your brother."

"And we already said it never mattered because we didn't know," Emily said. "What mattered was that you pushed us away, you hated us for something we didn't know anything about. You made our childhood miserable."

"As your mother made mine. You think it was easy growing up in this house knowing that she didn't want me here, pretending to be my mother but all along wishing I'd never been born?"

"I was only five," Emily said. "I hadn't done anything to you."

"Guilty by association."

"That's just cruel," Angel said. "So that's why you did the same to me? To punish me because Grandma didn't want you?"

David looked at Angel. "No. It wasn't like that."

"Well?" Angel said when David didn't say more.

"I was so happy when you were born," he said. "But as you got older, I noticed things, like you're left-handed, your hair is the same colour as his." He pointed to Bradley. "I started to suspect that your mother had cheated on me, that you weren't mine."

"I was just a baby. You were the only dad I knew," she said, tears gushing down her cheeks. "I loved you."

David's face suddenly became pained and he couldn't look at Angel any longer. "I am sorry that I couldn't look past that."

"So you did to her what Mom did to you?" Bradley said.

"I couldn't love her knowing that she wasn't mine."

"So you did to her what Mom did to you?" Bradley said again. "And you can't forgive Mom?"

"How many times do I need to tell you she wasn't my mother?" he said, his voice rising in anger. "Irene wasn't my mother. She didn't want me."

"And you didn't want me," Angel said and ran out of the kitchen.

Bradley made eye contact with Cassandra just as she was sliding off the stool to go after Angel. "Should I come too?" he said.

"I'll be fine," she said. "You're needed here."

Cassandra was right, but he still felt the urge to go comfort Angel. It was a weird feeling, this sudden need to protect his daughter. It was like he shared her pain.

"I didn't mean to," David said.

"Yeah, sure," Bradley said. "If you really want to make things right, read Mom's letter."

ೞ ೞ

Cassandra rushed down the hallway after Angel, her heart aching with the pain she had caused her daughter. David's inability to truly love Angel was her fault, for being unfaithful and then holding on to the truth all these years. She had not just lied to everyone, she had lied to herself in order to believe she was doing the right thing.

A life of mistakes she could never right.

Angel stepped out onto the porch and Cassandra followed. She took a couple of hesitant steps and then wrapped her baby into her arms and spoke soothing words to her, like she used to do when Angel was younger. The worst thing in the world for a mother was to see your child hurting, and when you were responsible for that pain, it totally crushed your heart.

"It's my fault," she whispered to her daughter. "I shouldn't have hidden the truth from you, or from David. I'm sorry, honey, so so sorry."

"I j-just . . . I just wanted a d-dad," she said. "A dad to love me."

"I know, sweetie. And I took that possibility away from you both."

"B-but I k-know how he f-feels," she said, and waited until her sobs died. "As angry as I am with him, and you, I know how he felt when he was eight. But I can't hate him like he hated Grandma. I don't want to. He's my uncle, he made mistakes."

"That's awfully mature of you," Cassandra said. "You're a much better person than I was."

"It's a choice," Angel said.

Cassandra kissed her daughter's temple. "Yes, you're right. Life is full of choices. Good and bad."

"I forgive you," Angel said.

Cassandra felt her throat grow thick. "If only I could forgive myself."

"You will."

Cassandra hugged Angel tighter. She wasn't so sure, but the first thing she was going to do was apologize to David. Angel was right. It was a choice, but it was also much more. She was tired of being angry with him, of blaming him. The blame lay with her. Apologizing would free her and hopefully get her one step closer to forgiving herself.

"I love you," Cassandra said.

"I love you too, Mom."

A car suddenly pulled away from the curb and Cassandra reacted instinctively. She let go of Angel, rushed down the steps, and ran across the dying lawn while waving her hands, but the car kept going. She stood at the edge of the road, her stomach in knots as she watched another big mistake being made.

It had to be Kate leaving in an Uber.

Kate and her baby.

Bradley's baby.

Cassandra's chest tightened. Why was Kate leaving? It didn't make sense. If she'd told Bradley, there was no way he'd let her go. She was sure of that. Which meant she hadn't.

Why?

While she and Kate had been alone in the sitting room, Cassandra had agreed with Kate that she should tell Bradley. Sooner the better. As much as she had wanted to see what the future might hold for her and Bradley, Cassandra had known it wasn't meant to be. That was another decision she had made since finding out about Kate. She would always love Bradley, but they couldn't be together.

Bradley should be with Kate.

And their baby.

"Mom?"

Cassandra turned around. "I think that was Kate."

"Leaving?"

"I think so," she said.

"She just got here," Angel said. "Why is she leaving already?"

Cassandra made her way back to her daughter and stood beside her, smiling. Cassandra had been lucky to have lived and breathed the joy of loving her child unconditionally, and although she couldn't ever undo her mistakes, she could make sure she didn't repeat them. She wanted Bradley to experience seeing his child be born, watch it smile for the first time, crawl for the first time, walk for the first time. She wanted him to experience all he'd missed with Angel.

It might not right her wrongs, but it was a start.

"I have something to tell you," Cassandra said. "Something really good this time, something that's going to change our lives, again."

THIRTY

Bradley, Henry, and Emily waited to see if David was going to read the letter, but he seemed content to just sit there and pretend it didn't exist. The day had been too long, and Bradley's patience was running out. He was drained, his shoulders and neck were tight, and there was a throbbing in the back of his head that would turn into a headache soon.

Angel's wellbeing interrupted his thoughts.

His life with Kate made him second-guess his decision.

"Read it," Emily said, pulling Bradley back to reality. "Since he won't."

His sister was right. The sooner they got this done, the sooner they could all get on with it. He heard footsteps and turned to see Angel and Cassandra come into the kitchen. Relief must have crossed his face because Cassandra smiled and nodded.

No sign of Kate.

He just hoped that she hadn't left.

Bradley waited for Cassandra and Angel to get closer, but when they stayed where they were, at the kitchen's entryway, he reached for the torn letter.

And read it.

CB ED

July 10, 2018.

I haven't been feeling well over the last few weeks. I often feel tired, sometimes my eyes get blurry, and I've been getting migraines a lot more frequently than I ever used to. I know I should go to the doctor, but your dad and the bakery keep me so busy that it's probably what has dragged me down.

I need to talk to Emily about her taking the bakery over completely so that I can take care of Dad. He is your dad, all three of you.

But David, you are not my son.

I know this won't come as a surprise to you because of what we agreed upon when you loaned me the money for the bakery renovations, but it will be for Bradley and Emily, which is why I'm mentioning it. I wish I had been a better mother to you, David, and the Lord knows I tried, but it was never good enough. I know that I hurt you, but please believe me that I never meant to hurt you purposely.

My sister Margaret, 'Peggy', was five years older than me. I'm sure Bradley and Emily are wondering why I'm mentioning her. I will get to that.

Anyway, Peggy was twenty in 1967. The drugs, the love, the peace, the rock and roll. She lived it. She breathed it. She became its victim.

Those times, the Haight-Asbury years, were such a draw for her, and she wanted to go to San Francisco so badly to soak it all in. The hippie vibe, it called her. By 1968, she'd become a total pothead and would steal money from the bakery whenever we turned our backs on her, which she used to buy more drugs. My mother forbade her from entering the bakery, so she snuck in at night, after it was closed.

One day, she was gone, and we didn't hear from her for years. If it weren't for the note she'd left, we would have feared she'd been murdered.

Broke your grandmother's heart that she had failed with one of her kids. She couldn't understand what in God's name she had done wrong. She believed Peggy's behaviour was some sort of punishment.

Life moved on.

We all did.

Peggy, being the oldest, was in line to learn the family business and inherit the bakery. That had been the family tradition. The oldest daughter took over at some point. But in this case, that responsibility was relegated to me.

It wasn't what I'd wanted, but my sister had already broken my mother's heart, so I wasn't about to do the same. I was always the sensible Irene. Peggy was the beautiful free spirit who needed to spread her wings and find her calling, and I was plain old Irene who could be depended on.

So I learned how to bake and run a business like my mother had, and surprised myself with how quickly I learned and how well I did.

I know you're probably thinking I couldn't have done that well since I came to ask you for money two years ago, David, but back in the 1970s, that bakery was thriving. The equipment was still in great shape and the place still didn't look dated. It had a bit of a 1950s feel because that was the last time things had been renovated by my grandmother when my mother was just learning to run the place. But overall, the bakery drew business from all the surrounding communities. Keep in mind that Ottawa wasn't sprawled out like it is now, and people had quite a drive to come to Forest Creek, but they did. Saturdays were crazy busy because we weren't open Sundays. Stores weren't allowed to open on Sundays back then.

Which I didn't mind.

We went to church, gathered at Grandma's house—the house that all three of you call home—and lived our lives as best we could.

But my mother always worried about Peggy. It was 1977 by then and we hadn't heard from her in nine years. Your dad and I had been dating for a few years and we were both getting on in age. I'd been busy with the bakery and hadn't paid much attention to the years going by, but then in June of 1978, he proposed. We set a date for the following June, and Grandma and I started to plan my wedding.

I was happy. I had a man who loved me and a family business that was doing well. Not bad for a high school graduate in those days when women were mostly secretaries or worked other low-paying jobs.

I was a success.

My parents couldn't have been prouder. Their dependable and sensible daughter had turned out just as they'd expected, and she was going to marry a good man who had a good job and would give them the grandchildren they wanted.

Life was as near perfect as it could be.

And then Peggy came back.

I had to take a break before writing the rest of this letter because I suddenly became upset. Peggy always had a way of doing that to me.

So, my big sister, after ten years of doing who knew what, showed up at the bakery one afternoon in the summer of 1978 and started acting like nothing had changed, like she hadn't been gone for the past decade.

Ten years since we'd seen her. She had left a hippie and come back as a thirty-year-old punk with short black hair, a studded collar around her neck, a row of piercings in either ear, and a loop in her nose that I couldn't stop staring at as I tried to imagine how painful that must have been.

Honestly, I'd given her up for dead. And I think your grandmother had too, which was why she'd put all of her energy into planning my wedding.

So Peggy was back, older but as gorgeous as ever, maybe even more so, but just as wild and irresponsible as when she had been twenty. Your grandmother got her to help out at the bakery, but I could tell right away that it wasn't for her, and probably never would be. Maybe that's why she had left—to make sure that Grandma didn't try to mold her into a bakery girl, and, as I like to think, maybe she left to make sure that I got the bakery knowing that I'd be perfect for that life.

I never asked her and she never said.

Peggy and I, we had a complicated relationship. Being five years apart didn't help. She was fifteen and dating boys and smoking cigarettes while I was ten and still playing with my dolls. My father was constantly crossing himself, praying that she didn't get pregnant by one of those bad boys from Ottawa that she seemed to hook up with constantly. My mother brooded silently, blaming herself for her sins. What sins those might have been, she never said.

Uncle Tim was between Peggy and me and he was the brain of the family. He never paid much attention to anyone, preferring to live in his books. Then again, he became a well-known heart surgeon in Ottawa so it's pretty hard to blame him for not getting involved with the drama that followed Peggy like a bad smell.

As for Uncle Joey, the baby of the family, Peggy might as well be someone he didn't know, which basically he didn't. He was only seven when she left.

But Peggy and I . . . Maybe it's because we were girls, but there was something between us during the last year that she was here, something that felt like jealousy. I could never quite figure it out because I'd just turned fifteen when she disappeared, hitching a ride to California with one of those boys Dad worried about.

Thank goodness she had the common sense to leave a note so that Mom and Dad wouldn't think she'd been murdered.

Gone to San Fran. Don't worry. Be back someday.

Your grandmother never shed a tear, but I know she was hurting because she closed up for nearly a year, and only when the date of the day Peggy had left came and went and she still hadn't returned, Grandma Alice started to open up again. It's about the time I started to work at the bakery and I think Grandma was happy that I was showing interest. I think she'd been worried that she'd be the last woman in the family to run the bakery and that when she got too old, we'd have to sell it.

As soon as I graduated high school, I worked at the bakery sixty hours a week. Soon after, your father and I started to date and both Grandma and Grandpa approved of such a fine young man.

I'm sorry if the letter isn't as straightforward and linear as I intended it to be. Forgive an old woman her roaming thoughts.

So back to 1978. Peggy has returned home. I'm planning my wedding, and life is as good as can be when Peggy is around, meaning there's plenty of drama. David, your room was her room, and at thirty, she was back living in it. And there seemed to be a constant flow of boys coming and going, which drove my parents nuts. Of course, Peggy was quick to remind them that she was thirty years old and it was 1978 and if she wanted to have boys—men—spend the night with her, because she hated sleeping alone, it was her choice.

She was old enough, in case they hadn't noticed. Which of course prompted my mother to tell her she hadn't raised a tramp and if she wanted to sleep with men under her roof, then she should find herself a fine young man like Irene's Henry.

Unknown to me, though, Peggy took my mother's words to heart and seduced your father over the course of the next couple of months.

You were born nine months later, David, on July 15, 1979, a month after I got married to your father. I didn't find out until my mother brought you to me at six weeks and said that you were my responsibility. When I asked her, she said I should speak to my *fine* husband. The way she'd said that left me feeling uneasy and I waited a whole week before I asked him.

By then your mother was dead.

I guess I shouldn't have been surprised to find out that Peggy was a heroin addict, but I was. I'd hoped, even prayed, that my sister had changed, which is why she had come back. The men that would come and spend the night would pay her with her fix.

I bawled like a baby at her funeral. And now I was stuck to raise her baby. Me, a newlywed of not even three months, obligated to care for my dead sister's baby.

So one night after feeding you your bottle and putting you to bed, I poured two fingers of whiskey in a glass and went to ask my husband what he knew about Peggy's baby. I'd brought the whiskey because I'd sort of figured I wasn't going to like the answer.

Henry was sitting at the small kitchen table—that's before we added the kitchen extension. He was nursing a beer and tears were flowing down his face. When I sat down across from him, I could see his lower lip quivering.

I just sat there and waited. Never said a word. He knew why I was there.

He told me that he was sorry for being such a weak and foolish boy. He and Peggy had gone to school together and they'd even gone on a few dates but that was before she got into drugs. He'd wanted no part of that. But now she had been back and she had seduced him. If you ask him, and if he can remember, he'll tell you that Peggy threatened to tell me they'd had sex even though they hadn't. That's the way she could be. And she wouldn't take no for an answer and he honestly hadn't had much experience. She'd promised to teach him everything he needed to know to make sure he didn't disappoint me, and like the foolish man that he was, well, by now we all know what happened.

This is probably more than what you kids want to hear, but if you're going to hear my side of the story, then I have to include this.

So, he told me what happened, and then I asked him how he knew that baby was really his, what with all the men that had come over every night, and he told me that Peggy had stopped taking the pill when she seduced him, and didn't sleep with anyone afterward. She'd *planned* to get pregnant by my Henry.

And come to think of it, the men did stop coming over that fall, and by the new year she was showing and we'd all assumed it was one of those men from Ottawa that had gotten her pregnant. But since she wasn't telling, my parents figured they had no choice but to help Peggy get through it as best they could.

She was actually good through the pregnancy and she even helped me pick out my wedding dress, and in return, I helped her get ready to become a mother. I think she let me because I was learning everything that I was going to need to know to care for her baby. I truly believe that her death wasn't an accident.

Peggy was a broken soul who had tried to fit into the punk lifestyle once the hippies had all moved on, but it wasn't working. She was getting old, and she knew it. There was nowhere for her in this world and I think she wanted to leave a little piece of herself behind, as a reminder that she had been here, that she had contributed somehow.

And I think she'd wanted my Henry to be the father because she had hated the idea of her baby having no parent at all (that's something that I've just recently started to mull over because in my heart, I want to believe that my sister was good. Broken, but good).

I'm an old woman now, and the years have erased the anger and betrayal I've always felt had been done to me by my sister and my Henry. I'm also aware now that because of their sin, I made you pay for it, David, and that's one regret that I will never ever be able to live down. You were nothing but a baby who hadn't asked to be born into the world this way, and I had the chance to make sure that their sin never touched your beautiful little heart, but it was *my* heart I should have been worried about, *my* heart that was full of darkness. It was my heart that was broken and I was never able to find the peace that would allow me to love you like you deserved. David, my beautiful lovely firstborn, I am your mother and cannot tell you how very very sorry I am that I made you feel anything but loved.

I hope that you can forgive me as I've learned to forgive your father.

And in some way, my sister, your mother, Margaret.

Love, Mom.

THIRTY-ONE

B radley put the letter down and eyed David. He could see his brother's internal battle as emotions crossed his face in rapid-fire succession—anger, denial, doubt, pain—and even though Bradley had read it twice, a similar storm of feelings went through him. This wasn't easy to hear and even harder to accept. Not every day you found out this sort of secret from your parents.

A world of lies.

"Mom—" Bradley started to say.

David grabbed the four shot glasses sitting empty on the countertop and threw them one by one at the far kitchen wall.

"No, no, no, *no!*" he yelled as each glass left his hand. "She doesn't get off that easily. She can't tell me she loves me *now*, she can't tell me she's my mother *now*. She doesn't get to ask for forgiveness *now*."

Bradley was about to say something but he saw Emily shake her head. They'd read the letter earlier and had had time to let it soak in, but for David, even if he had known some of this truth, it was still raw, unfiltered, and unwanted words from Irene.

Truths about David's real mother.

Regret from the woman who had raised him.

It was hard enough to grasp this now, as grownups. Bradley couldn't imagine how an eight-year-old David could have made sense of this, or whatever part of this truth he'd heard back then. Didn't matter; he got David's anger, his unrelenting drive to hurt them all, but it couldn't go on like this.

It had to stop.

Today.

Now.

But was it enough to break his brother's wall of hate and anger, that shield he'd put around himself on that Saturday morning when he was eight? As painful as it was to face all these secrets, Bradley hoped that David could forgive Irene, forgive Peggy, forgive them all.

Bradley looked at his watch: eight-thirty. That was all? His body ached from the long day. He looked at Emily and saw the same weariness in her posture. Over by the kitchen doorway, Cassandra and Angel also looked dead tired.

"You let that anger all out," Henry said. "She did love you, she really did. I think that's why she was so tormented by it. She didn't want to because of the way her sister had manipulated both of us. But in the end, you were Irene's as much as you were mine. We are a family."

"You don't get to tell me that now," David said, failing to hide his pain. "Not after all the years I've devoted to hating her, hating you all."

"But it was always a one-sided hate," Bradley said. "We never hated you. We were afraid and sometimes hurt, but we never hated you."

"We love you," Emily said. "Mom loved you."

David looked at them one by one, his clenched jaw throbbing. Bradley could see him holding on to that hate, but he thought—and maybe it was just wishful thinking—that it was slowly slipping away from his brother. Bradley wasn't much for religion, but right now he was nudging his dead mother to do some sort of magic, to help them out somehow.

To help David out.

Earlier, David had been the same old brother—despicable, hateful, unchanged—but right now, seeing him like this, lost, tormented, broken, tore at Bradley. And gave him hope—weak, but there. He could see glimpses of what might be, but also feared to want it, just in case David didn't break free of his hatred.

In the end, Bradley knew, it really came down to what his brother wanted. That letter was ugly. It painted his biological mother in different shades of black, and maybe David saw himself just like her, unable to fit into his world. Bradley couldn't pretend to know how David felt right now. They had all learned things from their past, from their parents, that showed them as the imperfect people that they were, and that was always difficult for kids to accept.

Parents didn't have a life before the kids came along, they didn't have flaws, they didn't hide secrets.

Parents didn't lie.

Bradley knew that wasn't true, but kids didn't need to know any different. Kids needed to believe in their parents' perfectness for as long as they could. And for him and Emily, that had lasted a very long time.

Not so for David.

They had all found out that their family wasn't exactly what it had pretended to be. His parents, as well as his aunt Margaret, had been far from perfect. They'd been young, foolish, full of dreams and full of fears. Pretty much the same as he'd been when he'd run off to Vancouver. Pretty much the way he felt right now. Maybe nothing had changed. Maybe everything had changed.

"Dad," Angel said, standing in the doorway, and Bradley knew that she wasn't talking to him. "I know how it feels to be told a lie all your life. You might not be my biological dad, but growing up, you were my dad and all I ever wanted from you, *needed* from you, was love, the same love that I gave you, the same love Grandma gave you in the end."

Angel took a hesitant step forward.

David watched her.

Bradley watched them.

Cassandra watched them.

Emily watched them.

Even Henry watched them.

This moment belonged to Angel and David, both broken, both hurt, both needing to heal. In a way, they were more alike than Bradley and Angel might ever be, and if there was anyone better suited to come save his lost brother, Bradley couldn't think of one.

Because there was no one better to save his brother than the daughter that they shared.

Angel.

C8 80

Bradley stood beside Emily, watching his older brother hugging Angel, his niece, his daughter. The whole thing was messed up but he knew they'd figure it out in time. All that mattered right now was that Angel had been able to break through to David.

It was the first step.

There was plenty of healing to be done, not just for David, but for all of them. The family lines had been blurred forty years ago and Bradley didn't know if they'd ever be able to right them, but hopefully, in time, they would.

All because of Aunt Peggy, someone none of them had ever really known, but the secret she had forced upon Irene had shaped the lie that they had all lived.

If there was anyone to blame, it was Aunt Peggy, but Bradley didn't see much point in that. Nothing could be changed. It was best that they all take this little victory and try to move on. No one would ever know his mom's true feelings, and all they would ever have was the letter. In the end, it really didn't matter.

"Do you think we've got our brother back?" Emily whispered. "Is this nightmare over?"

"I hope so," he said. "I wish Mom hadn't waited until she was gone."

"Maybe it's better this way," she said. "Frees David. She's not here for him to hate."

"I guess."

"Angel is something else," Emily said. "Able to see past her own pain to reach out to him. I really think he did love her. Does love her."

"We're all lucky to have her," he said. "Not sure either one of us would have gotten through to him."

"Probably not."

"It'll be great to spend time with her," he said. "Get to know her."

"Are you staying?"

He shrugged. "I'd like to. We all need each other."

"And Kate?" Emily said.

Bradley looked at Cassandra, who was standing on the other side of the kitchen, and he knew without a doubt that he loved her. How could he not? They shared a past that had created a beautiful daughter.

But Kate had saved him from that past. She had been the only one who had been able to make him fall in love again. Which he had. Which he was.

"I have to talk to Cassandra."

He made his way over to her.

"Angel did it," Cassandra said.

"You did an amazing job," he said. "You should be proud of her."

"Every day."

He stood beside Cassandra, admiring their daughter talking to David. He couldn't hear, but he didn't need to. David didn't look angry, which was strange but so nice, and the house didn't feel full of tension. Just an hour ago, he'd given up hope that things would ever change. It really did feel like an angel had saved them.

Bradley eyed his father, thinking of what his dad's *foolishness*, as his mom had said in her letter, had set in motion. The past was better remembered as cherished memories.

"I have to tell you something," he said.

"I know," she said. "It wouldn't have worked, you and I."

For the second time in the last little while, relief passed through him. "I'm sorry. I love you, but not the way I love Kate."

"You should be with her."

"Thank you." He leaned in and kissed her cheek.

"You'll have to hurry though, if you want to catch the plane back to Vancouver."

"She left?"

"I saw an Uber drive away a while back."

"Keys," he said to Emily. "I need to borrow your car."

"Hook by the front door."

Bradley dashed down the hallway, snatched Emily's car keys, and ran toward his sister's little puke green Hyundai.

THIRTY-TWO

B radley dropped the keys as he was about to unlock the driver's side door and swore under his breath. It never failed; whenever he hurried, things happened to slow him down. Annoyed, he fished them from the ground, stuck the key in the hole, and unlocked the car.

He couldn't lose Kate.

Not now. His past was finally where it belonged. It had taken too much of his life to find that out, but now that he had, all he cared about was the future. And that included Kate. It felt good to finally know that he had no more doubts. He could love her without wondering.

As painful as today had been, it had liberated them all. He really hoped it was the beginning David needed, and the closure Cassandra wanted, but most of all, he looked forward to getting to know Angel.

Which is why he really wanted to stay here, but if Kate was dead set against it, he'd go back to the west coast and stay in touch with his daughter as best he could. Angel was an adult, she could come visit. It wouldn't give them as much time together, but he'd be okay with it. She was off to college in a couple of days and a boyfriend was probably on the horizon. She had her own life to live.

And he had his.

Preferably with Kate.

Just as he pulled the car door open, he heard a squeaky sound.

"Going somewhere?" Kate said as she swayed gently back and forth on the old swing.

He turned and relief pulled a smile across his cheeks that was so big it hurt. The fear of having lost her had scared him more than he realized. What had he been thinking earlier? The craziness of today had muddled everything, blurred every line, made him second-guess his whole life, his whole future.

"You didn't leave?" he said and let out a loud sigh. He slammed the door shut. "Cassandra thought she saw you get into an Uber."

"I did call one," she said. "But just as it got here, I started to feel sick and barely had time to run to the side of the house and throw up in the bushes. Lilly decided to take it and go home instead of waiting for her mom to come get her. She's a funny girl."

"Poor her," he said. "Wasting her whole day with us."

"She's a good friend," Kate said. "She was glad to have been here when Angel needed her."

"It's been an eventful day," he said and made his way to the swing set. He didn't trust it to hold his weight so he kneeled on one knee in front of her. His eyes met Kate's and all he wanted was to pull her into his arms and never let her go. It had only been a day, but it felt like forever since he'd kissed her, smelled her, touched her. All he'd needed was a road trip back home to make him come to his senses.

"Forgive me?" he said.

She gave him her hand and he helped her up. "Why should I?"

"Because I love you," he said.

"And?"

"And I want to spend the rest of my life with you."

"And?"

He searched her eyes for a clue. "I'll go back with you to Vancouver. Angel can visit."

She gave him a quizzical frown.

"Did I say something wrong?"

"You don't know?"

A blank stared crossed his face.

"Cassandra didn't tell you?"

"Tell me what?"

Kate hesitated for a moment. "I'm pregnant."

He couldn't speak. This was the last thing he'd expected her to say, but then again, yesterday morning came to mind. He remembered that she'd told him to relax, that she wasn't pregnant. He couldn't blame her for holding on to the truth after the way he'd reacted.

"Did you hear me?"

He nodded but still couldn't utter a word.

"Brad?"

"Yesterday morning," he finally said, "*that's* what that was all about?"

"You're a dumbass."

"And earlier."

"Dumbass twice."

Yesterday, the idea of having a baby had freaked him out, but after today, he couldn't have asked for a better surprise. Everything that he'd missed with Angel, he'd be able to have with this baby.

Two kids.

He never would have thought his life could change so much in twenty-four hours. The thrill of discovering he had a daughter had been a high he'd doubted could be matched, but he'd been wrong.

"Wow!" he said.

"That's better."

Bradley couldn't keep his eyes off of Kate, the street light leaving the left side of her face in shadows. He didn't need to see it all to know how beautiful she looked. He pulled her into his arms but there was a bit of awkwardness.

"You okay?" he said as they parted.

"I'm getting used to vomiting," she said. "The next little while will be interesting."

"You won't be alone," he said. "What if we stayed?"

"Here?" she said. "My career, your career, they're back in Vancouver."

"I know but, listen." He didn't say any more.

"Listen to what?"

"It's peaceful here, perfect to raise a baby."

A sad smile touched her mouth, but didn't linger. "I'm a city girl."

"Ottawa is minutes away."

Kate bit her upper lip. "What would I do? I'd grow restless here."

He felt his hopes evaporating. Being home again, he'd realized how much he missed Forest Creek, how much he missed Emily. And to really fix his relationship with David, being here would help. And of course, there was Angel.

"You stay," she said. "And get things right with your family. The baby won't be here for another thirty weeks, plenty of time for you to figure things out. I'll be fine."

"There's nothing to figure out," he said and took both of her hands in his. "You're the one I want, not Cassandra. Yes, I kissed her and I'm truly sorry I did. I wish I hadn't but, in a way, I think it's what made me realize that she wasn't you. We're friends and that's all we'll ever be. Yes, we have a daughter together, but Cassandra is not who I really want to be with."

"You're just saying that because of the baby," Kate said and pulled her hands from his. She took a couple of steps forward and looked out across the front yard. She crossed her arms. "If I weren't pregnant . . . you'd be staying no matter what."

"I'd already made up my mind that I wanted to be with you before you told me," he said. "Given a choice, I'd prefer that *we* stay here. My family needs me. This house needs me."

"You're asking me to choose between you and my career," she said. "I'm selfish. I want both."

"I do too."

He wanted to wrap her into his arms again, but a bit of a wall stood in the way. He wasn't sure where they stood. A few minutes ago, he'd been relieved that she was still here, but he wondered now whether *she* was the one saying goodbye.

"I know I'm asking a lot," he said.

Kate turned her head to face him. "And what if I say no? Will you really come back with me?"

"It will be hard, but not as hard as letting you go," he said, grabbing her hand and giving it a gentle squeeze. "I know asking you to give up your life in Vancouver for suburbia is selfish of me, but it would be such a great place to raise our baby. And he or she would get to know Angel."

Kate looked away.

"Stay the week," he said. "Stay until we say goodbye to Mom, and make sure David doesn't get back on that ledge. Get to know them. I've missed Emily and I can't just run off so soon and leave her to take care of everything and everyone."

Kate continued to stare out into the night. He didn't ask for permission, he simply wrapped her into his arms and after a second or two, she leaned into him.

He breathed in the night.

They stood in silence like this for a few minutes.

Kate took his left hand and put it on her stomach.

Tears ran down his cheeks.

"I'll stay the week," she said. "But I can't promise to stay longer."

THIRTY-THREE

The hot late June sun was already punishing the ground below, sucking any moisture left in the earth and making everything dry and hard. There was an attempt at a breeze, but it barely rustled the leaves on the old maple tree in the front yard, offering no relief from the heavy and clammy air. Three moms pushing baby strollers were complaining about the early heat wave and couldn't wait to have their morning walk done so they could go back to air-conditioned homes

It was not quite nine in the morning.

Bradley wiped his brow and unwittingly left a dirt mark across his forehead, complementing the one he'd smeared on his left cheek a few minutes ago. He stood back and scrutinized the new front garden he'd spent the past week gutting and redoing. After tearing down the front porch in early May to rebuild it, the garden had not survived.

He'd found out something about himself over the last two months that he'd never known: he was quite the handyman. David had asked him if he wanted to hire someone to redo the porch, but Bradley had decided to take it on. There was plenty of information on the internet, how-to books at all the home centres, and lots of expert advice if he just asked.

Besides, he'd spent the winter watching home renovation show after home renovation show, and they all made it seem so easy that he'd started to believe that he could do it.

He eventually found out that it wasn't so easy, but that didn't stop him. He made mistakes, banged a few fingers, nursed plenty of cuts, but after five weeks of working from sunup to sundown, the front porch was completely reconstructed. He went with composite decking board to avoid future rot, used western red cedar for the columns that he stained a rich dark walnut, and he installed a front railing made of glass that gave the illusion, when you were sitting on the brand-new two-person swing chair, that the deck was just an extension of the front lawn.

That too had been completely redone after the irrigation system was installed. He'd thought of doing that too, but Emily had convinced him to get professionals to install the system so that he could concentrate on the deck and the gardens. He was glad he'd listened to her. They were all getting better at listening to each other.

"Looks great, Dad," Angel said as she came out from the house with a cup of coffee in her hand.

"I can't disagree with you," he said. "Where's your mom?"

"Helping Aunt Emily at the bakery," Angel said. "I think she's really taking to it. Not crazy about getting up at four, but I've never seen her this happy."

Bradley gave the bakery a quick glance. They'd finally decided to brand it properly and change its name to Sarah's Bakery. Below that, Angel had convinced them all to add a little slogan.

Forest Creek's Yummy Treasures.

Bradley thought Great-Grandma Sarah would have approved. They'd actually found boxes and boxes of old recipes and journals in the bakery's basement that Emily was slowly making her way through, and each time she found something she thought she could use, she muttered to herself that Great-Grandma Sarah was full of yummy treasures.

Angel was a clever girl.

"Today's the day," Angel said.

Bradley turned back to his daughter. She was already done with her first year of college, and best of all, he'd been here for her nineteenth birthday. It had been a long and cold winter, and there had been snow on the ground in early April, but that hadn't stopped them from sitting around a small bonfire in the back yard.

"Let's hope so," he said. "We won't know until later."

"I feel good," she said. "David will come through."

She had told Bradley that she couldn't call him Uncle David, not after everything that had happened. It didn't feel natural. When he'd asked her how come she had no issue calling him Dad, she'd rolled her shoulders and told him that *that* felt natural.

He didn't argue, mostly because he really did like to be called Dad. It was something that he had never expected to experience, but now, after all these months of hearing it almost every day, it gave him a real sense of accomplishment.

"Do you want a coffee or something?" she said.

"I could use a bottle of water," he said.

Angel went back into the house. It had become the communal home. Everyone crashed here regularly. Turned out the place was in worse shape than it looked and they all chipped in whenever possible. They had discovered a leak in the upstairs bathroom just before Christmas and Bradley had jumped at the opportunity to get his feet wet—literally—in home renovation.

He'd gutted the entire room, brought it back to the studs, and then stole some space from Emily's old room to create a stunning spa-like ensuite.

It had become the pride of the house.

He also wanted to turn the dining room into an office since it was in the front of the house and not convenient at all, and he wanted to knock down another wall in the back to make the eating area even bigger to accommodate them all when everyone gathered on Sundays. He was still waiting on the architect to come back with plans.

"Catch," Angel said and tossed him a water bottle. He cracked the cap open and downed more than half of it. "Don't get dehydrated again."

"I won't," he said. Yesterday had been very hot and by nighttime his feet and hands had been cramping so bad he couldn't move until the cramps passed. "You're just like your mother."

"You Knighton boys need to be kept in check."

He smiled. After Angel had convinced David that day back in September, she had decided that as much as she loved the bakery, maybe she had a knack for working with people, so she had switched to the Social Services Studies program at Algonquin College. She wanted to work with underprivileged kids and youths.

Bradley and Cassandra had both felt it was a wonderful idea. If she could get David to change the course of his life, then the kids under her care would be in great hands.

"How's Grandpa doing?"

"I made him his favourite breakfast, so I've got a few minutes. I think we'll work on that puzzle for a while," she said. "Or until he grows frustrated."

They'd found a great place for Henry twenty minutes away in Stittsville, but last night Emily had brought him home for the weekend. This allowed Angel to work with her grandfather as much as she could, which was good practice, but they also all hoped that keeping his brain engaged might help somehow, maybe even slow his degeneration. They'd all read everything they could find about the disease, and asked plenty of questions to the numerous doctors they'd met, but truth was, nobody really knew if keeping the brain challenged helped. The way they all saw it, it certainly couldn't hurt. And as Angel cared for her grandfather, Bradley had seen her grow not just as a person, but as the potential social worker she was going to be.

Both he and Cassandra were so proud of her, but she'd had to tell them to tone it down because, really, their constant gloating of how well she was doing, how great she had become, how special she was had become nauseating.

Of course, there was a grin that accompanied that reprimand.

Cassandra, too, was moving on, helped by getting involved in the bakery, and mostly by being forgiven by Angel. She'd also discovered during her numerous conversations with her daughter that as much as she and her mother had believed they'd been better off without her father, some lingering insecurities had settled deep into her psyche. It didn't absolve her of all her lies, but it helped her understand why she had hidden them for so long.

Which helped her move on and stop blaming David for everything. She and David had managed an amicable separation, and were still waiting for their divorce request to be approved.

As for David, it had taken him most of the winter to finally accept what Irene had written in her letter. It hadn't been easy for him, but with the support of his family and some professional counselling, he was making good progress. And Josée had slowly been introduced into the family, which seemed to ease his own reintegration into the familial stronghold.

Things weren't perfect for the Knighton family, but they were the best they'd ever been, and every day that went by they got a little better.

"Have I told you—?" he started to say.

"About a million times," Angel said and rolled her eyes. "I'd better get back in there and see what Grandpa is doing."

Bradley followed Angel with his eyes and then he turned to his right as he heard footsteps going up the driveway. This was the best part of his day.

"There's Daddy!" Kate said as she came up the driveway pushing a stroller. "Yes, Daddy!"

Every morning, Kate left for an hour-long walk, a compensatory substitute for the five-kilometer run she'd been accustomed to for the last fifteen years but had to give up for now. The pounds weren't coming off fast enough for her, and no matter how often Bradley told her that she looked fantastic, she just waved off his compliment like a typical wife.

"You'd say anything to sleep with me," she'd say playfully.

"I think it's working because I get to sleep with you every night," he'd say back.

They'd gotten married on Christmas day, here at the house. Her family had flown in from Vancouver and Bradley had insisted that they all stay with them. It had been a bit cramped, but a lot of fun too.

Bradley and Kate had talked and talked and talked that night back in September, going back and forth on whether she would stay, could stay, wanted to stay. It was asking a lot to give up a career she loved and excelled at, but by the end of the week, she had told him that she was starting to enjoy the slow pace and tranquility of Forest Creek. It was a nice change.

She'd also told him that she already felt part of the family, and was starting to think he might be right about their baby being close to Angel.

"Would be great for them to know each other, even if there are nineteen years between them," she'd said.

Plans to move to Forest Creek had been set in motion the day after they had buried Irene. It had been a beautiful service, sunny but not too hot, the house full of family and friends, turning the day into a real celebration of life.

A new beginning for them all.

Shortly after the move, Bradley came up with a plan for the bakery that he ran by Emily and David, after Kate told him she thought it was brilliant. She even offered to invest some of her savings into the idea.

Everyone was on board instantly.

First came the name change to Sarah's Bakery, which they then incorporated. Next on the plan was to start buying other bakeries in Ottawa until they had about a dozen or so.

"I never would have thought my little brother was such a shrewd businessman," David said as often as he could.

In February, they had bought a bakery in Stittsville, and in March, one in Bells Corners. But today was the big day Angel had referred to earlier. About a week ago, they had made an offer to Louis Brasseau to buy his three bakeries, and he'd asked to have until today, noon, to decide.

"Hey, little buddy," Bradley said as he scooped his son out of the stroller. "How's my little man doing this morning?"

"Place looks better and better every day," Kate said. "You've done an amazing job, honey."

"Surprised?"

"Not about your abilities," she said and paused. "Surprised that I was able to give up city life for a little piece of suburbia."

"It's not bad, is it?"

Kate tickled Callum's neck. They had named him after Great-Grandma Sarah's husband. It had seemed appropriate to honour them both, since so much of their lives traced back to Bradley's great-grandparents.

She leaned over and kissed Bradley.

"I could get used to it," she said.

Did you enjoy
The Little Lies We Hide?

You can make a big difference. Reviews are incredibly powerful. There is no better way to let other readers know if a story is good. And since I can't compete with authors who have the financial backing of a big publisher, your review means that much more to me.

I'd be extremely grateful.

Best places to leave your review is where you typically buy your books and ebooks, and also on BookBub and Facebook. Nothing is better than word-of-mouth.

If you're not part of my Insiders Group, you can join and receive updates about future novels, special promos or giveaways, and reviews about books I've read and want to share with you. I really value that you've welcomed my books into your life and will never spam you. You'll be able to unsubscribe from my Insiders Group anytime you want, but I hope you'll stick around because more stories are coming.

And you'll get a FREE ebook when you sign-up.

Story behind *The Little Lies We Hide*

My father passed away on Nov 16, 2005, at the age of just seventy-two. When he died, he was diagnosed with lymphoma and was also suffering from Alzheimer. Growing up, I had rarely seen my dad miss work because he was sick. He never was.

So here I was at the age of forty-two, not knowing how I was going to face life without my dad in it. After about seven years of not writing, I wrote furiously for months. What I ended with was a book titled *Horses on the Roof.*

But it wasn't fiction. It was a personal journal.

So, I wrote a very different version, but it still wasn't fictionalized enough.

So, I wrote another version and thought it was pretty good but it needed a lot of work.

That's when I put it aside and wrote *Beautiful Midnight* and *It Happened to Us* almost without a break.

Losing my dad was the hardest thing I'd ever experienced and I needed the passage of time to easy the loss. And I knew that I would come back with Henry someday.

Henry isn't the main character in *The Little Lies We Hide* and that's probably why I was able to write him into the story. My dad did think there were horses on my brother's house (he and my mom were living with him at the time), and some of the other scenes were loosely based on some of the things my dad did and said. He had very similar hallucinations as Henry.

Sharing these very personal and emotional memories with you was something I wasn't sure that I could do, but to make Henry as memorable as I wanted him to be without being the protagonist, I decided it made sense.

I hope I did his memory justice.

My dad was a good man, a great father, and writing this still brings tears to my eyes, even fourteen years after losing him.

I will miss him forever.

Excerpt from

THE TREES
HAVE BUDS

ONE

S arah woke up to a dreary autumn morning with the odd
sense that the perfect harmony that had unexpectedly
found her less than three years ago would someday soon
be impossible to hold onto—thin and misty like the fog that
wisped by her bedroom window.

Jack was in the shower, getting ready for work. Sarah had gotten up with the intent to join him, but that fear she'd been
harbouring lately, like she was a fraud and soon Jack would figure
it out and cast her aside like the nobody she used to be, paralyzed
her.

Giving up her former life had been easier than she'd ever
dreamed of, but it was never far away, almost like an impercepti-
ble mosquito buzzing around her head and keeping her awake at
night.

Sarah hated it when Jack went to work and left her alone.
She'd always loathed being alone, mostly because she had spent
the majority of her life alone with her mom, moving from place
to place. Always the new kid at school, on the perimeter of other
kids' lives, watching friendships from the boundary of the

playground or the lunchroom, never venturing closer, never becoming one of them.

She watched others live while she waited to be invited to join. By the time others kids warmed up to her, she was gone, her mom hooking up with another *boyfriend* and off they'd go to a new place until her mom outstayed her welcome and Mr. Boyfriend dumped her sorry ass and they found themselves with nowhere to live once again.

Sarah put her fingers to her lips but the cigarette that had been a fixture in her hand since she was twelve had become a part of her old life. She had been all too happy to give that up when Jack had suggested that it might be best for her health.

And his.

He didn't smoke and she had figured it was as good a time as any to give up the habit anyway. Besides, at almost twenty dollars a pack, it made little economical sense.

But still, while her mind agreed with the common sense of quitting smoking, at times her fingers seemed to have a mind of their own. There was still the odd time she had a craving, especially on mornings like this when she was feeling completely out of her element and could feel her anxiety come at her from everywhere, desperately trying to suffocate the happiness she felt she so deserved.

The shower stopped and Sarah knew Jack would be on autopilot now to get ready for work. She'd only get in the way and she really didn't want to pick a fight this morning just because she was feeling insecure.

Again.

Thanks to her mother.

And her mother's *boyfriends*.

So many men.

So many towns.

So many disappointments.

Sarah closed her eyes and took several deeps breaths. Remembering to breathe had helped her get through some really bad moments, but today it wasn't really helping. Maybe because this morning wasn't really a bad moment. She was married to the most amazing man she had ever met and had never been this happy.

Well, things could be better with Hailey, but she was a teenager going through adolescent stuff and clearly had no intention of sharing any of that with Sarah. If anyone could understand the troubles of teenagerhood it would be Sarah, but Sarah had not yet managed to earn her stepdaughter's trust or respect.

She really had no clue how to be a mother and she hadn't had much experience with friendships either, so when she was left alone with Hailey, both seemed to keep to themselves while waiting until Jack came home.

Being a firefighter, he'd be gone for the next twenty-four hours.

No wonder Sarah was feeling anxious.

CB ❧

Sarah was still standing in front of the window which looked across an expansive farmer's field when Jack crashed out of the bathroom—Jack never seemed to do anything with delicate finesse, always seeming to be destroying as he moved about. Sarah had remarked this early in their relationship and he'd simply laughed it off, telling her when your life was spent rushing into burning buildings to save lives, delicate finesse wasn't going to get the job done.

"No," she'd said. "I guess it wouldn't."

Still, it wasn't like their house was burning so he really didn't need to act like he had to rush in and out of rooms as if it were.

Stop it, she told herself. *You're doing it again, finding faults where there are none to be found. Are you trying to ruin this beautiful life that basically fell into your lap?*

Sarah felt Jack wrap his arms around her, his naked body against her bare skin.

"Good thing we don't have neighbours," he whispered into her ear.

"It's such a great view from up here." Dawn was just pushing the night away. "Except right now, even if we did have nosy neighbours, that fog blocks everything. It makes me feel like we're cut off from the world."

Jack kissed her neck and she felt him against her lower back— he was a big man, nearly a foot taller than she was and she wasn't short—and reflexively, she reached behind and grabbed him.

"You don't have time," she said sadly.

Jack spun her around and kissed her like it was their first time, deep and long and eagerly. No one had ever kissed her like that before she had met him and she wondered why that was—why hadn't anyone before Jack ever made her feel like she was that desirable?

She felt a tear sneak out of her right eye.

"Hey, what's wrong?" he said after their kiss ended.

"Nothing," she said. "I'm just so happy."

He looked at her with a frown.

"Are you and Hailey getting along?" he said. "Do I need to talk to her again?"

Sarah shook her head. "We're good."

He looked at her a little longer and she could feel his gaze trying to reach her lie, but then she started to run her hand up and down and next thing she knew, he'd led her onto the bed and loved her until they were both spent and he was running super late.

"I'll grab something at Tim's," he said as he rushed out the front door. "Love you, babe."

"I love you more," she said.

Sarah stood just outside the open front door and watched Jack back his car out of the garage and into the little two-car parking area off to the side of the driveway designated for guest parking. He gave her that big smile she loved so much and then blew her an air-kiss before heading towards the main road. Their driveway was so long that Jack owned a tractor-snowblower because there was no way anyone could shovel that much snow in the winter without getting a heart attack. She saw the tail lights turn bright red, and then Jack aimed the car towards town and out of Sarah's sight.

She then closed the door and began to shake.

ℭℬ ℬ

Sarah let herself slide down against the wall until she was sitting on the floor. She pulled her knees up against her chest and wrapped her arms around them, making herself as small as she could.

Small things went unnoticed.

She hated when this happened. The shaking, the sweating followed by chills, that invisible hand around her throat cutting off her airwaves, as if she had no control over anything. It would be easy for her to blame her mother, or at least her upbringing for these sudden panic attacks, but she'd basically been taking care of herself since she was barely ten and had never made excuses for anything.

Her mom wouldn't have cared anyway, so complaining about things wouldn't have mattered. Nothing would have changed. She had learned to live by being unseen and unheard.

The panic attack would pass. It always did. She just didn't understand why she was still getting them, especially now. She had never been more loved, cared for, safe.

Which was probably the problem.

She was afraid of losing it all.

Her eyes stung.

The day her mother died when Sarah was seventeen didn't even bring a tear to her eye. She'd been too busy trying to figure out how to survive.

Sarah had no idea who her father might be and she had no brother or sister.

At seventeen, she'd been all alone.

Grieving for a mother who had dragged her around like she was a used piece of luggage had been a luxury she couldn't afford; her new reality was that she'd become an orphan, was homeless, and no one in the world cared what happened to her.

She never returned to school.

What was the point? She was still just in grade ten because of all the moving around, and she was tired of being made fun of by the other kids when they found out she was old enough to be in grade twelve. Being called stupid and worse had long ago made her despise school anyway.

And it wasn't like she could afford to go to college after graduating. Besides, there was only one thing she'd been meant to do, and although the thought hadn't ever crossed her mind until that day, she'd known that following in her mother's footsteps had been the only option she'd really ever had.

Jack had saved her from that life. She couldn't imagine life without him and every time he went off to work, she felt like that seventeen-year-old who'd suddenly found herself all alone.

Something rough and yet wet touched her bare feet repeatedly and through the cascade of grief pouring out of her eyes, she saw the one true thing that really belonged to her.

"Hey Peanut," Sarah said as she scooped her little Maltese into her arms and buried her face into its fur. Jack had brought her home last July. One of the guys he worked with had a dog who'd had a litter and Jack had surprised Sarah by bringing a little puppy home. Not that she'd ever expressed any desire to have a dog, but Peanut was so cute and friendly and lovable that Sarah had simply fallen in love with her. "Mommy is all right. I'm just being my silly old self."

Peanut acknowledged her mommy's silliness by licking Sarah's tears from her face.

"You'll never leave me, will you?" Sarah said and was greeted by more kisses. "Of course, you're not. You love your mommy, yes you do."

Sarah held Peanut up against her chest, feeling the Maltese's warmth and comfort. Slowly, her shaking stopped, the chills vanished, and she was able to breathe again as the pressure around her throat eased and disappeared.

Sarah put Peanut down and pulled herself up. She took a deep breath and straightened her nightgown. "I bet you're starving."

She let the dog out to do her business in the back yard and she took Peanut's bowls to the sink and gave them a quick wash before filling one with water and the other with dry lamb and rice kibble. Peanut came in and dashed toward her food while Sarah went to make a cup of coffee and put a couple pieces of bread into the toaster. She smothered peanut butter on her toast but after a couple of bites she found that she didn't have much of an appetite. She sat at the kitchen island with her cup of coffee in her hands, watching Peanut eat, wondering how she was going to fill the next twenty-four hours until Jack came home.

She heard the old pipes rattle as the upstairs shower came to life. Her heart began to beat a little faster.

Her stepdaughter was up.

Connect with François Houle

www.francoisghoule.com

www.facebook.com/francoishouleauthor

www.bookbub.com/authors/francois-houle

Acknowledgments

My wife and daughter mean the world to me and their support inspires me every day. My daughter is a college student now (2019) and it's been wonderful to watch her become a very independent and strong young woman.

She definitely challenges me to see things from different points of views.

I'd like to say a special thank you to my editor Ethan James Clarke of SilverJay Editing. He has a wonderful eye and provided awesome suggestions that helped make this story that much stronger.

I want to thank Noah Sabourin (aka: DJ Noah of Live 88.5) for answering all my questions around how radio stations work. Hopefully I got it right.

I also want to thank my realtor, Nim Moussa, who did an awesome job of selling two of our previous houses and always answers my real estate questions. If I got it wrong, it's my fault, not his.

And most importantly, I want to thank you for coming along on this journey with me. I hope you enjoyed reading *The Little Lies We Hide* as much as I did writing it.

Until next time, take care and happy reading!

Also by François Houle

About François Houle

François Houle's first novel *It Happened to Us* spent multiple weeks in 2019 as an Amazon top 100 best seller in two categories. His fiction explores themes that are universal such as family and friendships, love and grief, and anything else that makes us all human. Reviews often refer to his books as "beautifully written," "heartbreaking and heartwarming," and "intense and emotional."

François is one of five boys so it's no surprise that family is a strong theme in his books. A lot of the inspiration for his first two novels *It Happened to Us* and *Beautiful Midnight* came from the passing of his father in 2005.

François grew up in a small town outside of Montréal, moved to Toronto when he was ten, and currently lives in Ottawa. An avid reader from a young age, he tried to create a comic book when he was twelve, penned hundreds of song lyrics as a teen-ager, and wrote his first novel in 1985, a sci-fi influenced by the novel *Dune*. Several horror novels followed, and although none of these books will ever be published, they were important in his development as an author.

In 1985, at the age of 22, he graduated from college with a Programmer/Analyst diploma and then went into the ice cream business with his family, owning three Baskin-Robbins franchises for about 6 years. In 1991, he started his IT career, and from 2003 – 2017, he was a Certified Professional Résumé Writer and operated a part-time business writing résumés, which helped while his wife took a sabbatical from work to stay home and care for their two kids.

If you'd like to stay current with what he's working on, please like his Facebook page and join his Insiders Group at *www.francoisghoule.com*.

Fun Facts About Me

1. I'm a big hockey and football fan.
2. I love alternative music (*The Twilight Sad* is one of my all-time favourite bands).
3. I enjoy woodworking.